THE ASSISTANT

ALSO BY ROBERT WALSER

FORTHCOMING FROM NEW DIRECTIONS

ROBERT WALSER

The Assistant

Translated from the German by Susan Bernofsky

A NEW DIRECTIONS PAPERBOOK ORIGINAL

New Directions gratefully acknowledges the support of Pro Helvetia, Swiss Arts
Council.

Manufactured in the United States of America
New Directions Books are printed on acid-free paper.
First published as a New Directions Paperbook Original (NDP1071) in 2007
Design by Erik Rieselbach
Published simultaneously in Canada by Penguin Books Canada Limited

Library of Congress Cataloging-in-Publication Data
Walser, Robert, 1878–1956.
[Gehülfe. English]
The assistant / Robert Walser ; translated from the German by Susan Bernofsky ;
with an afterword by the translator.
p. cm.
ISBN-13: 978-0-8112-1590-9 (alk. paper)
ISBN-10: 0-8112-1590-3 (alk. paper)
I. Bernofsky, Susan. II. Title.
PT2647.A64G3613 2007
833'.912--dc22   2007006865

New Directions Books are published for James Laughlin
by New Directions Publishing Corporation
80 Eighth Avenue, New York 10011

Second Printing

THE ASSISTANT

ONE MORNING AT EIGHT O'CLOCK a young man stood at the door of a solitary and, it appeared, attractive house. It was raining. "It almost surprises me," the one standing there thought, "that I'm carrying an umbrella." In earlier years he had never possessed such a thing. The hand extending down at his side held a brown suitcase, one of the very cheapest. Before the eyes of this man who, it seemed, had just come from a journey, was an enamel sign on which could be read: C. Tobler, Technical Office. He waited a moment longer, as if reflecting on some no doubt quite irrelevant matter, then pressed the button of the electric doorbell, whereupon a person, a housemaid by all appearances, came to let him in.

"I'm the new clerk," said Joseph, for this was his name. The maid instructed him to come inside and go right down there—she pointed the way—into the office. Her employer would appear presently.

Joseph descended a flight of stairs that seemed to have been made more for chickens than for people, and then, turning to the right, found himself in the inventor's office. After he had waited a while, the door opened. Hearing the firm tread upon the wooden steps and seeing the door being thrust open like that, the one waiting there had at once recognized the boss. The man's appearance only served to confirm the certainty that had preceded it: he was in fact none other than Tobler, master of the house, the engineer Tobler. His face bore a look of astonishment, and he seemed out of sorts, which indeed he was.

"Why is it," he asked, fixing Joseph with a punitive glare, "that you're already here today? You weren't supposed to arrive until Wednesday. I haven't finished making arrangements. What were you in such a hurry for, eh?"

For Joseph, that sloppy "eh" at the end of the sentence had a contemptuous ring to it. A stump of a word like that doesn't exactly sound like a friendly caress, after all. He replied that the Employment Referral Office had indicated to him that he was to begin work on Monday morning, that is, today. If this information was in error, he hoped to be forgiven, as the misunderstanding was beyond his control.

"Just look how polite I'm being!" the young man thought and secretly couldn't help smiling at his own behavior.

Tobler did not seem inclined to grant forgiveness right away. He continued to belabor the topic, which caused his already quite ruddy face to turn even more red. He "didn't understand" this and that, certain things "surprised" him, and so forth. Eventually his shock over the error began to subside, and he remarked to Joseph without looking at him that he might as well stay.

"I can't very well send you packing now, can I?" To this he added, "Are you hungry?" Joseph replied imperturbably that he was. He immediately felt surprised at the serenity of his response. "As recently as half a year ago," he thought quickly, "the formidableness of such a query would have made me quake in my boots, no doubt about it!"

"Come with me," the engineer said. With these words, he led his newly acquired clerk up to the dining room, which was on the ground floor. The office itself was located below ground, in the basement. In the living and dining room, the boss spoke the following words:

"Sit down. Wherever you like, it doesn't matter. And eat until you've had your fill. Here's the bread. Cut yourself as much as you'd like. There's no need to hold back. Go ahead and pour yourself several cups—there's plenty of coffee. And here is butter. The butter, as you see, is here to be eaten. And here's some jam, should you happen to be a jam-lover. Would you like some fried potatoes as well?"

"Oh yes, why not, with pleasure," Joseph made so bold as to reply. Whereupon Herr Tobler called Pauline, the maid, and instructed her to go and prepare the desired item as quickly as possible. When breakfast was over, approximately the following exchange took place between the two men down in the workroom, amidst the drawing boards and compasses and pencils lying about:

As his employee, Tobler declared in a gruff tone of voice, Joseph must keep his wits about him. A machine was of no use to him. If Joseph planned to go about his work aimlessly and mindlessly, with his head in the clouds, he should kindly say so at once, so that it would be clear from the start what could be expected of him. He, Tobler, required intelligence and self-sufficiency in his employees. If Joseph believed he was lacking in these attributes, he should be so kind as to, etc. The inventor appeared prone to repetition.

"Oh," Joseph said, "but why shouldn't I keep my wits about me, Herr Tobler? As far as my abilities are concerned, I believe and most decidedly hope that I shall be able to perform at all times whatever you see fit to ask of me. And it is my understanding that for the time being I am up here (the Tobler house stood atop a hill) merely on a provisional basis. The nature of our mutually agreed-upon arrangement in no way prevents you from deciding, should you consider this necessary, to send me away at a moment's notice."

Herr Tobler now found it fitting to remark that he certainly hoped it would not come to that. Joseph, he went on, should not take umbrage at what he, Tobler, had just declared. But he'd thought it best to get down to brass tacks at the start, which he believed could only be beneficial to both parties. This way, each of them knew what to expect from the other, and that is the best way to handle things.

"Certainly," Joseph concurred.

Following this consultation, the superior showed the subordinate the place where he "could do his writing." This was a somewhat too cramped, narrow and low-to-the-ground desk with a drawer containing the postage box and a few small books. The table—for in fact that's all it was, not a real desk at all—abutted a window and the earth of the garden. Gazing past this, one could glimpse the vast surface of the lake, and beyond it the distant shore. All these things were today enveloped in haze, for it was still raining.

"Come with me," Tobler said abruptly, accompanying his words with a smile that to Joseph appeared almost unseemly, "after all, it's time my wife had a look at you. Come along, I'll introduce you to her. And then you should see the room where you'll be sleeping."

He led him upstairs to the second floor, where a slender, tall figure came to meet them. This was "her." "An ordinary woman," was the young clerk's first hasty thought, but then at once he added: "and yet she isn't." The woman observed the new arrival with an ironic, indifferent look, but unintentionally so. Both her coldness and her irony appeared congenital. She held out her hand to him casually, even indolently; taking this hand, he bowed down before the "mistress of the house." This is the secret title he gave her, not to elevate her to a more beautiful role but, on the contrary, for the sake of a quick private affront. In his eyes, the behavior of this woman was decidedly too haughty.

"I hope you will like it here with us," she said in a strangely high, ringing voice, frowning a little.

"That's right, go ahead and say so. How nice. Just look how friendly we're being. Well, we'll soon see, won't we." These are the sorts of thoughts Joseph saw fit to entertain upon hearing the woman's benevolent words. Then they showed him his room, which was situated high up in the copper tower—a tower room, as it were, a noble, romantic location. And in fact, it appeared to be bright, airy and friendly. The bed was nice and clean—oh yes, this was a room in which one could do some living. Not bad at all. And Joseph Marti, for this was his full name, set down on the parquet floor the suitcase that he had carried upstairs with him.

Later he was initiated briefly into the secrets of Tobler's commercial enterprises and made acquainted with the duties he would have to fulfill generally. Something odd was happening to him—he understood only half of what was said. What was wrong with him, he thought, and reproached himself: "Am I a swindler, just full of empty talk? Am I trying to deceive Herr Tobler? He is asking for 'wits,' and today I haven't got my wits about me at all. Maybe things will go better tomorrow morning or perhaps even this evening."

He found the lunch that was served quite delicious.

Worrying again, he thought: "How is this? Here I am sitting and eating food that tastes better than anything I have eaten for months perhaps, and yet comprehend none of the ins and outs of Tobler's enterprises? Is this not theft? The food is wonderful, it reminds me vividly of home. Mother made soup like this. How firm and succulent the vegetables are, and the meat as well. Where can you find food like this in the city?"

"Eat, eat," Tobler encouraged him. "In my household everyone eats heartily, do you understand? But after lunch there's work to be done."

"As you see, sir, I am eating," Joseph replied so bashfully it all but enraged him. He thought: "Will he still be prodding me to eat a week from now? How shameless of me—to be so taken with this food, which belongs to other people. Will I justify my outrageous appetite with equally prodigious productivity?"

He took second helpings of each dish on the table. It's true, he had arrived here from the lower depths of society, from the shadowy, barren, still crannies of the metropolis. It had been months now since he had eaten well.

He wondered if anyone noticed, and blushed.

Yes, the Toblers had clearly noticed at least something. The woman gazed at him several times with almost a pitying expression. The four children, two girls and two boys, kept glancing at him surreptitiously, as at something utterly alien and strange. These openly questioning and probing glances dismayed him. Glances like these cannot help but remind a person that he has only just come to perch in this unfamiliar place, and draw his attention to the coziness of these unfamiliar surroundings which are in fact a home to others, and at the same time to the homelessness of the one sitting there now, whose obligation it is to make himself at home as quickly and eagerly as possible in this snug unfamiliar tableau. Glances like these make one shiver in the warmest sunshine, they pierce the soul with their coldness and loiter coldly within it for a while before departing just as they arrived.

"Very well now, back to work!" Tobler exclaimed. And the two of them left the table and made their way, the clerk following his master, back down to the office so as to carry out this command and return to their labors.

"Do you smoke?"

Indeed, Joseph was a passionate smoker.

"Take a cheroot out of that blue package there. Feel free to smoke while you're working. I do the same thing. And now look over here: this right here—and make sure you look it over carefully—is the required paperwork for the 'Advertising Clock.' Are you good at figures? All the better. Above all it's a matter—what are you doing? Young man, ashes belong in the ashtray. Within my own four walls I like things to be shipshape. All right, well, above all it's a matter of—grab a pencil over there—of, shall we say, putting together and precisely calculating the profitability of this enterprise. Have a seat over here, I'll give you all the details you'll need. And be so kind as to pay attention, I don't like having to repeat myself."

"Will I be good enough?" Joseph thought. It was at least helpful that he would be permitted to smoke while performing difficult tasks. Without the cheroot, he would honestly have started to doubt whether his brain was properly put together.

While the clerk was now writing, with his employer peering over his shoulder from time to time to observe his progress, the latter strolled up and down the length of the office holding a crooked, long-stemmed cheroot between his beautiful, blindingly white teeth and calling out all sorts of figures that were copied down industriously by a still somewhat inexperienced clerical hand. The blue-tinged smoke soon entirely enveloped the two figures working there, while outside the windows the weather appeared to be clearing up; now and again Joseph glanced up through the windowpanes and observed the changes quietly taking place in the sky. Once the dog barked outside the door. Tobler stepped out for a moment to calm the creature. After two hours of work had passed, Frau Tobler sent one of the children to announce that afternoon coffee was served. The table had been set in the summer house, as the weather had improved. The boss took up his hat and said to Joseph that now he should go have coffee and afterward prepare a fair copy of everything he'd written down hastily so far, and by the time he was finished, it would no doubt be evening.

Then he departed. Joseph watched as he descended the hill through the downward-sloping garden. What a stately figure he cuts, Joseph thought, and remained standing there for quite some time, then he went to have coffee in the pretty, green-painted summer house.

While they were partaking of this refreshment, the woman asked him: "Were you unemployed?"

"Yes," Joseph responded.

"For a long time?"

He told her what she wished to know, and she sighed each time he spoke of certain pitiable human beings and human circumstances. She did this perfectly casually and superficially, and moreover held each sigh in her mouth somewhat longer than necessary, as if she were basking in this pleasant sound and sentiment.

"Certain people," Joseph thought, "appear to take pleasure in contemplating unfortunate matters. Just look how this woman is making a show of pensiveness. She sighs just the way others might laugh, just as gaily. And this is the lady it is my duty to serve?"

Later he flung himself into his copy-work. Evening fell. The next morning it would be seen whether he was self-sufficient or a zero, intelligent or a machine, someone with his wits about him or utterly mindless. For today, he decided, enough. He cleared away his work and went to his room, happy that he could be alone for a little while. He began, not without melancholy, to unpack his suitcase, all his worldly possessions, piece by piece, recalling the countless moves during which he had availed himself, so many times now, of this same little suitcase. One could become so fond of simple objects, the young clerk felt. How would things go for him here with Tobler, he wondered as he placed the few linens he possessed into the armoire, taking care to do so as tidily as possible: "For better or worse, here I am, whatever happens." Silently vowing to make an effort, he tossed onto the floor a ball of old threads, bits of string, neckties, buttons, needles and scraps of torn linen. "If I am to eat and sleep here, I shall apply myself mentally and physically as well," he murmured. "How old am I now? Twenty-four! No longer particularly young." He had emptied the suitcase and now placed it in a corner. "I have fallen behind in life."

As soon as he thought that it was approximately time for this, he went downstairs to dinner, then to the post office in the village, then to bed.

In the course of the next day, it seemed to Joseph that he had succeeded in acquainting himself with the nature of the "Advertising Clock," for he had managed to comprehend that this profitable enterprise was a decorative clock which Herr Tobler was intending to franchise to railway station managers, restaurateurs, hotel owners, and the like. A genuinely quite fetching clock like this, Joseph calculated, would be hung up, for example, in one streetcar or several, in particularly conspicuous locations, so that all those riding and traveling would be able to set their pocket watches by it and always know how early or late in the day it was. The clock is really not bad, he thought in all seriousness, especially as it has the advantage of being associated with the institution of advertising. To this end, the clock was embellished with a single or double set of eagle wings, made of silver or even gold seemingly, that could be delicately adorned. And what else would one wish to adorn them with other than the precise addresses of the firms that had availed themselves of these wings or fields—"fields" being the technical term—for the profitable advertisement of their services and wares. "A field of this sort costs money; and it is imperative, as my master Herr Tobler quite rightly points out, to approach only the most successful business and manufacturing firms. The fees are to be paid in advance, according to contracts still to be drawn up, in monthly installments. Moreover, the Advertising Clock can be displayed virtually anywhere, both locally and abroad. It appears to me that Tobler has pinned his greatest hopes on this enterprise. To be sure, manufacturing these clocks and their copper and tin ornamentation will cost a great deal of money, and the painter in charge of the inscriptions will demand payment as well, but the advertising fees, it is to be hoped, and hoped with a high level of probability, will be arriving on a regular basis. What was it Herr Tobler said this morning? He had inherited a goodly sum of money but now has "thrown" his entire fortune into the Advertising Clock. What an odd thing to do, throwing ten or twenty thousand marks into clocks. It's good that I've made note of this word "throw," it seems to me to be actively in use and is moreover an exceedingly direct verb that I will perhaps soon have occasion to incorporate in my correspondence."

Joseph lit himself a cheroot.

"Quite a pleasant spot in fact, this technical office. To be sure, most aspects of the business practices employed here still mystify me. I have always had trouble comprehending new and unfamiliar things. I'm aware of this, oh yes. Generally people take me for smarter than I am, but sometimes not. How peculiar everything is!"

He took up a sheet of paper, crossed out the letterhead with two strokes of the pen and quickly wrote the following:

Dear Frau Weiss!

In point of fact you are the very first person I am writing to from up here. Thoughts of you are the first and easiest and most natural of all the many thoughts presently buzzing around in my head. No doubt you were often surprised at my behavior when I was your tenant. Do you still remember how you often had to shake me out of my dull, hermit-like existence and all my wicked habits? You are such a dear, good, simple woman, and perhaps you will permit me to adore you. How often—indeed, every four weeks or nearly—I came to see you in your room with the succinct request that you be patient with regard to my monthly rent. Never did you humiliate me, or rather, you did, but only with your kindness. How grateful I am to you and how glad I am to be able to say these words. What are your esteemed daughters now doing and how are they living? The bigger one will no doubt be getting married soon. And Fräulein Hedwig, is she still employed at the life insurance company? So many questions! Are these not utterly foolish questions, given that it's been only two days now since I parted from you? It seems to me, dear, revered Frau Weiss, as if I'd lived beside you for years and years and years, that's how lovely, long and peaceful the thought of having been with you feels. Can a person make your acquaintance without also being compelled to love you? You always told me I should be ashamed to be so young and yet so lacking in enterprise, for you always saw me sitting and lying in my dark room. Your face, your voice, your laughter were always a comfort to me. You are twice as old as me, and have twelve times as many worries and yet appear so young, even more so now than when I was still living with you. How could I always have been so tight-lipped in your presence? Incidentally, I still owe you money, don't I, and I'm almost glad of this. Exterior ties can preserve the life of inner bonds. Never doubt my respect for you. How foolishly I am speaking. I am living here in a lovely villa, and in the afternoons, when the weather is fine, I enjoy the privilege of drinking coffee in the summer house. My boss has stepped out for the moment. The house stands upon what one might call a green hill, and the train tracks run beside the road at the bottom, quite close to the lake. My lodgings are most agreeably situated in an, it appears to me, rather regal high tower. My master seems to be an honest man, if somewhat pompous. Possibly there will be scuffles of a personal nature between us one day. I do not wish for this to happen. Really I don't, I would prefer to live in peace. Farewell, Frau Weiss. The image I retain of you is beautiful and precious; it can't be put in a frame, but neither can it be forgotten.

Joseph folded up the sheet of paper and placed it in an envelope. He was smiling. The memory of this Frau Weiss had something so friendly about it, he didn't quite know why. And now he had written to a woman who, based on the impression he had given her of his person, would hardly be expecting so swift and affectionate a letter and would certainly not be prepared for it. Had this happenstance acquaintance had so great an influence on him? Or did he love to surprise and bewitch people? But the letter, once he had glanced over and inspected it, appeared appropriate to him, and he set off for the post office, as it was in any case time for this.

In the middle of the village, a young man covered in soot from head to toe suddenly stopped short before Joseph, gazing at him in laughter, and held out his hand. Joseph made a show of astonishment, for he really could not remember where and when in his previous existence he might have encountered this black figure. "So you're here, too, Marti?" the man cried out, and now Joseph recognized him: this man had been his comrade during the military training he had only just completed. He greeted him, but then pretended he was on a pressing errand and took his leave.

"Ah, the military," he thought, proceeding on his way, "how it forces people from all imaginable walks of life to join together in a single shared sentiment. In the entire country, there is no elegantly brought up young man, provided he is healthy, who will not one day suffer the fate of being compelled to leave his exclusive environment behind and make common cause with a random assortment of equally young common laborers, farmers, chimney-sweeps, clerks and even ne'er-do-wells. And what common cause it is! The air in the barracks is the same for everyone—it is deemed good enough for the baron's son and fitting for the humblest farmhand. All distinctions in rank and education tumble mercilessly into a large and to this day still unexplored chasm, that is, into camaraderie. Camaraderie rules the day, for it is what ties all these various things together. No one thinks of his comrade's hand as dirty, how could he possibly? The tyrant Equality is often unendurable or at least can seem so, but what an educator it is, what a teacher. Fraternity can be distrustful and petty with regard to trifles, but it can be great as well, and indeed it is great, for it possesses all the opinions, the feelings, the strength and drives of everybody. When a nation is able to guide the minds of its young people into this chasm—which is large enough to contain the earth and thus easily has room for a single country—it has then succeeded in barricading itself off in all directions, on all four borders, with fortresses that are impenetrable, for they are living fortresses equipped with feet, memories, eyes, hands, heads and hearts. Young people truly are in need of rigorous training . . ."

Here the clerk interrupted his train of thought.

Verily, he was speaking and thinking just like a general, he thought, laughing. Soon thereafter he was home again.

Joseph had been working at an elastic factory when he was called up. Now he thought back on this pre-military time. Before his eyes, an old elongated building appeared, a black gravel path, a narrow room, and the severe, bespectacled face of the supervisor. Joseph had been engaged there, as they say, provisionally, on a non-permanent basis. He and his entire person appeared to constitute merely a sort of frill, an ephemeral appendage, a knot tied for the nonce. When he took up this position, he already vividly saw before him the moment when he would leave it again. The apprentice learning the elastic trade was "above" him in every way. Joseph was constantly having to seek the advice of this person, who wasn't even fully grown yet. But in fact that didn't bother him at all. Oh, he had already gotten used to so very many things. He performed his work absent-mindedly, that is, he had to confess that he appeared to have lost track of many absolutely essential bits of knowledge. Certain things that other people were able to assimilate at astonishing speed took so strangely long to sink into his skull. What could he have done to change this? His main consolation, a thought constantly on his mind, was the "non-permanence" of his position. He lodged at the home of an elderly, pointy-nosed and pointy-mouthed spinster who occupied a most peculiar room, which was painted light green. An étagère held several old and modern books. The spinster was, it appeared, an idealist—not one of the fiery sort, but rather one who was frozen stiff. Joseph quickly learned that she maintained an assiduous amorous correspondence with—as he was able to ascertain from a lengthy epistle carelessly left lying upon the round table one day—either a book printer or architectural draftsman, he could no longer quite remember which, who had emigrated to the canton of Graubünden. He quickly read the letter, sensing as he did so that the injustice he was thereby committing was only a slight one. The letter, incidentally, was hardly worth being read on the sly, one might just as well have pinned up copies all over the city, so few secrets did it contain, so very little that an outsider might have been puzzled over. It was modeled on the most ordinary sorts of books, it contained travel descriptions sketched in broad strokes and adorned with crosshatching. How splendid the world was, he read in this letter, when one took the trouble to ramble through it on foot. It then went on to describe the sky, the clouds, the grassy slopes, the nanny goats, cows, cowbells and the mountains. How significant all these things were. Joseph occupied a tiny room at the rear of the building, where he read books. Any time he set foot in his little chamber, bookish pursuits began flapping wildly about his head. He was reading one of those huge novels you can keep reading for months. He took his meals at a pension filled with pupils from a technical school as well as apprentices in the mercantile trades. It cost him great effort to converse with these young people, and so he remained largely taciturn at meals. How mortifying it all was. In this, too, he was hanging by a thread, just a button that no one took the trouble to sew back on again, as the jacket itself no longer had much wear in it. Yes, his existence was nothing more than a hand-me-down jacket, a suit that didn't quite fit. Just outside the city lay a round hill of moderate height covered with vineyards and topped with a crest of forest. Well, that was certainly a charming spot for taking walks. Joseph regularly spent his Sunday mornings up here, recreation that invariably found him entangled in far-off, almost pathologically lovely reveries. Down at the factory, things were decidedly less agreeable, despite the incipient spring that was beginning to unfurl its tiny fragrant wonders on all the bushes and trees. One day the boss gave Joseph a proper dressing-down, indeed, in reprimanding him, he even went so far as to call him an imposter, and for what reason? Oh, it was just another instance of mental indolence. Empty heads, to be sure, can do considerable harm to a business venture, either by failing to perform the mathematical operations properly or else—and this is worse by far—neglecting to perform them at all. Joseph had found it so difficult to verify a calculation of interest that had been made in English pounds. He was lacking certain skills necessary to complete this task, and rather than admitting this openly to the supervisor, which he was ashamed to do, he placed his mendacious confirmation at the bottom of the page without having truly checked the calculations. He penciled in an M beside the final figure, which signified the firm and stable fact of its having been confirmed. But one day, a suspicious question on the part of the supervisor revealed that Joseph's verification had been faked and that he was in fact incapable of solving equations of this sort. After all, the currency in question was the English pound, and Joseph had no idea how to handle it. He deserved, his superior declared, to be thrown out in disgrace. If there was something he didn't understand, there was nothing dishonorable about that, but if he feigned understanding where there was none, that was outright theft. There was no other name for it, the supervisor said, and Joseph should be thoroughly ashamed of himself. Oh then, what a thunderous heart-pounding he had felt. It was as if a black wave were devouring his entire being. His own soul, which had always appeared to him anything but wicked, was now constricting him on all sides. He was trembling so violently that the numbers he was writing came out looking monstrously unfamiliar, distorted and huge. But an hour later he was again in such good spirits. He strolled to the post office, it was lovely weather, and walking along like that, he had the sudden impression that everything was kissing him. The small, sweet leaves all seemed to be fluttering toward him in a caressing, colorful drove. The people walking by, all of them perfectly ordinary, looked so beautiful he would have liked to fling his arms around them. He peered contentedly into all the gardens, and up at the open sky. The fresh white clouds were so beautiful and pure. And then the lush, sweet blue. Joseph hadn't forgotten the unpleasantness that had just transpired, he carried it with him, still with a sense of shame, but it had been transformed into something both carefree and wretched, both unchanging and touched by fate. He was still trembling a little and thought: "Must I be drubbed with humiliations before I can take true pleasure in God's world?" At the end of the workday, he stepped casually into a cigar shop he knew quite well. This shop was home to a woman who was possibly, well, probably, and in point of fact beyond all doubt, a whore. Joseph was in the habit of sitting down on a chair in her shop evening after evening, smoking a cigar and chatting with the owner. She'd taken a liking to him, that was plain to see. "If I please this woman," he thought, "then I am doing her a good turn by sitting beside her on a regular basis," and he acted accordingly. She told him the entire story of her youth and various lovely and unlovely things about her life. She was already growing old, and her face was rather hideously painted, but good eyes shone out of it, and as for her mouth: "How often it must have wept," Joseph thought. He always behaved nicely and politely in her presence, as if the appropriateness of this conduct went without saying. Once he stroked her cheek and noticed the joy she felt at this caress; she blushed and her mouth trembled as if she wished to say: "Too late, my friend." In earlier days, she had waited tables for a while, but what does any of this matter, seeing as the entire ephemeral frill was detached just a few weeks later. The boss gave Joseph a bonus as a farewell present despite the incident with the English pound, and wished him luck in the barracks. Now comes a railway journey through the vernally enchanted countryside, and then there is nothing left to know, from then on a person is nothing but a number—you are given a uniform, an ammunition pouch, a sidearm, an actual rifle, a cap and heavy marching shoes. You no longer belong to yourself; you are no longer anything more than a quantity of obedience and a quantity of drills. You sleep, eat, do calisthenics, shoot, march and allow yourself periods of rest, but all these things take place according to the rules. Even feelings are scrupulously monitored. At the outset, you feel as if your bones will break, but bit by bit the body steels itself, the flexible kneecaps become iron hinges, the head empties of thoughts, arms and hands become accustomed to the gun that accompanies the soldiers and recruits everywhere. In his dreams, Joseph heard orders being shouted and the staccato din of gunfire. For eight weeks things continued in this way; an eternity it wasn't, but sometimes it felt like one.

But what does any of this matter now that he is living in the home of Herr Tobler.

*

26

Two or three days is not such a terribly long time. It's not long enough to familiarize oneself completely with a room, let alone with an in fact rather imposing house. Joseph was in any case a slow learner, at least that's what he imagined, and what we imagine is never entirely lacking in underlying justifications. The Tobler house, moreover, consisted of two separate parts: it was both a residence and a place of business, and it was Joseph's duty and obligation to acquaint himself with both aspects. When family and business are situated in such immediate proximity that there is, as it were, physical contact, it isn't possible to become well-versed in one while overlooking the other. The responsibilities of an employee in such a household do not lie explicitly in one realm or explicitly in the other—they are dispersed. Even the hours for the discharge of duties are not precisely calibrated, but rather may at times extend deep into the night, or occasionally cease abruptly in the middle of the day for a while. He who enjoys the privilege of drinking afternoon coffee out in a summer house in the company of a woman who is certainly not half bad has no cause to become cross when he is called on to complete some urgent task after eight in the evening. He who enjoys such delicious lunches as Joseph must attempt to repay this kindness with redoubled effort. He who is permitted to smoke cheroots during business hours needn't grumble if the lady of the house asks him to take on some quick household chore or familial task, even when the tone of voice in which the request is made should happen to sound more imperious than timidly supplicant. Who is able to enjoy only pleasant and flattering things all the time? Who

27

would be so presumptuous vis-à-vis the world as to expect from it nothing but pillows to recline upon—never stopping to consider that these velvet and silken pillows, filled and stuffed with the finest down, cost money? But Joseph never expected any such thing. It is important to remember that Joseph had never had much cash in his possession.

Frau Tobler found there was something curious about him, something as it were out of the ordinary; she did not, however, form a good opinion of him, even approximately. He struck her as rather ridiculous in his worn-out, faded suit, which had been dyed a dark green color, but even in his behavior she thought she could discern something odd, an opinion which, in certain respects, was quite correct. His irresolute demeanor was odd, as was his obvious lack of self-confidence, and his manners were odd as well. On the other hand, it must be observed that Frau Tobler, a bourgeoise of highly authentic lineage, was quick to find many things odd if they appeared even only the slightest bit alien to her world-view. This being the case, however, let's not allow ourselves to get too worked up over such a woman finding such a young man odd, but rather report on their conversation. We shall return to the little summer house and to the hour of five o'clock:

"What a magnificent day it is," Frau Tobler said.

"Oh yes," the assistant responded, "it really is splendid." Still seated at the table, he half turned to gaze off into the blue distance. The lake was a pale, pale blue. A steamer dispersing musical sounds was gliding past. One could just make out the handkerchiefs being waved about by the people enjoying this excursion. The smoke from the steamer flew toward the back of the boat where it was absorbed into the air. The mountains on the distant shore were scarcely discernable through the haze that this utterly perfect day had spread across the lake. The peaks appeared to have been woven out of silk. Indeed, the entire round vista was blue; even the nearby greenery and the red of the rooftops had a bluish tinge to them. You could hear a single droning sound, as if all the air, all that transparent space, were quietly singing. Even this droning and buzzing sounded and looked blue, or nearly! How tasty the coffee was again today. "Why does it make me think of home, of my childhood, when I drink this peculiar coffee?" Joseph thought.

The woman began to speak of her holiday that past summer at Lake Lucerne. This year, alas, there'd be nothing of the sort. It was out of the question. And then it was also so very beautiful here as well. You didn't need a summer holiday when you could live in such a place. At bottom, one was almost always presumptuous in one's wishes, always desiring something or other, which of course was perfectly natural—Joseph nodded—but at times this resembled outright arrogance.

She laughed. "How strangely she laughs," the subordinate mused and went on thinking: "One might, if one was set on it, take this way of laughing as the basis for a geographical study. This laugh precisely designates the region from which this woman comes. It is a handicapped laugh, it comes out of her mouth in a slightly unnatural way, as if it had always been held a little in check in early years by an all-too-strict upbringing. But it is a lovely feminine laugh, even a tiny bit frivolous. Only highly respectable women are permitted to laugh in such a way."

Meanwhile the woman had continued to speak, describing that really quite idyllic and agreeable holiday. A young American had rowed her out onto the lake each day in a skiff. What a chivalrous young man he was. And then, of course, it was so delightful, so refreshing for a married woman like herself to be able to spend a few weeks all alone, and in so very beautiful a place. Without her husband, without the children. There's no need to imagine this in an indelicate light. To just do nothing all day long but eat splendid food and lie in the shade beneath such a magnificent, broad-limbed chestnut tree, just such a tree as stood in that spot where she took her holiday last year. Such a tree. She kept picturing it, and herself lying beneath it. She'd also had a tiny white little dog, she always brought it to bed with her. Such a clean, delicate little creature. Well, this animal only served to reinforce the charming impression she was being invited to indulge in: that she was a lady, a true lady. Later she'd had to give the dog away.

"I must go back to work," Joseph said, rising from his seat.

"Are you really so very diligent?"

"Well, one does what one considers one's duty." With these words he withdrew. In the office he was confronted by an invisible-visible apparition: the Advertising Clock. He sat down at his desk and resumed his correspondence. The mailman came to collect a C.O.D. charge; it was a trifling sum, Joseph paid it out of his own pocket. Then he wrote a few letters on behalf of the Advertising Clock. What great investments had to be made in pursuit of such a clock!

"It is like a small or large child, this clock," the clerk thought, "like a headstrong child that requires constant self-sacrificing care and doesn't even thank one for watching over it. And is this enterprise flourishing, is the child growing? Little progress can be seen. An inventor does love his inventions. Tobler has become quite enamored of this costly clock. But what will other people think of it? An idea must entrance those who hear of it, fill them with enthusiasm, otherwise it will be difficult to put into practice. As for myself, I firmly believe in the possibility of bringing this idea to fruition, and I believe in it because it is my duty to believe in it, because I am being paid to do so. But come to think of it, what sort of salary am I to receive?"

Indeed, no arrangements had yet been made in this regard.

For the rest of the week, all was calm. What might possibly have troubled the peace? Joseph was obedient and took pains to display a cheerful expression. And what cause did he have to be particularly grumpy? For the time being he appeared to have every cause to feel content. After all, he hadn't exactly been coddled in the military either. He probed ever deeper into the nature of the Advertising Clock and was already of the opinion that he had fathomed it in its entirety. What did it matter that two bills to the tune of four hundred marks apiece had gone unpaid? It was simple enough to postpone the due date of these items for a month; Joseph even found it gave him tremendous pleasure to be permitted to write to these dunning accounts: "Please be patient a short while longer. The financing of my patents will soon be completed, and at such time, it will be possible for me to resolve these overdue obligations promptly."

He had several letters of this sort to write, and felt pleased at the facility with which he was mastering the style of business correspondence.

Already he had explored much of the village. Strolling to the post office was always quite enjoyable. There were two ways to get there: either by taking the broad road that led along the lake, or by crossing over the hill between orchards and farmhouses. He almost always chose the latter route. All these things appeared quite simple to him.

On Sunday Tobler presented him with a good German cigar along with five marks pocket money so that he could "treat himself to something" now and again.

The house stood there so beautifully in the bright sunshine. To Joseph it appeared a veritable Sunday house. He walked down through the garden, swinging his swim trunks in one hand, and descended all the way to the lake, where he undressed in a leisurely fashion in a dilapidated bathing shack whose cracked boards admitted the sunlight, then he threw himself into the water. He swam far out, he was in such good spirits. What swimming person, provided he is not about to drown, can help being in excellent spirits? It appeared to him as if the gay, warm, smooth surface of the lake were taking on a rounded, vaulted shape. The water was simultaneously cool and tepid. Perhaps a faint breath of wind came whispering across it, or else a bird flew past above his head, high up in the air. Once he came close to a small boat; a single man was sitting in it, a fisherman peacefully fishing and rocking away his Sunday. What softness, what shimmering light. And with your naked, sensation-filled arms, you slice into this wet, clean, benevolent element. With every stroke of your legs, you advance a bit further in this beautiful deep wetness. From below, you are buoyed up by warm and chilly currents. You plunge your head briefly beneath the water to irrigate the excitement in your breast, squeezing shut your mouth and eyes and breath, so as to feel this delightful sensation in your entire body. Swimming, you want to shout or at least cry out, or at least laugh, or at least say something, and you do. And then from the shores of the lake echo these sounds among high, distant shapes. These wonderful bright colors on a Sunday morning such as this. You splash about with your hands and feet, stand upright in the water, floating and, as it were, balancing upon a trapeze, all the while keeping your arms in motion. There's no sinking then. Now you press your closed eyes once more into the fluid, green, firm, unfathomable entity and swim to shore.

How splendid that was!

Meanwhile lunch guests had arrived.

The story behind these guests is as follows: Joseph's predecessor in his position was a certain Wirsich. This Wirsich had won the Toblers' hearts. They recognized in him a person capable of great devotion and deeply valued his efficiency. He was an extremely precise individual, but only in a state of sobriety. As long as he was sober, he was endowed with practically all—indeed one can say with all—the virtues desirable in a clerk. He was exceedingly orderly, he possessed knowledge of both a commercial and legal nature, he was industrious and energetic. He was skillful at representing his employer at any time and under most any circumstances in a confidence-inspiring, convincing way. On top of this, he wrote a fair hand. Quick-witted as he was, and possessed of a lively interest in all things, this Wirsich had found it child's play to further his employer's business interests with autonomy and to the latter's complete satisfaction. His book-keeping skills, moreover, were exemplary. But all these fine qualities could sometimes vanish altogether at a moment's notice: when he had been drinking. Wirsich was no longer a young man, he was around thirty-five years old, and this is an age at which certain passions, if their bearer has not yet learned to govern them, often take on a horrific appearance and terrifying dimensions. The consumption of alcohol regularly (that is, from time to time) turned this man into a wild irrational beast with which, quite understandably, it was impossible to reason. Time and again, Herr Tobler showed him the door, instructing him to pack his things and never return. Wirsich would in fact leave the house, cursing and shouting imprecations, but then, as soon as he was himself again, he would reappear with a contrite poor-sinner face on the very threshold that just a few days before, in the madness and folly of his inebriation, he had vehemently sworn he would never again cross. And miracle of miracles: Tobler would take him back again each time. He would harangue him mercilessly on these occasions, as one might discipline poorly behaved children, but then he would say that Wirsich could stay, that they would draw a veil over what had occurred and give him one last chance. This happened four or five times. There was something irresistible about Wirsich, which was particularly in evidence whenever he opened his mouth to utter a plea or an apology. In such cases he appeared so utterly penitent and distraught that the Toblers were overcome with a feeling of warmth, heat even, and they forgave him, without themselves knowing why. And then there was that peculiar and, as it appeared, profound impression that Wirsich always succeeded in making upon persons of the opposite sex. It can be assumed with reasonable certainty that Frau Tobler, too, was susceptible to this bizarre spell, this inexplicable magic. She respected Wirsich as long as he was even-tempered and sane, and she felt a compassion that even she found inexplicable for the ruffian and brute. His very looks were as if made to be judged by women. His sharp masculine features, supported in their sharpness and assurance by his pallid skin, his black hair, and his large, deep-set dark eyes, were just as involuntarily appealing as a certain dryness that adhered to all the rest of his bearing and nature—a homespun quality that generally gives the impression of kind-heartedness and strength of purpose, two features no sensitive woman can resist.

And so it happened that Wirsich was always taken back again. What a woman says to her husband over lunch in a light, laughing, luxurious tone of voice never fails to influence him, particularly, in this case, as Tobler himself had "always been quite fond of this unfortunate individual." Wirsich's mother regularly came to call each time her son was reinstated, to give thanks on his behalf. Her, too, they were fond of. People do, by the way, tend to cherish those upon whom they have been able to impose their power and influence. Wealth and bourgeois prosperity like to dispense humiliations, or, no, that's going too far, but they do have a fondness for gazing down on the humiliated, a sentiment in which we must acknowledge the presence of a certain benevolence, and of a certain brutality as well.

One night Wirsich went too far. He returned home from an evening spent at The Rose, a public house on the main road into town that was heavily frequented by all sorts of vagabonds including unsavory women, drunk out of his mind, blustering and shouting, and demanded to be let in. When he was refused entry, he availed himself of the crooked stick he was carrying to shatter the pane of glass set into the front door and then as much of the lattice as he could manage. He also threatened in a terrifying, unrecognizable voice to "send the whole place up in flames," as he expressed himself in the ferocity of his ravaged mind, bellowing so loudly that not only the whole neighborhood must have heard him but even those living farther off in the surrounding countryside, and indulging in the most shameful execrations of his benefactors. He had almost, with the help of that physical strength possessed by every unconscious, unfeeling brute, succeeded in breaking down the door—lock and bolt were already wobbling alarmingly—when Herr Tobler, who, it seemed, had at last lost all patience, thrust open the door from within and fell upon the drunkard with a hail of violent blows that knocked Wirsich to the gravel at his feet. In response to Tobler's unambiguous demand that he instantaneously make himself scarce, as he would otherwise be subjected to further and similar blows, Wirsich raised himself up on all fours to crawl out of the garden. Several times the figure of the drunkard—in the moonlight, those standing above him were able to observe each of his monstrous gestures— tumbled to the ground again, then again stood up and finally thrust itself, much like a clumsy bear, out of the garden altogether, making for the main road, where it was lost from sight.

Two weeks following this nocturnal incident, Tobler held in his hands a voluminous letter of apology from Wirsich wherein the miscreant apparently pledged in well-nigh classical style to mend his ways and requested that Herr Tobler offer him employment one single last time, as otherwise Wirsich would find himself reduced to the most bitter adversity. Both he and his elderly mother implored that the old, agreeable benevolence he had enjoyed might be his once more—just one last time—even though, as he openly admitted, painful as this was for him, he had already forfeited many times over his right to expect kindness. Wirsich, the letter concluded, was filled with such longing for the household, for the entire family he had come to love and cherish, for the site of his erstwhile employment, that he had to tell himself that either he would be permitted to hope for a rebirth of his former existence and be filled with good cheer, or else the bolt had snapped shut behind him once and for all, and all that remained to him was despair, remorse, shame and bitterness.

But it was too late. The bolt had, in fact, snapped shut and locked: he had already been replaced. The very next morning following that appalling nocturnal scene, Tobler had betaken himself to the capital and paid a visit to the Employment Referral Office, where he had engaged Joseph. The aforementioned letter arrived in the Tobler household on the same day Joseph did.

Meanwhile, the guests who had arrived for Sunday luncheon were none other than Wirsich and his mother.

Feeling fresh from the exertion of swimming, Joseph greeted his predecessor warmly. Before the old woman he made a slight bow. It was immediately obvious that the mood at the lunch table was one of dejection. Very little was said, and the few comments ventured were of a general nature. A sense of misery and gingerliness had cast a pall over the white tablecloth and the fragrant steaming food upon it, as well as over the faces of the people seated there. Herr Tobler's eyes were popping, but as for the rest he was cheerful and friendly and in a benevolently condescending tone of voice encouraged his guests to dig in. Every meal tastes good after a swim, and in the open air, beneath a blue sky like this, almost anything one might eat would taste delicious, but today's meal struck Joseph as utterly glorious, simple as it was. The others, too, seemed to be enjoying it, not least the old woman who, for the occasion, had donned an air of refined worldliness. Where might this down-at-heels lady be living, and how? In what rooms, in what surroundings? How shabby and gaunt she appeared. She looked, as it were, thrifty, scanty or skimpy, particularly beside the voluptuous, upper-class Frau Tobler, who had been born and raised amid plenty and warmth. Frau Wirsich and Frau Tobler. Indeed, if distinctions exist in this world, these were differences of the purest, truest sort.

Frau Tobler always looked a bit haughty, but how charmingly this faint, unwavering trace of haughtiness flattered the lines of her face and figure. One wouldn't have wanted to wish it away, it belonged to her appearance, just as a resonant, ineffable magic belongs to a folk song. This song rang out delicately in the very highest notes, Frau Wirsich understood and felt this quite distinctly. How paltry was the sound of the one song, how rich that of the other. Herr Tobler was pouring out red wine. He wanted to fill Wirsich's glass as well, but his mother quickly covered her son's glass with her old bony hand.

"Ah bah, why ever not? He's got to drink something, too," Tobler exclaimed.

The eyes of the old woman instantly filled up with tears. Seeing this, all of them shuddered. Wirsich wanted to whisper something to his mother, but some stiff stony force, against which he was helpless to defend himself, paralyzed his tongue. He sat there mute as a mullet, gazing down at his own timid eating. Frau Wirsich had withdrawn her hand, thereby declaring, as it were, that now of course it was a matter of complete indifference to her whether her son drank or not. Her gesture said: Go on, fill his glass: All is lost in any case. Wirsich took a few small sips from his glass, and he seemed to be filled with an insurmountable dread of that thing that had toppled him from a position in the world that had in fact been quite comfortable.

O Frau Wirsich, how your tear-sullied eyes utterly overshadow those few resplendent worldly mannerisms you've adopted. You had so intended to confine yourself to the most delicate gestures, and now your grief has gotten the better of you. Your old hands, as creased as a worried forehead, are trembling considerably. What is your mouth saying? Nothing? Ah, Mother Wirsich, one is required to speak in respectable company. Just look how a certain other lady is observing you.

Frau Tobler was glancing casually over at Frau Wirsich with

concerned but cold eyes, at the same time stroking the curls of her youngest child, who sat beside her. A genuinely prosperous woman! On one side, childish affection and trust were beaming up at her, while the other was given over to the woes of a sister human being. Both sides, the sweet and the sorrowful alike, were flattering to this woman. In a soft voice, she spoke a few words of comfort to Frau Wirsich, which the latter fended off, if humbly, by shaking her head. Now the meal was over. Herr Tobler passed around his cigar case, and the gentlemen smoked. This sunlight, this wonderful scenery of mountain, lake, meadow. And then this narrow, wary conversation among this little cluster of people. Certainly it was important to be merciful to others, they were people too. This sentiment was clearly visible in the expression of the lady of the house. But precisely this silent insinuation of the desire to act with mercy was utterly merciless. It was devastating.

The two women then chatted about the Tobler children; both seemed delighted to have found a topic free of the slightest hint of offense. Besides which the conversation evolved quite naturally. They just forgot themselves for a little while. From time to time the old woman's eye would come to rest on Joseph's figure, face and bearing, as if to study their merits and shortcomings and mentally compare them with those of her son. The boys soon leapt from their seats to go play in the garden, and the girls followed them, leaving the grown-up ladies and gentlemen alone at the table. Meanwhile the maid had arrived with a wooden tray in her hand to clear away the plates. Everyone got up. Tobler instructed Joseph to "go fetch the glass ball." The glass ball was the pride of the Villa Tobler.

This ball was suspended by narrow chains and hinges within a delicate iron frame and was parti-colored, so that all the images of the world reflected in it—in a perspective that appeared round and, as it were, stacked one thing atop the other—shone green, blue, brown, yellow and red. It was approximately as large as a larger-than-life human head, but together with its stand it surely weighed a good eighty or ninety pounds and was difficult to lift. During rainy weather, the ball could never be left standing out of doors. It was always being carried outside and in, inside and out. If it ever happened to get wet, Tobler would rant and rave. To see the ball wet pained him; after all, there are people who treat certain inanimate possessions as if they were endowed with life and expect others to do the same. So Joseph quickly ran to fetch the lovely colorful glass ball, for he had already had occasion to observe Tobler's great fondness for it.

After he had satisfied the desires and the fair-weather whim and pleasure of his master, he adroitly slipped off, out of sight of the others, charged up the stairs and disappeared into his tower room. How peaceful and quiet it was up here. He felt liberated, though he didn't quite know from what. But it was enough merely to have this feeling; the true causes, he thought, were surely present, hidden somehow and somewhere, but what were causes to him? There appeared to be something golden hovering about him. He gazed at himself for a moment in the mirror: Oh, he still looked quite young, not at all like Wirsich. He couldn't entirely suppress a laugh. He felt moved to pick up the photograph of his departed mother. The photograph was just standing there on the table. Why shouldn't he pick it up and look at it? He gazed at it for what seemed a long time, then returned it to its place. Then he took yet another picture, a more recent one, from his jacket pocket; it was the portrait of a dance student, a girl he had met "in the city." That entire distant metropolis filled with people—this grand, animated image—how distant it now appeared to him, as if it had vanished a long time ago. He couldn't help interrupting these thoughts with an involuntary laugh. He was taking ponderous steps up and down the room, smoking of course. Was it really always necessary to carry about such a torpedo in one's mouth? How splendidly the fresh mountain and lake air was streaming through his elevated four walls. And this is where Wirsich had lodged? The man whose face was stricken with suffering? Joseph bent his breathing head out the window, into the world's Sunday and noonday freedom. And to think that I have five marks pocket money and am able to stick my head out such a majestically constructed and situated window!

Down in the office, meanwhile, the mood was more subdued than majestic. The tone in which Herr Tobler and his former clerk, Herr Wirsich, were conversing there was very, very muted, almost muffled.

"You've got to admit yourself," Tobler was saying, "that for the time being there can be no question of reinstating our former reciprocal relations. It was you who forced me to break things off, I would have liked to keep you on. I have no reason to send Marti away, he's doing a good job. I'm sorry, Wirsich, please believe me, but you have only yourself to blame. No one instructed you to treat me, your employer, like a stupid school-boy. You're going to have to make your peace with the consequences of your actions. I will be glad to do everything my sense of propriety allows to help you find another post elsewhere. Have another cigar. Here, take one."

Was it really true, then, that there was nothing to be done?

"No, there isn't, not any more. And really you need only remind yourself of all those things you bellowed at me that glorious night, and you will see that there can no longer be any sort of relations resumed between us."

"Oh, Herr Tobler, it was only the liquor, it wasn't me!"

"What nonsense, the liquor and not you! That's just the thing. I myself thought five or six times: That isn't him. Of course all these things are you. Human beings do not consist of two separate entities, otherwise life on earth would in truth be far too simple. If everyone was just allowed to protest "It wasn't me" every time he did something stupid, what meaning would the concepts order and disorder retain? No, no, for God's sake let people be who they are. I have gotten to know you in two quite different guises. Do you believe the world is obliged to think of you as a child, a little lapdog? You are a grown man, and expected to know what is proper and fitting. I see no cause to take into account secret passions, or whatever those things are called that the philosophers go on about. I am a business-man and the head of a household, and cannot help but feel an obligation to bar my doors to idiocy and impropriety. You were always such an industrious worker, why did you have to subject me to such scurrilous behavior? You would laugh at me, simply laugh at me, and with good cause, if I were foolish enough to take you back again. So now I've given you my opinion, let's speak no more of it."

"So everything is finished between us?"

"For the time being, yes."

With these words, Tobler walked out the door of the office and into the garden, where he shot his wife a meaningful glance and then took up position beside his beloved glass ball. Cigar between his teeth, he gazed down contentedly at his property, thereby presenting, unbeknownst to himself, a flawless tableau of seigneurial midday leisure.

Wirsich, who was still standing rooted in the office, right where he happened to be standing when Tobler left him, was surprised there by Joseph. Each stood looking the other up and down, wide-eyed. But then they found it appropriate to strike up a conversation about the ongoing developments in Tobler's technical enterprises, a conversation that quickly devolved into an intolerable series of gaps and pauses and eventually broke off altogether. Wirsich was trying to make a show of self-possession, of standing above the factual circumstances, and so he reeled off all sorts of advice and practical hints for his successor, who was not, however, particularly taken with them.

And now the afternoon coffee hour had come to an end. It was time for the two visitors to bite the bullet and take their leave. Everyone shook hands, and then, if you were one of those still standing up on the hillside, you could observe two persons unsteadily walking and making their way along the gleaming garden fence, adorned at one-meter intervals with gilded stars, in the direction of the main road. It was a melancholy sight. Frau Tobler heaved yet another sigh. A moment later, she burst into laughter at something or other, and it was plain to hear how the sigh and the laugh shared one and the same timbre, one and the same tone.

Joseph, who was standing off to one side, thought: "There they go, the man and the old woman. From up here, they are no longer visible, and already they are half forgotten. How quickly one forgets people's gestures and bearing and deeds. Now they are hurrying as best they can along the dusty road to get to the train station on time, or the ferryboat. On this entire long walk—for ten minutes is a long time for two people filled with defeat and worry to walk—they will no doubt exchange scarcely any words at all, and yet they will be speaking a quite comprehensible language, a silent, all too comprehensible one. Sorrow has its own special way of speaking. And now they are buying their tickets, or perhaps they already have them, it's a well known fact that round-trip tickets exist, and now the train comes roaring up, and poverty and uncertainty climb aboard. Poverty is an old woman with bony covetous hands. Today she attempted to make conversation at table like a lady but did not fully succeed. Now she is being carried off, seated beside Uncertainty, in whom, if she peers closely enough, she will have to recognize her own son. And the car is filled with pleasure-seekers out on Sunday excursions, and they are singing, hooting, chattering and laughing. One young fellow is holding his girl in his arms so as to kiss her again and again on her voluptuous mouth. How terribly painful the joy of others can appear to an aggrieved soul! The poor old woman feels she is being stabbed in the throat and heart. She might at any moment cry out loudly for help. On they go. Oh, this eternal clattering of wheels. The woman takes her red-colored handkerchief from her skirt pocket to hide the utterly foolish and conspicuous tears now flowing torrentially from her old eyes. When a person has grown as old this woman—no, such a person should no longer have to weep. But what do the things of this strange earth care for the precepts of noble propriety? The hammers come crashing blindly down, striking sometimes a poor child, sometimes—and you should take note of this, Frau Wirsich— an aged woman. And now mother and son have reached their destination and are preparing to leave the train. What must things look like now where they are living?"

He was awoken from this reverie by Tobler's melodious voice. What was he doing there all by himself? He should come and help finish off the red wine. A bit later, the master of the house said to him:

"Well. So Wirsich is gone for good now. I hope that a certain other someone will be more appreciative of the privileges a person enjoys who is permitted to live up here with us. There is surely no need for me to explain whom I mean by this 'certain other someone.' You are laughing. Go ahead, laugh, I don't mind. But one thing I will tell you right now: if you should have any sorts of urges, I mean to say on Sundays for example, for which a healthy young person certainly shouldn't be blamed, see to it that you go to the city, such desires are amply provided for there, more than amply. In my home, you must understand,

I will not tolerate anything of the kind. Wirsich made his presence here intolerable through precisely this sort of behavior. Decency is absolutely required."

Then they spoke of business matters.

Above all else, Herr Tobler said, it was crucial that funds be mobilized, this was the main thing. What they needed to do was interest a capitalist in their inventions, a factory owner perhaps, so that the patented technical articles could be put into production with no further delay. But in any case, anyone who brought pecuniary resources to their ventures would be welcome—he could be a tailor for all Tobler cared—and there would be no need for him to understand the first thing about their enterprises, that's what he was for, Tobler.

"Copy down this advertisement."

Joseph took a pencil and notebook from his pocket. The following was dictated to him:

FOR CAPITALISTS!

Engineer seeks contact with capitalists for the financing of his patents. Profitable, absolutely risk-free undertaking. Address inquiries to . . .

"And when you go down to the village tomorrow morning, you can bring home a fresh pack of cheroots, get the 500-count package. We've got to have something to smoke around here."

Little by little, evening arrived.

Two women appeared in the summer house, the owner of a firm that produced parquet floors and her daughter, a tall freckled girl, both of them living in the immediate vicinity. Together with these women and his own wife, Tobler began to play a card game that was well known and well loved in all the land. Usually this game was played only by men, but it was just beginning to become fashionable among women as well, particularly among women of the so-called "better sort," that is, women who did not need to work so very hard all day long—for these, after all, are the "better" ones.

These three women, Frau Tobler, the factory owner and her daughter, were outstanding card players, the young lady being the best and most "cut-throat" among them, and Frau Tobler the weakest. When the daughter played a trump, she always worked herself into a proper tizzy, as was fitting for lovers of this game. What's more, she would smack the tabletop with her girlish fist just like the most hard-boiled old gambler, and would often utter little maidenly shrieks whenever the game took a turn to her advantage. Her figure was angular and her face rather unlovely. Her mother's conduct was cultivated and wise. How could an older, well-situated woman like herself have displayed anything but impeccable manners?

Observing this card game that he had not yet had opportunity to learn, Joseph thought to himself, "It is interesting to watch the faces of these three women as they play. One of them, the oldest, is unperturbed, she smiles as she plays. My Frau Tobler, on the other hand, is utterly rapt. The game's magic has captivated her. Her face is glowing with her genuine, passionate love of the game. This makes her face more beautiful to a certain extent. But of course she is my employer, and it is in no way appropriate for me to find fault with her. With regard to this diversion, she is like an attentive child. But the third one, that man-maiden over there, Lord help us, that's one to watch out for! She rolls her eyes while she is bidding and playing, thinking who knows what sorts of outlandish things, and without a doubt considers herself the most beautiful, clever and best of women. Not even at a distance of two meters or in one's dreams would it be agreeable to kiss her. A depraved girl. Just look what a pointy nose she has. The slightest touch of it could freeze you to death. And in what a false tone of voice she speaks, laughs, laments and shrieks. I consider her a wicked, devilish person, and next to her my Frau Tobler is an angel."

He would have gone on musing in this way if something had not suddenly occurred to Frau Tobler, an idea she gave voice to at once: taking a boat ride on the lake that very night. It was such a beautiful evening, and the trifle it would cost wasn't even worth discussing. As the card game had just come to its conclusion, no one had any cause to object to the plan, not even Tobler himself, who grumbled his assent. Joseph, in his role as errand boy, was sent down to the village with instructions to procure a wide boat with three benches, "quickly now, and no dallying along the way," as night was already beginning to fall, and to paddle it along the shore until he was close to the villa. Everyone else would get into the boat at the bottom of the hill, where there was a sort of small harbor. The clerk had already set out to perform his errand. Tobler, for his part, declined to join them. Nor could one ask the old factory proprietress to clamber into a boat, but in their place Frau Tobler decided to bring the children along. The young lady declared herself willing not only to take part but to share the work of rowing, whereupon the lady of the house went off to prepare herself for the excursion.

The passengers were already waiting at the landing-place just downhill from the Tobler villa, standing upon the broad stone slabs of an old embankment that was no longer in use, when at last Joseph rowed up in the boat. All of them began to get in, Frau Tobler leading the way so that the children could be handed across to her one at a time. The two boys were being quite unruly; their attention was called to the dangerousness of their wild, reckless behavior, and they quieted down. The girls sat perfectly still, they held fast to the sides of the boat with their little hands. Joseph was the last to get in, as he had been holding the vessel steady by a rattling chain until the very last moment. And then they were suddenly underway. Joseph plied the oars, he was good at this, but they made only slow progress; no one, however, was demanding that things go any faster. How cool the world became all at once. Frau Tobler looked at the children, warning them to be good and under no circumstances to make any sudden moves, as otherwise a terrible catastrophe would occur and all of them would mercilessly drown. All four children listened to these strange words and kept still, even the boys, because they were feeling somewhat apprehensive now out in the middle of the night and on the murmuring water in this slowly gliding boat. Frau Tobler quietly remarked how beautiful it was here, and what a good idea it had been, or so it seemed to her, to have suggested the outing. It was nice to have a pleasure to enjoy for a change, and her husband would have done well to come with them. But, she added, he had no appreciation for such things. How cool it was, how lovely!

Describing a certain distance from the boat, Leo, the large dog, swam behind them in the dark glittering water. They called out to him. Above all it was the children calling out endearments to him. Beside Frau Tobler lay her little silk umbrella. A feathered hat adorned her oblong face. Her hands and arms were encased in long white gloves. The young lady was chattering her head off. But Frau Tobler, who was usually herself not particularly disinclined to do the same, gave only absentminded, monosyllabic answers. Something like a beautiful, happy nature reverie seemed to have made the ordinary concerns of daylight hours and their lengthy expostulation appear to her unimportant and unworthy. Her large eyes were quietly, beautifully shining along with the gentle motion of the boat. Was Joseph growing tired from rowing, she asked. Oh no, he replied, what was she thinking. The young lady wanted to swap seats with Joseph and take a turn at the oars, but Frau Tobler refused to allow it, saying it would make the boat unsteady. It didn't matter if they weren't going very fast, she said, the slower Joseph rowed, the longer their outing—which in any case was a short one—would last, and that's what would please her best, for it was so lovely.

This woman had been born into genuinely bourgeois circles. She'd grown up amid an atmosphere of utility and cleanliness, in regions where usefulness and sober-mindedness were the highest virtues. She had not had many romantic pleasures in her life, but this is precisely why she so loved them, for she treasured them in the depths of her soul. Just because a thing like this had to be kept carefully hidden from her husband and the world, so that she wouldn't seem a "hysterical goose," didn't mean pleasure had to perish; on the contrary, it continued to live its own peculiar life while buttoned up inside her. Some day, some little opportunity would come along to greet her and coax her with its large eyes, and then the thing that had been halfway forgotten would grow warm and come to life again, though just for a short while. A person who is allowed to display openly his love of and desire for pleasures, a person whose life circumstances make these pleasures easily and conveniently available, will find his soul and heart all too quickly deadened, and everything that once burned within them extinguished. No, this woman had no eye for color or anything of the sort, she knew nothing of the laws of beauty, but precisely for this reason she was able to feel what was beautiful. She had never had time to read a book full of lofty ideas, indeed, she had never given a single thought to what was lofty and what lowly, but loftiness itself was now paying her a visit, and the essence of deep feeling itself, attracted by her unknowingness, bedewed her consciousness with its wet wings.

Yes, it was cool and dark all around the slowly gliding boat. The lake was perfectly calm. The silence and peacefulness joined with human perceptions and the impenetrable blackness of the night. From the shore came flashes of scattered lights and a few sounds, among them a man's clarion voice, and now from the opposite bank the warm notes of an accordion could be heard. This music sent its notes twisting and entwining, a flowery or ivy-like thing, about the dark fragrant body of the lake's summer night silence. Everything appeared to have partaken of a strange contentment, gratification and meaning. Depth affixed itself to the unfathomable wetness. The woman dangled her hand in the water, she was saying something, but she seemed to be speaking her words into the water. How it bore them along, this beautiful deep water. Once another boat, steered by a man sitting alone in it, passed close by the Tobler vessel. Frau Tobler gave a faint cry of surprise, indeed almost of terror. No one had seen the other boat coming, it appeared to have thrust itself suddenly next to them from the far unknown distance, or else from out of the depths. The sky was completely covered with stars. How the stars lifted them up and bore them and spun them around. The woman said she was beginning to feel almost chilly, and she threw a shawl she had brought with her about her shoulders. To Joseph it appeared, as he gazed at her, as if she were smiling there in the darkness, but he wouldn't have been able to discern this precisely. "Where is our Leo," she asked. "There he is, there!" cried Walter, the boy. "He's swimming after us!"

Rise up and ascend, O depths! Yes, there they are—rising from the surface of the water, creating a new enormous lake out of the space between sky and lake. The depths have no shape, and there is no eye that can see what they are depicting. They are singing as well, but in notes no ear can catch. They reach out their long moist hands, but there is no hand able to grasp them. They rear up on either side of the nocturnal boat, but no knowledge in any way present knows this. No eye is looking into the eye of the depths. The water disappears, the glassy abyss opens up, and the boat now appears to be drifting along, peaceful and melodious and safe, beneath the surface of the water.

It must be admitted that Joseph has surrendered himself somewhat too completely to these flights of fancy. He hardly notices that their journey has come to an end when they strike land, or rather, a fat pole sticking out of the water close to the embankment where they had planned to disembark. Tobler, standing right next to them, shouts to his underling that he ought to pay more attention. He couldn't imagine, Tobler went on, in what part of the world Joseph had learned how to row and steer. But in fact no harm's been done, and all emerge from the boat unscathed. The rest of the night was spent in a charming beer garden filled with people, where Tobler came across some acquaintances, a railway conductor accompanied by his wife, and the two of them were soon being liberally engaged in conversation. The small, merry official's wife talked about her chickens and eggs and the brisk business she was doing with these two profitable articles. There was a great deal of laughter. Joseph was introduced to the others by Tobler in his capacity as "my employee." A young French girl who worked as a salesclerk in a department store scurried past the gathering. "Une jolie petite française," the conductor's wife said, evidently overjoyed at having an occasion to recite a few French words she knew by heart. This is always the case in Germanic lands, people love to be able to show that they understand French.

"Frau Tobler," Joseph thought, "knows no French at all, the poor thing!"

Later they all went home.

When Joseph had returned to his room and lit a candle, he

went to the window half undressed instead of going straight to bed and, standing there, gave voice to this soliloquy: "What is it that I am accomplishing? I can, if I like, lie down upon this bed at once without anyone disturbing me, and fall into a most healthy and probably deep slumber. At the beer garden they give me beer to drink. I can go for a boat ride with women and children, I have plenty to eat. The air up here is splendid, and as for the way I am treated, I would be a liar if I were to find fault with it. Sunlight and air and healthy living. But what is it I am giving in return for these things? Is it something real, something of substance, that I am able to offer? Am I intelligent, and am I truly offering up the full measure of my intelligence? What services have I provided Herr Tobler to date? With all due consideration, I am firmly convinced that my lord and master hasn't yet derived much benefit from me. Could I be lacking initiative, enthusiasm, flair? This is possible, for I came into this world equipped with an oddly generous portion of peace of mind. But does this do any harm? Of course it does, for Tobler's enterprises require the most passionate engagement, and equanimity can sometimes resemble the driest indifference. The fate of the Advertising Clock, for example—has it truly taken hold of all the fibers of my being? Am I consumed by it? I must confess that my mind's often occupied with quite different things. That, however, my good man, is treason. It is time to dive stalwartly headfirst into the affairs of others; after all, you are eating other people's bread, you go boating on the lake with other people's wives and children, lie upon other people's cushions and beds and drink other people's red wine. Keep your head up, and above all else, keep your nose clean. What I mean is, we aren't here in the Tobler household solely for the purpose of enjoying life. It is an honor to roll up one's sleeves. So get a move on!"

Joseph had meanwhile finished undressing; he put out the candle and threw himself on the bed. But for quite some time he continued to be plagued by reproaches for "his utter lack of wits."

In his dream, he found himself suddenly in the living room of Frau Wirsich. He knew where he was, and yet wasn't quite certain of it, the room was rather bright, but it appeared to him to be full of sea water. Had the Wirsichs become fish? To his astonishment he saw he was smoking a pipe, it was Tobler's pipe, the one he was so fond of. Tobler, too, seemed to be nearby, his metallic, masculine voice could be heard, the perfect voice for a boss. This voice seemed to be framing the living room or embracing it. Then the door flew open and Wirsich appeared, his face even paler than usual, and sat down in a corner of the room, which was ceaselessly quaking as a result of that voice surrounding it. That's right, the living room was quaking, it was afraid, even the windowpanes were trembling. And how bright it remained all this while. But this light was not daylight, it was not moonlight either, but rather a watery, glassy light. After all, they were underwater. Frau Wirsich was bending over some sort of needlework, but all at once the work in her lap dissolved into something glittering-sharp, and Joseph remarked: "Just look, tears!" What had made him say that? At just this moment, Tobler's voice crashed and thundered like a storm raging around this beggarly domicile. But the old woman just smiled, and when one observed this smile more closely, it was Leo, the dog that was smiling, still wet from the swim he'd just taken. The terrifying voice gradually gave way to a rustling sound— the way leaves, say, are in the habit of whispering and rustling in the warm quiet wind of a midsummer noon. Then Frau Tobler appeared wearing a dress of coal-black silk, there was no guessing why she was dressed in this manner. Slowly she approached Frau Wirsich with the noble bearing of a philanthropist, but suddenly her feelings seemed to have taken another turn, for she threw her arms about the woman's neck and kissed her. Tobler's voice growled something in response, but the words themselves were indistinguishable. No doubt, Joseph thought, he found this outpouring of his wife's emotions gratuitous. All at once the Wirsich lodgings were transformed into the shop run by that unattractively coiffed and painted cigar lady where he had once sat in a chair each day to hear her stories. This time, too, she was telling a story, a long monotonous sad tale, and curiously, although the story was long, it took up scarcely a moment. Am I only dreaming this, or am I really experiencing it, thought Joseph, and what does the cigar lady have to do with Frau Wirsich? Then a magnificently constructed, curvilinear golden boat sailed into the shop, the woman got in, and off she went, far far away, until she vanished in a black, glaring, acrid stretch of sky, but a tiny dot of her remained suspended high in the air. Once more the dream made a leap, a leap down into the Tobler workroom, there Joseph saw himself sitting in his shirtsleeves writing at his desk, and everything was looking at him questioningly, with a penetrating, inquiring look. What this everything was that was observing him he was unable to see clearly, but it was quite simply everything—it was, it seemed, the entire living world. Everywhere there were eyes that took a malevolent pleasure in his peculiar nakedness. The office was completely green with malicious joy, a piercing green. He tried to get up to escape from this locus of shame, but he was stuck fast in it; his heart filled with horror—and he awoke.

Feeling an oppressive thirst, he got up and drank a glass of water. Then he went over to the window, breathing and listening to the out-of-doors, everything was perfectly still: pale moonlight was bewitching and bewhispering the landscape. And it was so very warm. The small old working-class houses at the foot of the hill appeared to be sleeping in their shapes. Not a single speck of human light or lamplight anywhere! The surface of the lake was enveloped in haze and could not be seen. The tremulous cry of a bird briefly interrupted the nocturnal silence. Such moonlight, might it not serve as an allegory for sleep? What a silence this was. Joseph could not recall ever before having beheld such a thing. He almost fell asleep right there at the open window.

The next morning he was late for work.

Tobler grumbled his displeasure.

Joseph had the impertinence to reply that a few minutes one way or the other made little difference. This remark was a smashing success! For one thing, Joseph was treated to the sight of a livid face, and for another he was reprimanded as follows:

"It is your duty to appear at work punctually. My home and my establishment are not a chicken coop. Get yourself an alarm clock if you can't wake up. Besides which, are you willing or aren't you? If you are not prepared to put in an honest effort, let's put an end to things right now. The city is full of people who would be delighted to have such a position. You just have to take the train and go there. Nowadays you can scoop them up on the sidewalk. From you, on the other hand, I expect punctuality, or else—I don't even want to say it."

Joseph quite sensibly said nothing.

Half an hour later, Herr Tobler was comporting himself as the most benevolent master and most amicable of men. He even, overwhelmed by kind-heartedness, started addressing his assistant more informally, calling him Marti. Up to now it had always been Herr Marti.

In fact, the grounds for this amicability lay elsewhere. They were rooted in the notion of patriotism. The next day, you see, would be the first of August, and on this day fell the yearly jubilee celebrated throughout the country in honor of the magnanimous, brave deeds performed by the nation's forefathers.

Joseph had to run down to the village to purchase lamps, lanterns, little pennants and flags, as well as candles and combustibles to be used in firework displays. In addition, he was to commission, as swiftly as possible, a wooden frame two meters in height and length—oddly enough, it was the village bookbinder he was to entrust with this task, as he was skilled in work of this sort—along with two pieces of bunting, one bright red and one white. The cloth was to be stretched over the wooden frame, and the result would represent the nation's emblem, namely a large red square with a white cross in the middle, and all of this was to be set up that very night before the façade of the Tobler villa. Behind the frame and the image, they would place burning lamps so that the light would shimmer through the cloth and everyone off in the far and farthest distance would be able to see their two national colors illuminated.

An hour and a half later, all the requisite items were assembled. People suddenly began arriving to help decorate the house, people who were all at once present, and then the work began of affixing little flags everywhere and mounting lamps on the sills and niches, on ledges and windows and lattices. Even in the bushes and sturdier plants in the garden, incandescent devices were laid and hung and perched and clamped, so that nowhere on the entire Tobler property did a single spot remain that had not been secretly mined and prepared for the approaching fireworks. How happy Tobler looked. He was in his element. No one, it appeared, was better suited than he to putting on parties in high style. He kept coming out of the house to arrange something here or there or to twist a wire with the nippers, to rotate an electrical lamp hanging askew till it was straight, or to merely observe the work in progress. He appeared to have forgotten his Advertising Clock or at least put it temporarily aside. Naturally all these proceedings had a joyous, ceremonial and mysterious aspect for the children, who could not get their fill of marveling and asking questions and wondering what the significance was of all these things. Joseph was kept so busy with preparations for the holiday that he had no time left to reflect on whether the services he was providing Tobler were indeed services in the truest sense. Frau Tobler seemed to be smiling all day long, and as for the weather—

Speaking of this weather, Tobler remarked that if it continued to be so utterly glorious, they might as well plan something truly out of the ordinary. Given such an opportunity, there was no need to spare the little bit of expense this would necessarily entail. After all, this was a celebration in honor of their native land, and a man and individual must be in a sorry state indeed if no shred of patriotism was to be found in him. And certainly they were by no means overstepping the bounds of propriety, there was no need to exaggerate. But a person who no longer had an appreciation for things of this sort, one who spent his life shackled to his work and his cashbox, really did not deserve to have such a beautiful homeland, he could depart for America or Australia at any moment and find that a matter of complete and utter indifference. As for the rest, it was surely also a matter of taste. He, Tobler, just happened to like things this way, and that was that.

A large beautiful flag was fluttering at the top of Joseph's tower. Depending on how the wind was blowing, it would execute a bold proud arc with its light body, or else would double over on itself, abashed and weary, or curl and wave flirtatiously about its pole, whereby it appeared to be basking and admiring itself and its own graceful motions. And then all at once it would be blown high and smooth and wide, resembling a victorious warrior princess—a strong protectress—only to collapse again little by little, touchingly, caressingly. This splendid blue in the sky.

Getting much work done in the office appeared all but impossible. The mail (how surprising it was that there was mail delivery at all) brought a fairly steep bill related to the only quite recently executed construction of the tower's copper roof, the very same roof upon which such a pretty flag had been placed. The steep amount contained in this bill was so clearly expressed in the furrows on Tobler's brow, expressed with almost mathematical precision, that one might have been asked to read the exact figure presented there. Viewed as a contribution to the patriotic celebration, this item was anything but edifying.

"Let him wait," Tobler said, throwing the invoice right next to Joseph's thinking and corresponding head, which was bent down low to his desktop. Joseph replied through his nose with a single word: "Naturally!" as if he'd been in this business for long years already and was more than well acquainted with the circumstances, habits, torments, joys and hopes of his employer. Moreover, it seemed only appropriate on such a day to speak and act in a good-natured manner. With the weather so fine—

"What a hurry people are always in when it's a matter of presenting their bills," Tobler remarked. He was just busying himself at the drawing-board, working on the sketch for the "Deep Drilling Machine."

"If the Advertising Clock doesn't work out, then at least the drill will," he murmured in Joseph's direction, and from the correspondence desk an additional "Naturally!" rang out in answer.

"And in the very worst case, I still have the 'Marksman's Vending Machine,' that'll save the day," spoke the drawing-board, whereupon the commerce department replied:

"Of course!"

"Do I really believe these things I am saying?" Joseph wondered.

"And let us not forget the patented invalid chair," Tobler cried.

"Aha!" the assistant responded.

Tobler asked Joseph whether in fact he had a more or less clear notion of what these inventions entailed.

"Well," the amanuensis thought it permissible to say.

Had he written the letter to the national patent office?

"No, not yet." Joseph hadn't yet found the time for this today.

"So write it already, devil take it!"

When Joseph presented the document for his employer's signature, it turned out that the letter he had penned was incorrect, it got torn up and had to be written all over again. Nevertheless, he enjoyed the afternoon coffee break a great deal. What's more, he received a letter from his Frau Weiss in the city in response to his last communication. She wrote that he could take his time with the repayment of the debt he owed her, there was no great hurry. As for the rest, her letter was rather conventional, boring even. But had he been expecting anything different? Not at all. He had never, thank goodness, considered this woman particularly clever.

Today for the first time he noticed a scar on Frau Tobler's neck beneath her ears, and asked her what it was from.

She told him the scar was left over from an operation and that she would probably have to undergo a second operation in the same spot, since her illness had not yet been cured. She lamented: You shovel out so much money, just toss it down the ever-hungry jaws of the surgical arts, and then it turns out that no real healing has taken place. Yes, these individuals, the doctors and professors, she said, demand a small half-fortune for even the tiniest scalpel incision scarcely visible to the eyes of ordinary mortals, and for what? So that they can make some mistake or other, with the result that one is forced to go running back to them yet again, forced to undergo yet another course of treatment.

Was she in pain, Joseph wanted to know.

"In pain? Sometimes," the woman said.

Then she told Joseph about the operation. How she had been instructed to go into a large empty room in which nothing could be seen but a high bed or framework and four identically dressed nurses. Each of these nurses had looked exactly like the others, just as empty and unfeeling. Their faces resembled one another as closely as four stones of the same size and color. Then she was commanded, in a strangely harsh tone of voice, to climb up onto the bed-frame. She didn't wish to exaggerate, but in all truth she had to say that these proceedings had filled her with horror. There was not a trace, not a snippet of friendliness anywhere around her; rather, everything had left her with an impression of severity and callousness. Not a hint of a gentle look, not the slightest inkling of a comforting or calming word. As if a bit of kind-heartedness might have poisoned, infected or even killed her. In her opinion, this was taking prudence and propriety too far. Then she had been put to sleep, and from then on she naturally hadn't felt anything or known anything until it was over. And perhaps, she concluded her report, this was all as it had to be. Maybe she just perceived it as unnecessarily heartless. And a true doctor was perhaps not allowed to have a heart at all, who could say.

She sighed and ran a hand through her hair.

The thought, she went on, of having to—to lie down there a second time was abhorrent to her and distressing. And also for quite a different reason. Joseph could no doubt guess this easily enough. She found it difficult to bring up such matters with her husband now that their financial situation, as Joseph surely knew, was becoming ever more precarious. A woman could count herself lucky if she had no reason to require extraordinary expenses. Stupid money; how vile it was constantly to have to worry about such things. No, first—and here she smiled—she wanted to buy that new dress she'd been wanting a long time now before she'd give the doctors anything again. They could wait a while as far as she was concerned.

Joseph thought: "The husband wants to keep the metalsmiths waiting, and his wife the doctors."

The first of August!

An evening, a night and a day had passed without anything in particular. Now it was evening once more, the evening of the celebration. Already they were beginning to light the candles. From the distance, the soft thudding of guns fired in salute reached the ears of those assembled at the house. Tobler had provided several bottles of good wine. The mechanic working on the "Marksman's Vending Machine" had come from the neighboring village to attend the festivities. The two parquet ladies were there as well. They were sitting in the summer house and had already opened the bottles of wine. Tobler was glowing with anticipatory pleasure at this night of celebration, glowing already, and the darker the sky and earth became, the more fiery was the peculiar gleam that shone in his ruddy face. Joseph was lighting the candles and lamps, he had to duck down under each of the bushes in search of possibly over-looked lanterns. From the village, a murmur of singing and shouts could be heard, as if that place, scarcely a kilometer dis-tant, had become the scene of joyous revelry. More gunfire! This time the shots came thundering from the far shore of the lake. Tobler cried out: "Ah, they're getting down to business!" He called Joseph to him to give him "something to drink" along with some more copious pointers regarding the electrical illu-mination of the large national emblem. Tonight the clerk was a clerk in the service of the great, holy fatherland.

How the sonorous voice of Herr Tobler rang out on this great evening. Soon the sputtering, hissing rockets were zoom-ing up into the sky, or else a squib exploded. Entire glowing snakes, guided by the hand of the assiduous assistant, sprang up into the dark air—truly, it was starting to look like a tale from the Thousand and One Nights. Once more, bam, a shot in the distance. Down in the village, they were shooting as well. Tobler shouted down: "Well? Are you trying to catch up? You're always the last in line. That's just how you are, you barroom slugs!" He roared with laughter, brandishing a full glass of shimmering golden wine in his hand. His relatively small eyes were sparkling as if wanting to shoot off fireworks themselves.

Again and again, one rocket after the other, one sparkler and fiery snake after the other. The way Joseph was standing there, he resembled a heroic artilleryman in the heat of battle. He had assumed the noble-romantic bearing and stance of a fighter apparently resolved to give the last bit of his blood in the name of honor. This had happened without intention on his part, it was quite involuntary. At such moments, human beings can imagine for themselves all sorts of things, the image of something good and exalted and exceptional arrives of its own accord. All that is needed is a little wine and the thunderclap of gunfire, and already the illusion of the extraordinary has been spun tightly enough to let one go on dreaming an entire long, peaceful, humble night. Joseph's heart, like that of his master, was aflame with pleasure at the evening's festivities.

"Shoot, you lousy bastards!"

These words, shouted by Tobler in the direction of the village, were addressed to those few individuals who always permitted themselves a certain derisive tone when he began to speak of his inventions over a beer. His choice of words and the shout were meant to show these "milksops"—they received this title in yet another brief speech—how utterly he despised them.

"But Carl!"

Frau Tobler couldn't suppress a resounding laugh.

How intoxicatingly beautiful it was now. In the distant invisible mountains, hovering as if in midair, high up in the heavens, bonfires were ignited and burned. Horns, too, sounding huge and robust, now rang out from high up and far away, slowly expelling their metal breath and drawing it out for a long time.

This was beautiful, and everything that had ears was listening. Yes, if the mountains themselves were beginning to resound and speak, the tiny hisses and pops of the hasty little rockets must soon fall silent. Mountain fires burn quietly but for a long time, whereas the fizzling and spluttering of nearby fireworks can create quite a sensation for a brief moment but then soon vanishes without a trace.

Tobler was exceptionally pleased with the impression made by the large illuminated emblem with its bold red and white. For this reason he sent for another few bottles of wine and seemed never to tire of pouring it into various glasses. "Confound it," he exclaimed loudly, "on a day like this you've got to drain the cup dry!"

And so there was an assiduous clinking of glasses, and the sounds of chiming glass combined with the laughter ringing out at the various foolish stunts being hastily dreamed up and carried out. Cheeks were gleaming just as brightly as the looks in people's eyes. Naturally Frau Tobler had had the children put to bed long ago. A cork was secretly painted with red enamel and suddenly placed upon the nose of the old lady from the parquet factory in such a way that it remained stuck there. At this sight, Tobler was in danger of laughing himself sick, he had to hold his cheeks with both hands, as they were threatening to explode.

Finally the celebration jingled and grinned its way to an end with the last glass of wine raised to the lips of the revelers. The desire to play pranks began to ebb, it was quickly tumbling head over heels into slumber. The women all rose from their seats and went home, while the men lingered for another half hour in the summer house, gradually becoming earnest again.

The village of Bärenswil, the community housing the Tobler settlement, lies a good three-quarters of an hour by train from the canton's metropolitan capital. Like all the villages in the region, this town is situated in the most delightful surroundings and boasts a considerable number of stately aristocratic or public buildings, many from the rococo period. There are also notable factories here, such as silk manufacturers and ribbon weaving plants, which themselves have reached a considerable age. Industry and trade first set their more or less primitive wheels and fan belts in motion here approximately one hundred and fifty years ago, and they have been able to enjoy a continuously good reputation to this day, not only nationally but worldwide. The merchants and factory owners, however, did not merely remain trapped, stuck in the task of earning money. No, over the many years, and under the many different fashions of the day, they expended a great deal of money as well, and it is still plain to see that, in a word, they most certainly knew how to live. In various periods and various styles, they had all sorts of attractive villa-like buildings erected whose unobtrusive but charming forms can even today be admired and secretly coveted by the chance visitor. These newly prosperous individuals no doubt did a masterful job of residing within their little castles and homes with both consequence and taste: one cannot help but imagine these edifices as the site of the most beautiful and wholesome domesticity. But now the descendents of these old genteel merchant families are continuing to build in a dignified style. They like to tuck their houses away inside old gardens already distinguished by prodigious growth, for an appreciation of both distinctiveness and simplicity was given to them and passed on through the transmission of the ancestral blood. On the other hand, we can also see a great many indigent and miserable structures in Bärenswil or Bärensweil, which are home to the working classes; and even this other side, the opposite of wealth and delicate beauty, has a long-standing and natural tradition. In a manner every bit as solid and long and well-established as the affluent and tasteful villa the squalid hovel can go on existing; squalor will never die out as long as splendor and refined worldly living are still to be found.

Yes, Bärenswil is a pretty and pensive little village. Its alleyways and streets resemble garden paths. Looking upon it, one beholds not only urban but also small-town and rural characteristics. If you should happen to see a proud woman on horseback with a retinue, you needn't be dumbstruck with foolish astonishment; just have a look at the factory smokestacks and consider the money being made here, and also consider that money, as everyone knows, is capable of anything. Even coaches with rigorously uniformed footmen are not merely the stuff of legend hereabouts. Nor are they necessarily the property of countesses or baronesses either, for now and then it might appear fitting for the wife of a factory owner to travel in style, all the more so as the proud tradition of industry and trade is quite clearly represented among the landed and townhouse-dwelling gentry.

"A charming little hole in the wall" is how some cultivated

stranger might describe the town. Herr Tobler, on the other hand, had no longer said anything of the sort for quite some time, indeed, he cursed the "filthy hole," for the one and only reason that several of the Bärenswilers with whom he was in the habit of spending evenings at the "Sailboat" were not entirely convinced of the healthy foundation underlying his technical enterprises.

He would show them. Their eyes would be popping out of their heads one of these days, as he had begun to say fairly often now.

But why had Tobler moved here in the first place? What was it that had inspired him to choose this region as his domicile? The following somewhat unclear account seeks to address these questions. Only three years before, Tobler had been a low-level employee, an assistant engineer in a large machine factory. Then one day he had inherited a goodly sum of money and begun to concoct a plan to go into business for himself. A still relatively young and hot-blooded man like this tends to be somewhat hasty in matters of all sorts, including in the execution of secret plans, which is just as it should be. One evening, night or morn, Tobler read a notice in the newspaper announcing that the Evening Star Villa, for this was its name, had been put up for sale. Glorious lakeshore location, beautiful, majestic garden, excellent rail connection to the not terribly distant capital: Devil take it, he thought, that's the very thing! He set to work right away and purchased the property. As a freelance, independent inventor and businessman, he could live anywhere he pleased, he wasn't bound to any one spot.

A home of his own! This was the single driving force that had led Tobler to Bärenswil. Let a home be located where it may, just so it's a home of one's own. Tobler wanted to be his own lord and master, able to do and act just as he pleased, and this is what he became.

The morning after the night of celebration, Joseph had a look at the "Marksman's Vending Machine" down in the office, since this invention, after all, merited his attention. To this end he took up a sheet of paper upon which one could read and see the detailed description of this machine with its sketches and the instructions for its production. So what was the story of this second Tobler brainchild? The first he now knew almost by heart, and so it was high time, Joseph reasoned, to occupy himself with new material. And he was surprised how quickly he was able to familiarize himself with the inner and outer workings of this second invention.

The Marksman's Vending Machine proved to be a thing similar to the vending machines for candy that travelers encounter in train stations and all sorts of public gathering spots, except that the Marksman's Vending Machine dispensed not a little slab of chocolate, peppermint or the like, but rather a pack of live ammunition. The idea itself, then, was not entirely new: it was a concept that had been honed and refined, and cleverly translated to a quite different realm. In addition, Tobler's "Marksman" was significantly larger than most vending machines, it was a tall, sturdy structure of one meter eighty in height, and three-quarters of a meter across. The girth of the machine was that of a perhaps hundred year old tree. There was a slit approximately at eye level for tossing in coins or inserting the tokens that would be available for purchase. After inserting the money, you had to wait for a moment, then you pulled a lever located at a convenient height and simply reached down to retrieve the packet of bullets just deposited in an open cup. The entire thing was practical and simple. The inner construction was based on three interconnecting levers along with a sloping chute for the delivery of the bullets that were stored piled up in a sort of chimney in uniform packages of thirty, corresponding to the national standard issue; when you pulled the lever with its easily accessible handle, one of the packets stored in the chimney tumbled out with the utmost elegance, and then the machine went on working, which is to say that it remained still until a second marksman came along and prodded it once again to perform the operation described above, and then a third. But there was more! This vending machine had the additional virtue of being connected to the sphere of advertising, in that a circular opening located on the upper part of the machine displayed a new segment of a neatly painted advertising disk each time a coin was introduced or the handle of the lever pulled. This advertising method consisted quite simply of a ring of variously colored paper that interacted most closely and functionally with the entire system of levers in such a way that when a packet of bullets tumbled down the chute, it nudged a new advertisement into its exact location immediately behind the circular opening by causing the paper ring to rotate by one notch. This strip or ring was divided into "fields," and occupying and utilizing these fields cost money—and this money would brilliantly cover the costs of manufacturing the machine. "The Marksman's Vending Machine will be installed for use at the many shooting festivals held throughout the nation. As for the advertisers, one should, as in the case of the Advertising Clock, seek to obtain orders from only first-class firms. If it can be assumed that all of the fields of the ring will be filled with advertisements, and that can certainly be assumed, then Tobler (Joseph was so caught up in his train of thought that he started talking to himself) will earn a goodly sum of money, for the money brought in by the advertisements would greatly exceed the fabrication costs. For companies that reserve fields in several, let us say ten machines, a considerable discount will naturally apply."

A messenger from the Bärenswil Savings Bank came into the office.

"A bill, naturally," Joseph thought. He got up from his seat, accepted the document, looked at it from all sides, gave it a little shake, inspected it painstakingly, made a simultaneously thoughtful and important face, then told the messenger that it was all right, someone would come by.

The man retook possession of the bill and left. Joseph immediately picked up his pen to request, by letter, that the issuer of the bill be patient for another month.

How easily the words flowed. Also the bank would have to be telephoned right away. Dealing with these matters was becoming, it was to be hoped, fairly routine: Joseph just planted himself firmly and fixed his eyes on the sum that was owing, then he simply gazed at the messenger with a calm, indeed even somewhat stern expression. How the man was overcome with respect! People who wanted to extract money from Tobler would, in future, have to be dispatched quite differently, far more vigorously. This was Joseph's duty, dictated by his wish to spare Tobler any unnecessary unpleasantness. Under no circumstances should his employer be reminded of these repulsive bagatelles. Tobler was occupied with quite different things, and only the most crucial matters should vie for his attention. This is why, after all, Tobler had acquired a clerk, so that this with any luck intelligent and ingenious fellow would spare him all petty annoyances, would take up his post beside the door to intercept uninvited, starched individuals bearing bills and energetically send them on their way. Well, that's just what Joseph was doing. But to reward himself he was now smoking, yet again, one of the new cheroots that had just been sent up from the village.

He paced up and down within the confines of the office. Tobler had gone out on business and would probably not return home all day. If only that Herr Johannes Fischer did not choose this particular day to pay a visit—that would be exceedingly awkward.

This Johannes Fischer had responded by letter to their advertisement "For Capitalists," writing that he would in all likelihood be paying a visit to Bärenswil in the very near future to examine the inventions in question.

What a delicate, almost feminine handwriting the man had. Compared to it, Tobler's writing appeared to have been scratched out with a walking stick. Such a slender and delicate script already hinted at great wealth. Nearly all capitalists wrote just like this man: with precision and at the same time somewhat offhandedly. This script was the handwritten equivalent of an elegant easy bearing, an imperceptible nod of the head, a tranquil expressive hand motion. It was so long-stemmed, this writing, it exuded a certain coldness, certainly the person who wrote like this was the opposite of a hot-blooded fellow. These few words: concise and courteous in their style. The politeness and succinctness extended even to the intimate format of his blindingly white letter paper. This Herr Joseph Fischer had even been wearing perfume when he first introduced himself to them from a distance. If only he didn't come today. Tobler would deeply regret this, indeed, it might even happen that this annoyance would infuriate him, driving him into a frenzy. But in any case, Joseph had been given instructions to show and explain everything to the gentleman when he arrived, and Tobler had particularly impressed on him that he was under no circumstances to allow this Herr Fischer to depart again but must attempt to detain him until Tobler's return. It might well be that this apparently quite elegant stranger would accept a cup of coffee, for it had by no means been established that he was too fine for this. Such a charming summer house as the Toblers possessed was certainly worthy of serving as a spot of peaceful contemplation and pleasure for anyone at all, even for persons of the highest rank and grandeur. This capitalist, then, need only come trotting along; after all, Joseph felt, adequate preparations had been made for his visit.

All the same he felt rather apprehensive.

How pleasant he found his life here, by the way, when Herr

Tobler was out. After all, the presence of a boss—even if he was the nicest person in the world—required one's constant vigilance. When the boss was in good spirits, one felt perpetually afraid that something might transpire that would transform his lordship's cheerful mood into its diametrical opposite. When he was nasty and vicious, one had the more than bitter duty of considering oneself the lowliest scoundrel because one involuntarily saw oneself as the miserable cause of the master's ill-humor. When he was even-tempered and composed, it was clearly one's function to avoid inflicting even the slightest, most threadbare little injury to this equanimity, so that not even the tiniest crack or crevice might appear woundingly upon its surface. When the master was in a jesting mood, one instantly became a poodle, as the task at hand required one to imitate this droll creature and nimbly catch all the jests and jokes in one's mouth. When he was kind, one felt like a miserable wretch. When he was rude, one felt obliged to smile.

The entire house was a different one when the master was absent. Frau Tobler, too, seemed to be a quite different woman, and as for the children—particularly the two boys—their relief at the absence of their strict father was visible at quite some distance. A certain anxious quality was gone when Tobler was away. Gone, too, was a sense of gravity and tension.

"Am I an utterly spineless clerk?" Joseph thought. Then Silvi arrived, the older of the two little girls, and called him to lunch.

In the afternoon—Joseph was just sitting over his coffee and chatting with Frau Tobler—a gentleman entered the garden and walked through it to the house.

"Go to the office, someone's coming," the woman said to the assistant.

Joseph ran off in a hurry and had just reached the door to the office when the stranger intercepted him. In a pleasant voice, the newcomer asked whether he had the honor to be standing before Herr Tobler in person. No, Joseph replied, feeling somewhat embarrassed, Herr Tobler was off on a business trip, and he himself was only the clerk, but, please, if the gentleman would be so good as to come in.

The gentleman said his name. "Ah, Herr Fischer!" Joseph exclaimed. He bowed before Herr Johannes Fischer somewhat too gladly, somewhat too gleefully, and at once was conscious of his error.

The two of them now entered the drafting office, the capitalist leading the way, where Herr Fischer immediately began to make inquiries with regard to technical matters, while looking around him in all directions with a certain air of superiority.

Joseph elucidated the Advertising Clock. He brought out a real-life model of the same, placed it on the table before the eyes of his guest for inspection and at the same time set about illuminating the profit potential of this creation to his visitor, who was avidly observing everything around him.

The stranger, who appeared to be listening with interest, asked as he surveyed the eagle wings attached to the clock whether there might have been some slight miscalculation—as easily could happen in such cases—in determining the amount of revenue that would be raised through these advertisements. Had, he asked, any such commissions already been secured?

He pursued his line of questioning with equanimity. And he appeared to have become somewhat pensive, which Joseph, perhaps too hastily, interpreted as a good sign.

The employee replied that this sum could hardly be seen as inflated, on the contrary, and that a most satisfactory quantity of commissions had already come in.

"And the clock costs how much?"

Joseph attempted to clarify this, too, to Herr Fischer, in the course of which—he himself did not know why—he began to stutter. Uncertain as to how he should comport himself, he was about to light a comforting cheroot, but then dismissed this sudden craving as not entirely seemly. He blushed.

"I can see," Herr Fischer said, "that this appears to be an admirably planned and, it seems to me, already quite well organized enterprise. Might I be permitted to take a few notes?"

"Please do!"

Joseph had in fact intended to say: By all means, please do. But his voice and lips were refusing him the service necessary for speaking nicely. Why? Was he agitated? In any case, and this he felt distinctly, he had prepared himself very well to propose that the gentleman might find it agreeable to have a cup of coffee in the garden.

"My wife is waiting at the bottom of the hill," the other remarked offhandedly. He was writing some things in an elegant notebook. All at once he was finished. Joseph had the unflattering impression that the capitalist hadn't put particular effort into these aids to memory. He was about to open his mouth to say that he would just dash down the hill in a jiffy and invite the lady waiting there to join them.

Herr Fischer said that he regretted not having been able to meet Herr Tobler in person. This was a shame, but he hoped that this pleasure would not be denied him for long. In any case, he thanked Joseph most kindly for the considerate information he had provided. Joseph tried to get a word in.

"What a pity," the other resumed. "I would with the greatest probability have been able to commit to something definite. The Advertising Clock is quite appealing to me, and I am of the opinion that it will bring a profit. Would you be so kind as to communicate my regards to your employer? I thank you."

"We could also . . ." —Was that Joseph who was unable to speak any better?

Herr Joseph Fischer had made a brief bow and departed. Should Joseph run after him? What was he at this moment? Should he smite his own forehead? No, it appeared that what he had to do was return to the summer house and the nervously, expectantly waiting woman, and tell her how irresponsibly he had failed to "keep his wits about him."

"This is unfortunate, most unfortunate," he thought.

When he arrived at the summer or coffee house, Frau Tobler was just in the middle of giving Walter, the boy, a good thrashing. She was weeping, and remarked how awful it was that she had such monstrous children. This scene filled the clerk's heart with melancholy: On the one hand a weeping, enraged woman, and on the other an ironically waving and leave-taking capitalist, and as a backdrop the foreboding of Tobler's disapproval.

He sat down again at the place he'd hurriedly left ten minutes before and poured himself another cup of coffee. He thought: "Why not have some when it's there? All the self-denial in the world cannot avert the approaching storm that is about to break over my head."

"Was it that Herr Fischer?" the woman asked. She had dried her eyes and was peering down toward the main road. And indeed Herr Fischer was still standing there. He and the lady with him appeared to be enjoying the view of the Tobler property.

"Yes," Joseph replied. "I tried to make him stay, but it was impossible, he said he absolutely had to leave. But in any case we have his address."

He was lying! How shamelessly the falsehoods rolled off his tongue. No, he had not done everything in his power to detain Herr Fischer. If he now claimed to have done so, this was simply a cheeky, frivolous lie.

Frau Tobler said worriedly that her husband would be angry with them, she knew quite well how he reacted to these things.

Both were silent for a while. Silvi, the girl, was sitting on a garden stone, singing faint, foolish notes. Frau Tobler ordered her to be silent. How warm it was, sunny, all yellow and blue. The financier could no longer be seen.

"You must be a little frightened," said the woman and smiled.

"Oh, a little fear," Joseph replied defiantly, "that's the least of it. Besides, Herr Tobler can send me away if he wants to."

He shouldn't speak like that, she said, it was neither right nor proper, and in fact such comments could only cast a rather poor light on his character. Naturally he was a bit frightened now, that was plain to see. But he should calm down, "Carl" would certainly not devour him. There would be a mild thunderstorm this evening, that was all, and for this he should prepare himself.

She gave a bright, pretty laugh and went on speaking.

She had, she said, always had an excellent understanding of the respect her husband was able to inspire in other people. For those who did not know him well there was something almost terrifying about him, this was true, and she was speaking now in all earnestness and knew very well what she was saying. But she herself didn't have the slightest fear of Tobler.

"Really?" Joseph said. He was calmer now.

"Really I don't," she prattled on. She'd have to be a fool to be capable of deceiving herself in this regard. Even her husband's most horrendous fits of rage appeared to her more comedy than tragedy, and she always burst into laughter—she herself didn't rightly know why—whenever he treated her unkindly. She had never thought this a peculiar trait in herself, it had always seemed perfectly natural, but she knew quite well that there were people whose eyes and mouths would pop open with astonishment were they to witness such a thing, at the thought that an apparently anything but independent woman like herself could dare to find the behavior of her husband comical. Find it comical? Oh, sometimes she found it not the least bit amusing when Tobler would come home and take out on her the whole collection of bad feelings the world had impressed on him; on such occasions, she found it necessary to ask God to give her the strength to laugh. As for the rest, one gradually became accustomed to being rebuked and scolded, even if one was only an "anything but independent" woman.

Even a woman of this sort could now and then give serious thought to the things of this world, for example she was thinking just now that the tumult awaiting the two of them this evening would not last particularly long but rather, as was always the case with storms of this nature, would soon die down.

She got to her feet. There was something serene and ironic about her at this moment.

Joseph ran quickly up to his tower room. He felt a need to be alone with himself for a moment. He wanted to hastily "put his thoughts in order," but he was unable to find a suitable and calming train of thought that might have accomplished this. And so he made his way back down to the office, but even there he couldn't shake off this sinister, shameful feeling. In an attempt to overcome it, he made a bee-line for the post office, although it wasn't time yet. Marching and using his legs calmed and comforted him, and the sight of the friendly, picturesque world reminded him of the triviality and insignificance of his agitation. In the village he drank a glass of beer to get the humorous tone back in his voice; a certain insensibility this evening would serve him well, he thought. When he returned home, he immediately set about watering the garden with the help of a long rubber hose. The thin stream of water described a beautiful high arc in the evening air and fell splattering upon the flowers and grasses and trees. If there was something that could calm a person, it was watering the garden: during this work he felt a peculiarly cozy and cohesive sense of belonging to the Tobler household.

He who'd just been so diligent in tending the garden could

surely not become the object of particularly dire imprecations.

For dinner there was baked fish. It was utterly impossible to have eaten baked fish just a moment before and then immediately afterward find oneself the most miserable of human creatures. These two things simply could not be reconciled.

What a beautiful evening it was yet again. How could one have caused Tobler's enterprises to incur losses on such a splendid evening?

The maid carried a burning lamp into the summer house. No, in the light of such a pretty, friendly lamp, it was quite reasonable to expect that Herr Tobler would not take the missed visit of Herr Fischer too violently to heart.

Finally Frau Tobler requested that Joseph give her a ride on the swing. She seated herself on the plank, Joseph pulled back on the ropes affixed to it, and the swing commenced its back-and-forth motion. This was such an attractive sight that the thought of Tobler now arriving to disturb all these images was light-heartedly cast aside.

At around ten o'clock in the evening, Frau Tobler heard footsteps ascending the gravel path in the garden—they were "his."

How strange it is: the moment one hears the footsteps of a familiar person, it is as if the one approaching is already there in the flesh, and so his real appearance somewhat later is no longer ever a surprise, no matter what he's looking like.

Tobler was tired and irritable, but this was not surprising, he was always like this when he came home. He sat down, heaved an audible sigh—he was portly enough that climbing the hill had cost him some effort—and demanded his pipe. Joseph leapt into the house like a man possessed to fetch the desired item, happy to be able to avoid his employer for at least half a minute.

When he returned carrying the smoking utensils, the state of things had already changed. Tobler looked dreadful. His wife had quickly told him everything. She was now standing there—displaying unheard-of pluck, it seemed to Joseph—gazing calmly at her husband. He was looking like someone who doesn't dare curse for fear he will do so too immoderately.

"So Herr Fischer was here, I am told," he said. "How did he like our products?"

"Very much!"

"The Advertising Clock?"

"That one he especially liked. He said that it appeared to him to be a most excellent enterprise."

"Did you draw his attention to him the Marksman's Vending Machine as well?"

"No."

"Why not?"

"Herr Fischer was in such a big hurry, because of his wife, who was waiting down at the garden gate."

"And you left her waiting there?"

Joseph was silent.

"Why did I have to hire such a dunderhead as a clerk?" Tobler shouted, incapable of holding back for another instant the rage and professional misery consuming him. "Now I must suffer the misfortune of being betrayed by my own wife and a good-for-nothing assistant. Not even the devil could do business under these circumstances."

He would have shattered the petroleum lamp with his fist if Frau Tobler had not, thank goodness, moved it slightly to one side the moment before his hand came crashing down.

"You don't have to get so worked up," his wife cried, "and I forbid you to say I am betraying you. I haven't forgotten where my parents' house is, and if you keep acting this way, I'll go back to them. Joseph doesn't deserve to be abused like this either. Send him away once and for all if you think he has harmed you, but don't make such scenes."

As an "anything but independent" woman, she had naturally been weeping as she spoke these words, but what she said most certainly had the desired effect. Tobler became calmer almost at once, and the "storm" began to die down. Together with Joseph, Tobler began to deliberate as to what could be done to keep the assets of Herr Johannes Fischer from slipping through their fingers. They would have to telephone him first thing in the morning.

In the lives of certain businessmen, the telephone plays a major role. Mercantile coups are, as a rule, most successful when they are initiated telephonically.

The very thought that they could telephone this Herr Fischer the next morning caused their hopes, both Tobler's and Joseph's, to revive. How could it be possible, given the availability of such resources, that this business would come to nothing?

And Tobler, after announcing his arrival by telephone, would at once board the train and set off for the capital so as to pay this "escaped bird" a personal visit.

Tobler's voice was still trembling darkly long after he had

become cheerful and merry again, as if the agitation went on burning inside him. The three of them sat up until all hours playing cards. Joseph had to learn this card game too, they insisted; a man wasn't a man if he didn't know this game.

The next morning, as agreed, a telephone call was made. Tobler threw himself into the railway carriage with such optimism in his face! In the evening, his face was dejected, wrathful and sad. A bargain had not been struck. In the place of liquid assets, there was a new bitter scene played out in the nocturnal summer house. Tobler sat there like the very image of a suppressed cloudburst and indulged in unlovely and blasphemous curses. For instance, he said that as far as he was concerned, the entire earth could sink into a quagmire, it would make absolutely no difference; he was already wading through an endless morass!

When he went so far as to cry out that both he himself and everything around him should go straight to hell, Frau Tobler ordered him to control himself. He, however, turned on her so savagely that she collapsed face down upon the table, but she immediately then rose up to her full height and withdrew somewhat primly.

"What you just said hurt your wife," Joseph made so bold as to remark, suddenly feeling a sense of gentlemanly chivalrousness.

"Hurt her—what rubbish! It's a tiny world being injured there," Tobler replied.

Then the two of them sketched out a new advertisement to be placed in the international dailies. Their draft contained phrases like "Glorious enterprise" and "Maximal profit at absolutely no risk." They resolved to send it along to the advertising agency the very next day.

Sunday arrived once more, and once more Joseph was given five marks pocket money. Once more he enjoyed the privilege of being able to report for work in the office at his own discretion. This in particular had something decidedly poetical about it. There would be an excellent meal again today, perhaps roast veal, deliciously golden-brown, with cauliflower from the garden, followed perhaps by applesauce, which tasted so splendid up here. Also he would be handed one of the better cigars. What a way Tobler had of laughing and looking down at one mockingly as soon as it was time to hand out cigars. Just as if Joseph were a handyman to whom one might say: "Here, have one— you must enjoy smoking a good cigar now and again." As if Joseph had just finished painting a trellis or repairing a lock, or as if he had just pruned a tree. That was the way one rewarded an industrious gardener with a cigar. Was not Joseph Herr Tobler's "right-hand man," and was a right-hand man in fact sufficiently rewarded if given something nice to smoke on Sundays?

He stayed in bed somewhat longer than usual, he opened the windows and, lying there, allowed himself to be shone upon and blinded by the white early-morning sun, for this sunshine was demanding to be savored, along with other things as well, for example the thought of breakfast. How sunny and Sunday-like it all was. Sunny days and Sundays would appear to have been joined in brotherhood since time immemorial, and even the cozy thought of a peaceful breakfast appeared to have been woven of something sunny and Sunday-ish, this was clear. How could it have been possible to be feeling, let's say, crabby on a day such as this, much less ill-humored, much less melancholy. There was a sense of mystery in everything, in every thought, in one's own legs, in the clothes lying on the chair, in the wardrobe, between the blindingly white bleached curtains, in the washstand, but this mystery was not unsettling, on the contrary, it radiated calm and peace and smiles. In fact, there were no thoughts in one's head at all, though one didn't quite know why—somehow it seemed essential that this be the case. So much sunshine was collecting in and around this absence of thought, and wherever it was, the sunshine recalled to Joseph's mind the vision of opulently laden breakfast tables. Yes, this silly but almost sweet Sunday feeling began with a simple thought.

He got out of bed, dressed himself more painstakingly than usual, and went out onto the rectangular platform that was at his disposal. From here one could see into the crowns of the trees in the orchard next door. How peacefully and blindingly sunny it all looked. Pauline, the maid, was just setting the breakfast table out in the open air. This was a sight the assistant could no longer resist; he raced downstairs in the direction of coffee, bread, butter and preserves.

Later he went downstairs to the office. There wasn't much to be done, but he sat down all the same—drawn by the almost pleasurable force of habit—at his desk, which resembled a kitchen table, and began his correspondence. Ah, how lightheartedly he seemed to be flirting today with the usually so solemn pen. The words "telephonic communication" appeared to be clothed in Sunday finery, just like the weather and the world outside. The turn of phrase "and I shall take the liberty" was as blue as the lake that lay at the feet of the Villa Tobler, and the "most sincerely" closing the letter seemed fragrant of coffee, sunshine and cherry jam.

He went out the office door into the garden. What a Sunday feeling this was, to be able simply to interrupt one's work at will to go have a quick look at the garden. How fragrant it all was, how warm it was already, despite the early morning hour. In half an hour or so, one might go for a swim, it "wouldn't really make much difference." Yes, today one might say these words calmly to Tobler's face, and he would be of quite the same opinion as Joseph. The not making much difference, after all, was the whole difference between Sunday and a workday. The entire garden appeared enchanted, bewitched by the heat, by the buzzing of bees and the perfume of the flowers. This evening, the garden would have to be given a proper watering.

What a perfect clerk he was to have had such a thought. Joseph now carried the glass ball outside.

Then Tobler came up to him dressed in a truly elegant new suit and announced that he would be going on an outing today with his wife and children. After all, there was no point staying home all the time, and his wife deserved to have a little pleasure now and then. As for Joseph, Herr Tobler continued, he would no doubt want to go to the city to visit his friends there.

"Why don't you just let that be my business," Joseph silently responded to his master, "whether I visit any friends." But aloud he said, No, he would stay home today, that suited him better.

"You can do whatever you like as far as I'm concerned," Herr Tobler replied. Approximately half an hour later, the entire party—consisting of Herr and Frau Tobler, the two boys, the young lady from the neighborhood, and little Dora—had assembled before the house, prepared to depart; they would be traveling to a distant town to spend half a day at a cantonal singing festival. Frau Tobler had on a black silk dress that made her look fairly imposing. She instructed Pauline to keep watch over the house, and to Joseph she said casually that he might as well keep an eye on things too, since, as she'd been told, he was planning to stay home.

Finally they departed, accompanied by the howls of the chained dog, which seemed distraught at being left behind. Beside Joseph, Silvi, Dora's little sister, crouched on the ground. The girl appeared not in the least aggrieved at the injustice being done her. That she alone out of the four children was being left at home appeared to her an ordinary state of affairs. In fact she was accustomed to a variety of affronts and had lost all sensitivity to slights of this sort.

"Have a nice time at home, Marti!" Tobler had said to Joseph in parting.

"Yes, a nice time. Why don't you worry about your own nice time, Herr Carl Tobler, engineer," Joseph thought somewhat bitterly once he had made himself comfortable, book in hand, upon the turned-down bed in his pleasure chamber:

"Off they go, these curious employers of mine, along with that caustic angel from the parquet factory, off for a pleasant day of traveling and song, and little Silvi is left behind like a malodorous mound of refuse. This Silvi, it seems, is nothing more than a little trollop on whom this lovely Sunday weather would be wasted. Beautiful Frau Tobler cannot stand the girl, she finds her hideous, and so Silvi must stay at home. And then our most estimable entrepreneur! Just three days ago, his rage and disappointment were shaking him from side to side and around in circles, a pitiable sight, and today here he is telling me he hopes I have a nice time and that I should go visit my acquaintances and friends in the city. He's just afraid I'll get too friendly with Pauline, that's all."

He confessed to himself that he was being too bitter and forced himself to read his book. But as he was unsuccessful in this attempt, he laid the book to one side, went over to the table, picked up his own personal pen and a sheet of paper and wrote the following upon it:

Memoirs

I was just on the point of entertaining spiteful thoughts, but I shan't allow it! Then I tried to read, but I was incapable of this, the contents of the book failed to take hold of me, and so I laid the book aside, for it is impossible for me to read without feeling enthusiasm about what I am reading. So now I am sitting at this table with the intention of occupying myself with my own person, for there is no one in the world who is eager to receive news of me. How long has it been now since I have written a heartfelt letter? My letter to Frau Weiss clearly demonstrates to me how I have been knocked and jolted out of the realm of close, intimate human contact, and how utterly I am lacking in people naturally justified to expect me to keep them up to date as to my comings and goings. The sentiment behind that letter was a fictitious one, a feeling I dreamed up. The letter is true, but at the same time it was an invention, produced by a mind that was horrified to find itself entirely deprived of relationships of a simpler and more self-evident sort. Am I calm now? Yes. And it is to this noonday stillness that I am addressing these words. I am ringed about by Sunday tranquility—what a shame that I cannot disclose this circumstance to some person of consequence: it would make the loveliest opening for a letter. But now I should like to describe my own nature a little.

Joseph paused for a moment and then continued to write:

I come from a good family, but believe that my upbringing was rather too cursory. By no means do I wish to criticize my father or mother with these words, Heaven forbid; I merely wish to do my best to shed some light on the question of what is going on with my person and with the particular zone of the world charged with the task of enduring my presence. The circumstances under which a child grows up certainly play a large role in its upbringing. The whole region and community take part in raising it. To be sure, parental dictums and school are the main thing, but what am I doing occupying myself with my own exalted person like this? I'd rather go for a dip.

The assistant who was so poorly suited to diary writing laid aside his pen, tore up what he had written and left the room.

After his swim, there was lunch with Pauline and Silvi. The maid—a person of rather coarse sensibilities—was just attempting, amid constant laughter that presupposed Joseph's approval of her conduct, to instruct the child in manners, something in which the maid herself was notably lacking. This vain and heartless endeavor culminated in the demonstration and drill, repeated several times over, in the proper handling of knife and fork, whereby it was in no way expected that the lesson should be successful: in fact its success was not even desirable, since then the amusement provided by this harsh and entertaining exercise would have come to an end. The child sat there gazing with wide and, in point of fact, stupid eyes now at her taskmaster, now at Joseph, who was observing these proceedings calmly, and spilling her food in a rather unsightly manner, which caused Pauline to erupt in a renewed, exaggerated torrent of indignation calculated to appear serious to Silvi and comical to Joseph—as if satisfying two diametrically opposed worldviews with a single blow. Silvi was so sloppy that the housemaid, who had been given nearly absolute authority over the small creature by the child's mother, found it appropriate or considered it necessary to box the troublemaker's ears and shake her by the hair until Silvi began to scream, perhaps not so much because of the physical pain, though this was surely by no means insignificant, as on account of a last little stub of pride, of insulted humiliated childish pride, at having to submit to such abuse at the hands of an outsider, which is what Pauline was. Joseph kept his silence. Confronted with the child's fury and pain, the maid herself suddenly began to act gravely offended and insulted; this was because Joseph had refused to laugh, which she found utterly incomprehensible, and also because Silvi had not submitted to being misused without protest, which the maid, in her thoughtlessness and coarseness, had taken for granted. "I'll teach you to scream, you filthy little thing!" she cried or rather cawed, and seized the child, who had run away from her chair, thrusting her back into her seat so hard the child's body was slammed against the chairback. Once more Silvi was forced to take up fork and knife in her little hands, and properly at that, as her teacher and instructress commanded her with a severe and sharp cry, so as to finish, under duress, this melancholy and unappetizing meal. Her tear-stained eyes made her appear to Pauline even more stupid and lopsided than before, which prompted this pedagogical mastermind to burst into laughter. The sight of Silvi eating dejectedly appeared to exert a drastic effect on Pauline's laugh muscles. So humor had returned to the scene. A shameless set of jaws is quite an asset, and so Pauline of the broad forehead—upon which narrow-minded clodhopper astonishment was clearly depicted—inquired of Joseph, who was quietly looking on, whether he was angry or what else could be making him so tight-lipped. The audacity and pig-headedness of this flippant question produced such a feeling of revulsion in the one sitting there that he violently blushed. He would have had to attack the person sitting across from him physically if he had wished to convince her of the feelings he was experiencing. As it was, he merely murmured a few words and got up from the table, which only strengthened the maid's belief in her instincts which were telling her that Joseph was, all in all, difficult to get along with, an unfriendly person who had no doubt intentionally set about insulting her and spoiling her mood. This new venomous sentiment was soon taken out on Silvi, who received orders to clear the table, a labor that in truth ought to have been performed by Pauline herself. In her earnest attempt to carry out the orders of this oppressive tyrant, the child had to rise to the toes of her small feet each time she removed something from the table, using both hands to grip a bowl, a plate or a few pieces of cutlery, and in this way she carried everything, piece by piece, meekly and with caution, keeping her eyes on the kitchen virago, out to the place where the washing-up would be done. She did this as though she were carrying in her little arms and hands a small, thorny, damp crown, the crown of irrevocable childhood sorrow that she had cried shimmering wet with her own tears.

Joseph went up into the woods. The path that brought him here was very pretty and very quiet. Naturally he was occupied as he walked by thoughts of small, wizened, ill-used Silvi. Pauline appeared to him like a gluttonous bird of prey and Silvi like the mouse cowering beneath the talons of the cruel beast. How could Frau Tobler abandon her delicate little daughter to this dragon of a maidservant? But was Silvi really so delicate, and was the maid so fearsome a dragon? Perhaps things were not nearly so dire. It would be easy to fall prey to exaggeration if one insisted on always seeing on one side all the deviltry in the world, and on the other, all the sweetness and goodness. Silvi— the "filthy little thing"—was, it must be admitted, a tiny bit filthy, but Pauline was Pauline. Joseph found himself incapable of testifying on Pauline's behalf in his thoughts; the most favorable thing he could say of her was that her father was an honest signalman and farmer. But what did the household of a signalman have to do with the brutal pleasures of mistreating children? Certainly it might be that Pauline's father himself was capable of being half a raging bull—as far as anyone knew, it was quite possible! But this refined, nearly aristocratic Tobler lady, this mother, this woman descended from genuine bourgeois circles who had imbibed a delicate sensibility along with her mother's milk, this clever and in many respects even beautiful woman— what of her? What cause did she have to spurn and ill-use her own child? Joseph smiled over this quaint expression, "ill-use," it seemed so fully to represent the curious phenomenon it was describing. The word "spurn" made him think of something in a fairy tale, but one could "ill-use" poor, defenseless little children just as well today as many hundreds of years ago. Such a thing could even be accomplished in a Villa Tobler, the place where, as Tobler himself was in the habit of saying, two fairies so liked to disport themselves: decorum (I insist on decent behavior in my house) and cleanliness (devil take it, keep things tidy, do you hear). Could two such charming fairies tolerate something so unclean and, indeed, indecent as the on-going humiliation of a childish spirit in their presence, was this possible? It appeared to be! In fact, all sorts of things were, in the end, possible in this world when one took the trouble and love to reflect on this a bit while out for a walk through the meadows.

Joseph encountered almost no one at all. Two farmers were standing beside the path. Lush meadows extended to either side of it, covered with hundreds of fruit trees. Everything appeared so close together, and yet also so broad and green. Soon he came to the forest and after wandering about for a while discovered a small, narrow, wooded ravine with a stream running through it and made himself comfortable in the moss by simply allowing himself to plop down on the soft ground. The brook was murmuring so nicely, the sun was flashing through the leaves of the tall beech trees, so familiar, and so cozy, and succulent green enveloped the ravine as if with sweet delicate veils. This would have been a lovely, appropriate setting for a romantic tale. From somewhere or other on the plateaus surrounding him came the sounds of rifle fire, there must have been a shooting range somewhere nearby. As for the rest, how still it all was! Not a breath of air could slip into this green hidden world. The trees would have had to fall down first, but they were all tall old trees that could withstand a storm, ten storms even, and today there was no sign of wind or rough weather above the ravine. Some young lady from the age of chivalry, dressed in a velvet skirt and leather gloves, might come walking through the ravine just now, leading her white steed by the reins and wearing her full, golden hair hanging loose about her, Joseph would not have been terribly surprised by this pageant. That's what the place looked like, the perfect scene for chivalrous and womanly encounters. But what beautiful and chivalrous things might be found in the vicinity of the Villa Tobler? Pauline, for example, or else Tobler himself, the adventurous entrepreneur dressed for feats of derring-do? Enterprises there were, to be sure, any number of them, but what sorts of ventures were these? What did technical enterprises have in common with green wooded ravines, white steeds, noble dear female figures and courageous exploits? Did the knights and entrepreneurs of centuries past ride about on mounts resembling the "Advertising Clock" or the "Marksman's Vending Machine"? Did there already exist in those days "ill-used" children of the Silvi variety? Oh yes, but in those days such children were said to be "cast out" or "spurned," whereas today a certain individual, who was lying amid the most splendid greenery upon the moss, took it into his head to proclaim them "ill-used."

He laughed. Oh, how beautiful it was here. In the forest, every silence was redoubled. A broad ring of trees and bushes formed the first silence, and the second, an even more beautiful one, was formed by a person choosing a spot for his own. The way the brook was murmuring, you thought yourself already entangled in long cool daydreams, and when you gazed up into the green foliage, you found yourself in the midst of silver and golden and good world-views. The figures you invented yourself, drawn from a distant and close circle of acquaintances, were quietly whispering, they were saying something or perhaps only making faces while their eyes were speaking a profound, intimate language of their own. Feelings were stepping forward naked and courageous, and even the most delicately perceived sensation was met with a secret understanding suffused with longing. Lips and thoughts, requiring neither epochs nor roads on which to pass through life, kissed as soon as they recognized one another; you could see the joy burning upon these lips, and a friendly melancholy was singing from the thoughts that accorded well with brook, bushes and woodland silence. You only needed to think that evening would soon come, and at once all the familiar and unfamiliar landscapes appeared to be swimming in evening light. The forest above the dreamer's head rose and fell and gently rocked and danced in the gaze lifted toward it, and there was nothing for the gazing eye to do but dance as well. How beautiful it is here, Joseph said to himself several times over. Suddenly a scene from his childhood appeared before him with great vividness.

Back then, in the time of his youth, there had been a sort of ravine as well, but in fact it was more a sandstone hollow, but such a strange and delicate hollow as he never again beheld. This more or less round pit was situated at the edge of a large forest of beeches and firs and oak trees, he and his siblings discovered it one day while roaming about on an afternoon walk. This was also a Sunday in summer, perhaps it was even almost autumn. The children had run on ahead, thinking up games and trying them out, and behind them strolled their parents. The newly discovered hollow proved to be the most splendid of playgrounds, they decided to remain there and wait for their parents to catch up. The latter arrived, and they too found the place charming; there are spots in nature that simply enchant anyone who sees them, and this was one of them. The edges of the pit were overgrown with a veritable thicket of trees that was almost impenetrable, so that its discovery could in fact only have been made by curious children. There was, however, another reasonably wide opening in one spot where the pit could be comfortably entered. Mother sat down on a grassy bank and leaned her back against a fir tree. In the middle of the hollow was a small elevation of natural provenance that was so attractively set with young trees that it offered a most inviting spot for sitting and lying. Who could have failed to be captivated by it? This place, just as it was, appeared to have been created by the wistful hand of a nature-loving dreamer, but no, it was nature itself, its usual heedlessness notwithstanding, that was displaying here, so to speak, such delicacy of feeling by giving rise to this coziness and concord. All around the little elevation stretched and curved a pleasure ground, a woodland meadow strewn with the most fantastical grasses, herbs and wildflowers, which gave off a heady, romantic perfume. All that could be seen of the remaining world was a patch of sky that was truncated necessarily by the tall trees at the edge of the pit. The entire place resembled a corner in the rambling gardens of some manor house, not a chance woodland scene. The parents mutely observed their children running about, chasing one another up and down the steep sandy waves of the slope amid a din of laughter and shouts. These early voices. How wild they could all be then. The children were all happy that their mother was pleased with their hollow, that she was able to sit there quietly, caressed by all the advantages of so lovely a resting place. They knew the desires and needs of their mother's spirit. And soon the entire place seemed to be filled with this friendly, pensive pleasure and with the childish surmise, belief and hope that they'd found just the thing. A strange enchantment of spirit made their vivacious games significantly more beloved and rapturous. Since their mother appeared to be content, they could allow themselves a degree of exuberance that exceeded what was ordinarily permissible. Every bourgeois household contains some oppressive misfortune, but here all sense of misfortune had been put aside, indeed, the world itself appeared to have been forgotten. From time to time the children glanced over at their mother to see whether or not she was cross, but no, she was gazing straight in front of her with a kindly and otherwise reticent expression. This was a good sign, and the grassy little hillock itself seemed from then on to have become sentient. "She's in a good mood," the children whispered to the leaves of the rustling trees. When their mother was able to smile—which was such a rare occurrence—then the entire surrounding world smiled at them as well. Mother was already ill in those days, she suffered from an excess of sensitivity. How sweet the children found the peaceful repose of this woman, who was being gnawed at by unhappiness from all sides. Unhappiness appeared to be banished from this cozy little corner, and so a joyousness was whispering and sighing within each blade of grass upon this small secluded woodland meadow, and a friendly belief in every fir needle. In their mother's lap lay a few wildflowers, and her parasol lay beside her. Some book she'd been reading had slipped from her grasp. The face the children were afraid of looked so peaceful. It was all right, then, to frolic and shout and engage in boisterousness cavorting. Each of her features was saying: "Go on and frolic, it's all right now. Frolic all you want, it doesn't matter." And the entire charming place appeared to be festively, rapturously spinning along with them in the whirl of their game.

"That was a hollow, and this is only a wooded ravine, and the Tobler house is not far off, and it is an unforgivable sin to go on daydreaming when a person has left his twenty-third year behind him."

Joseph set off for home.

The Tobler house, how it stood there, solid and at the same time dainty, as though it were inhabited only by grace and contentment. Such a house was not easy to topple; industrious, skillful hands had assembled it to last with all its mortar, bricks and beams. Sea breezes could not knock it down, not even a hurricane. How could a few infelicitous business ventures harm such a house?

Now every house, to be sure, consists of two halves, a visible and an invisible one, and of an external structure and an inner support, whereby the inner construction is perhaps just as important, indeed perhaps sometimes even more important in bearing and propping up the whole than the external one. What good is it for a house to be standing there attractive and pleasing if the people who live there are incapable of propping and shoring it up? In this regard, commercial and economic errors are of the utmost significance.

To be sure, the Tobler house was still standing despite the fact that Herr Johannes Fischer had abruptly withdrawn his money-dispensing hand. Was there only a single person left on earth who was capable of floating a loan? If so, Tobler really would have to lose heart. But then how could it be that he was just now undertaking to have a grotto constructed in the garden? It would appear, quite simply, that the man had not yet suffered any losses whatsoever, otherwise he would hardly have been contemplating such a project.

Down on the main road, people often stopped in their tracks, raised their heads up and gazed unhurriedly at the villa, and when you looked down on them from above, you couldn't escape the impression that these chance observers were gladdened by the sight. But who wouldn't feel glad, being permitted to look upon such a charmingly situated dwelling? The copper tower was worthy of interest in its own right—Lord knows this tower cost enough. The thought that the invoice for this tower was at this very moment lying down in the office in the cubbyhole for unpaid bills would not be so swift to occur to a person immersed in the contemplation of this house, for house and garden made far too prosperous an impression.

No doubt the manager of the Bank of Bärenswil had found occasion to brood a little over the fact that it was customary in the Tobler household to send back bills presented for payment with the request for an extension. But he was careful not to express aloud these thoughts of concern and distrust that he had secretly begun to harbor. It might very well be just a passing crisis, and after all, a bank manager is not a washerwoman, but rather a man well acquainted with self-discipline who knows how destructive impertinent remarks can be for a striving and struggling businessman. To be sure, he was rather taken aback; he knit his brows a little in the privacy of his managerial office, raising his hand in the mildest of gestures, but he kept his peace—after all, he was laboring in the service of commerce and industrial development in this flourishing little town, and Herr Tobler was naturally a part of this, though recently things up at the Evening Star had appeared to be going a bit downhill.

Banks and financial institutions are generally possessed of re-fined, tight-shut lips, and such mouths speak only when the certainty of absolute insolvency is literally present. So Tobler could go on laughing up his sleeve in the best of spirits. The se-cret of his difficulties lay hidden in the Savings Bank of Bärens-wil as in a tightly sealed tomb.

A person who still felt moved to join in heart-thrilling cele-brations of gymnastics and song in the company of his wife and children must no doubt still have some secret source of credit flowing somewhere that he has not yet tapped only because he has not yet felt the need to avail himself of this last of all avail-able resources. A person possessing such a stately wife who is politely greeted on all sides when she walks through the vil-lage—how could he be badly off?

And things were indeed not so bad. Money might come raining into the technical office overnight, advertisements had been taken out, and for the moment all that was needed was pa-tience, the profits would most certainly materialize soon. What wealthy and enterprising man could resist an advertisement headed: "Glorious Enterprise"? And once someone had come so far and taken the bait, they would most certainly know how to keep him. They wouldn't go about things as they had with Herr Fischer, who, by the way, when one stopped to consider, had perhaps never intended to pursue the matter with appro-priate seriousness, and who therefore didn't deserve to be taken so seriously.

Had the Advertising Clock suddenly proved a washout? Not a bit of it. On the contrary, the elegant wings of its advertising fields shone brighter and more resplendently than ever, and the Marksman's Vending Machine? Hadn't the fabrication of the very first specimen been underway for weeks now? Didn't the most efficient and assiduous of mechanics turn up almost daily at the villa in order to play cards with Tobler? Other people played cards as well and enjoyed a glass of wine, and yet continued to prosper—why shouldn't Tobler prosper as well? There seemed no reason why he should not.

Moreover, Herr Tobler hadn't come to "this lousy Bärenswil" in order to become prematurely fainthearted, he could just as easily have done this elsewhere if there were truly no help for it, and done so perfectly well. No, his main concern at the moment was to set an example for all those pikes and herrings, to rub their curious snide little noses in what could be accomplished by a sanguine, hardworking man, even at a point when the very boards of his own home and workplace were threatening to collapse. And this is why Tobler, unconcerned as to what might be whispered into various ears at public houses down in the village, was having the garden dug up to build a grotto—who cared if it wound up costing a whole hay cart full of cash!

These Bärenswilers must not be allowed to triumph, that would be the last straw! It was crucial to use every means at one's disposal to spoil the pleasure it would give these people if Tobler were forced simply to toddle off into the distance like a jumping jack in a Punch and Judy show. No, things had not yet come to that. And to spite them all, Tobler was planning to send out invitations to a party celebrating the opening of the grotto—the moment it was even approaching completion—to the most respected citizens of the village, the ones who still had halfway decent intentions regarding him, so that they might see how firmly and serenely he looked upon and grappled with life.

A person who felt such responsibility for his family as Tobler did, who had a wife and four children to take care of, would not so swiftly be expelled from a place and spot he had come to acquire and inhabit. Just let a few of them come and try it—he would drive them off with blows glinting and flashing from his bare wrathful eyes. And if that wasn't enough for these bacon and sausage eaters, well then he might easily enough take a notion to seize one or the other of them with his own two hands and heave him over the garden fence, he would certainly not stand on ceremony in such a case.

But things were far from being in so dire a state. The firm of C. Tobler, Inventor still enjoyed unlimited credit among the craftsmen and businessmen of Bärenswil. Paperhanger and joiner, locksmith and carpenter, butcher and wine merchant, bookbinder and printer, gardener and furrier all delivered their labor and wares to the Evening Star Villa without demanding immediate payment, as they unquestioningly believed that their bills would be settled at a convenient future moment. There was no sign of any sort of whisperings or rumblings in the public houses down in the village, and by laying into the members of his household, Tobler appeared merely to be practicing in advance for such a situation, an occurrence which in any case would arise only when an individual or business transaction had provoked his ire.

The Tobler house was still releasing the odors of the most

fragrant cleanliness and respectability into its beautiful surroundings—and how! Framed by flashes of gleaming sunshine, raised up by a green hill that laughed wonderfully down at the lake and the level plain, surrounded and embraced by a truly magnificent garden it stood there: pure modest, lucid joy. It was no coincidence that strollers who happened to pass by gazed so long at it, for it was truly a delight to behold. Its windowpanes and white cornices gleamed so brightly, the beautiful tower beckoned with its coppery brown, and the flag that had been left standing atop it after that nocturnal celebration entwined with gaily majestic motions, with quiverings, coilings and flame-like furlings about the slender, sturdy pole. This house expressed two divergent sentiments in its construction and site: exuberance and serenity. To be sure, it was also just a tiny bit ostentatious, and it was different from the mansions of older vintage that were hidden deep within their dear, ancient gardens, but the villa was lovely, and a person who lived there and found himself plagued by the thought that he might be forced one day to leave it in dishonor would indeed have every right to be in low spirits, this was quite understandable.

But pursuing such trains of thought was something Herr Tobler did not permit himself.

Si-vi, Si-vi!

How piercing this sounded. And yet it didn't even cut properly. A crude kitchen knife that hadn't been sharpened in years would still be able to call out "Sivi" just as effectively as Pauline, who had a speech defect that prevented her from articulating the "l." But this housemaid had an excellent understanding of how to issue orders where Silvi was concerned. When it was Dora that was being addressed, Pauline's stentorian voice subsided to a whispery purr. She always called Dora "Do-li," for in this case the weakness of her tongue extended to the "r" in the nickname "Dorli," though she pronounced the "l," which was certainly curious, as she never managed to say it when crying "Si-vi." But "Si-vi" had a spiky sound to it, and the intention was to wound Silvi, to cause her pain even when merely shouting out her name; no one ever spoke lovingly to this little girl.

Even the child's own mother could not abide her, and so it was no doubt quite natural that all the others despised her a little, too. Dora, on the other hand, was made of sugar, at least this is what you thought at the outset, for cries of "Dorli, dear Dorli!" came ringing and piping solicitously out from every nook and cranny until it seemed there had to be a snow-white confectioner's shop just around the corner. Dora was almost not made of flesh and blood—everything about her was almonds, tarts and cream, at least that's how it appeared, for the air around her was always filled with pleasantries, sweets, curtsies and caresses.

When Dora fell ill, she was loveliness personified. She lay then, bedded in pillows, upon the daybed in the sitting room, a toy in her hand and an angelic smile upon her lips. Everyone went up to her and said flattering things to her, even Joseph did this, he was practically compelled to do so, he couldn't help himself, for this little girl was truly beautiful. She took after her father, with the same dark eyes, the same full face, one and the same nose, really his living image.

Silvi, on the other hand, was a not quite successful copy of her mother, a photograph reduced in scale but at the same time rather botched. Unfortunate child! What fault was it of hers that she had been photographed so poorly? She was thin and yet unwieldy. Her character, if one can speak of the character of a child, was inherently distrustful, and in her soul she appeared deceitful and false.

How delightfully open and sincere Dorli was, by contrast, in every fiber of her being. This is why she was so beloved among everyone in the household and indeed in the neighborhood as well. People gave her presents and did as she asked. Joseph carried Dora around on his shoulders in the garden, she need only say: do, and he did. She had such a nice way of asking. Heaven itself seemed to be lying upon her lips when she asked for something. Tiny white clouds would appear then to be drifting out of this childish Heaven, and somewhere, you couldn't help thinking, someone seemed to have started playing the harp. She asked and commanded all at once. A truly lovely request is always combined with a sort of irresistible command.

Silvi was incapable of asking for things, she was too shy and disingenuous, she never quite dared; in order to ask for something, one must have an irrepressible, powerful trust both in oneself and others. If one is to find the lovely courage to utter a fervent plea, one must from the outset be firmly, indeed adamantly convinced that the request will be fulfilled, but Silvi was convinced of no one's kindness, as she had been all too soon and incautiously inured to quite a different sort of treatment. A beaten-down slovenly little creature like Silvi can easily become more disagreeable to endure and more unsightly to behold with each passing day, for a small person like this will not only abandon all self-discipline and care, but indeed will exert herself—motivated by a secret, painful defiance no one would expect of such an undeveloped child—to goad the antipathy and disgust of those around her to ever higher levels by means of ever more loathsome conduct. In fact the case of Silvi was most peculiar: it was almost impossible to feel love for her when one was looking at her. One's eyes always condemned her at once. Only one's heart, provided one had one, would later speak in her favor, saying: Poor little Silvi!

Of the boys, Walter was the more favored, and Edi, the younger one, the more neglected. But in certain families boys are held generally in higher regard than girls, making it impossible for a less loved boy to be denied all kind, warm affection as might be the case with an "ill-used" girl. In the Tobler family, too, it was like this: Walter and Edi, taken together, had a higher value than their female counterparts Dora and Silvi. Walter and Edi were quite different in nature: the former was rambunctious, given to pranks, but still open-hearted, while Edi liked to hide in the nooks and crannies of the house just like Silvi, his little sister, and like her he spoke very little. Edi never made fun of Silvi's behavior, either; they had some sort of understanding that appeared all the more natural for being unspoken. They even played together. Walter would never have occupied himself seriously with Silvi. He made fun of her and mistreated her often, for he had been taught to think nothing of this.

One thing more that must be said of Silvi was that she wet her little bed almost nightly despite the fact that she was woken by Pauline at regular intervals and placed on the chamber pot. This physical flaw was primarily responsible for the severe treatment imposed on the little girl, for everyone was firmly convinced that she was merely too lazy to wake up and get out of bed. Pauline was under orders from Frau Tobler to strike the child every time without exception when her sheets were soiled, and if boxing her ears did no good, Pauline was to take the carpet beater to her—perhaps that would have an effect— and Pauline carried out her mistress's orders. And so in the middle of the night one often heard the most pitiable shrieks coming from the nursery, mixed with oaths and loudly shouted epithets which Pauline saw fit to apply to the youthful sinner. Every morning Silvi was made to carry the chamber pot she'd used during the night downstairs all by herself. This, too, was a directive from her mother, who was of the opinion that it was fitting for a soiler of bedclothes to see to such a task herself, as Pauline had her hands full with other matters. Then the wizened, disheveled little child could be found sitting with the aforementioned object, which she had, strangely, set down right beside herself upon one of the stair landings, looking for all the world as if she had been abandoned by all the good guardian angels that are generally said to look after poor, defenseless little children. When "to crown it all" she would become recalcitrant, she would be locked up in the cellar, and then there would be no end to the screaming and hammering against the locked cellar door, so that even the neighbors, simple working-class folk, couldn't help but notice the cries emanating from the villa.

Tobler knew little of all these things, he was so seldom at home—these days he had been traveling more and more often. Being so completely occupied with business concerns, he was scarcely able to devote himself to the upbringing and supervision of his children. A man like Tobler was happy to leave all domestic matters in the hands of his wife, for he himself, after all, was busy traveling and battling to defend the Advertising Clock and the Marksman's Vending Machine. Responsibility was the domain of men, so it was certainly quite reasonable to leave the love and everyday toil up to the wives. The husband did battle with existence, and the wife was in charge of good behavior and peaceful comportment at home. Will it be shown to us how Frau Tobler was managing these tasks? Perhaps.

Wherever there are children, there will always be injustice. The Tobler children formed a highly irregular quadrilateral. At the four corners of the square stood Walter, Dora, Silvi and Edi. Walter planted his feet down firmly and opened his impudent mouth to let out a vigorous laugh. Dora was sucking on her finger and glancing down at her servant Silvi, whose task it was to tie the princess's shoes. Edi was carving away at some piece of wood he'd picked up in the garden, utterly immersed in the work being performed by the pocketknife he was employing for this task. Where was regularity to be found here? How could one be fair to each little mind, each little heart? Pauline was gazing out the kitchen window. This person from a distant stratum of society appeared, astonishingly, to have no sense of justice, or else she simply misunderstood what justice was. Now the irregular quadrilateral was shifting, the children scattered—each to his or her own activity—into the hours and days and secret sentiments of childhood, and also into the space surrounding the Tobler household, into sorrows and joys, humiliations and caressing words, into the living room and the sphere of everyday life, into nights of sleep and the endless stream of childish experience. Perhaps they even exerted a certain direction-influencing pressure upon the rudder of the good ship of Tobler's enterprises. Who can know?

In the course of the week, which, by the way, passed without incident, two people paid a visit to the Evening Star Villa one evening, Herr and Frau Dr. Specker. It was a nice cozy evening, as they say. Once again, a deck of cards was brought out, and everyone played Jass. "Jass" was the name given far and wide throughout the land to a popular card game that even boasted a national flavor and flair. Frau Tobler who, as has been previously intimated, had already achieved a certain level of mastery in this game, was instructing Frau Dr. Specker in its trickier ins and outs, as this lady was far less well-versed in them. The evening saw a great deal of laughter and joking. Joseph had been pressed into service as sommelier, he was to run down to the cellar to fetch the wine and then pour the contents of the bottles into glasses, and it became apparent in the course of all this that he possessed a certain pride, which struck Tobler as ridiculous, but it was counterbalanced by his sense of social tact, so that his employer was able, with no trace of embarrassment, to present and introduce him to their distinguished guests. "This is my clerk,"

Tobler had declared in a loud voice, and at these words Joseph made a bow before the lady and gentleman from the village.

What sort of people were these anyhow? He was a doctor, and as for the rest still quite young, and his wife appeared to represent nothing more than the validation in female form that she was the doctor's wife, that was all. She was the wife of her husband and as such behaved in a quiet, shy manner all evening long. Frau Tobler was fairly different in this regard, you could see there was something cryptic about her—particularly when you compared the two women—only slightly, to be sure, but there was certainly nothing in any way cryptic or secret about Frau Dr. Specker. They ate little pastries to accompany the wine, and the gentlemen smoked.

"What a young, happy-looking fellow, this doctor," Joseph thought while at the same time trying to play as cleverly and trickily as possible. He had been invited to join the game. Several times the doctor addressed questions to the assistant: where was he from, how long had he been living in Bärenswil and with the Toblers, did he like it up here, etc., and Joseph answered him in as much detail as was allowed by the natural reticence that persons from the lower walks of life are wont to display on such occasions. Meanwhile he made some rather foolish plays, and now the most glorious speeches explaining the rules were being directed at him from all four sides of the table, as though the task at hand were converting a hard-headed and slow-witted heretic.

As for the rest, the conversation revolved around general topics, which, after all, is what made the evening so "cozy."

This same week also witnessed a minor incident of a moral and cultural nature in which Joseph's predecessor, Wirsich, figured prominently, causing this person who had been ejected from the Tobler household to become once more a recurrent topic of conversation for several days. This is what happened:

Along with Wirsich, the housemaid had been driven out of the Villa Tobler several weeks before, Pauline's predecessor, whom Frau Tobler had found to be a young creature of robust and mischievous—i.e., larcenous—leanings who, according to the allegations of her former mistress, to which one could certainly lend credence, had stolen from her entire linens and other things. She was also let go because of her lustful ways and sensual nature that had prompted her to enter into perfectly cheeky and shameless sexual relations with Wirsich, goings-on that could not remain hidden from her employers, as they were being indulged in so conspicuously and, in point of fact, indecently. Besides which, this domestic was prone to hysteria, which appeared to pose a danger for the children. She had often appeared suddenly on the stairs or in the kitchen wearing only a chemise, and when she was reproached for this, she would absolutely and positively insist, with tears pouring from her eyes and with her plump body heaving convulsively, that she'd been unable to endure having clothes on her back a moment longer, that she was dying, and whatever other cynical, silly nonsense it might have been. Since the Toblers knew perfectly well what sort of nocturnal visits this concupiscent person was in the habit of paying to Wirsich in his tower room, they quite reasonably and appropriately deemed it advisable to sever the employer-employee relationship with this unhealthy noxious person and send her on her way.

Now a letter from the hand of this very individual had just arrived at the Evening Star, addressed to Frau Tobler, and in it the former maidservant wrote in a disagreeably personal tone that rumors were circulating in the region where she lived, rumors to the effect that her former mistress had been having a love affair with Herr Tobler's subordinate, Wirsich, which she, the maid, was in no way willing to believe, being convinced, to begin with, that only calumnious and lying tongues could have been capable of making such wicked claims. But she had felt duty-bound to inform Frau Tobler, who had so long been her employer, of this abominable slander, in order to warn her, etc.

This letter, which was neither orthographically correct nor written in anything approaching a reasonable manner, transported its receiver into a state of the most passionate outrage, especially since the ostensible devotion of the domestic to her erstwhile employer expressed in it was just as fictitious as the presence of a nasty rumor about Frau Tobler's conduct. She showed the letter to Joseph, it was around noon and they were sitting out in the summer house, Herr Tobler was somewhere or other, and she asked him, once he had finished reading the document, whether he would assist her in composing the vigorous response this boldfaced liar deserved.

"Why not? Most willingly!" was Joseph's reply to the agitated, indignant woman. Since he said these words in a rather dry tone of voice—for he felt almost insulted at the zeal with which she was entangling herself in this matter related to

Wirsich—Frau Tobler believed he was less than willing to perform the favor she had requested, and so she declared that if he was not in fact willing, then she would certainly be capable of handling things on her own. After all, she had no intention of forcing Joseph to put himself out. It would appear that it gave him no pleasure to assist her, besides which his behavior towards her today was not as polite as one might wish.

"What do you mean by 'pleasure'?" Joseph retorted, nearly in a rage. "Give me strict orders. Tell me how you would like to have the letter written, and I'll go down to the office, and in a few minutes' time the work will be finished. There's no need for any particular 'pleasure' to play a role."

This was unmannerly of him. Feeling this, Frau Tobler measured Joseph with an astonished look and then turned her back on him. Without a word, Joseph returned to his workplace.

After a few minutes, Frau Tobler appeared in the office as well, still all worked up. She asked the assistant to give her pen and letter paper, sat down at her husband's desk, thought for a moment and began to write. Since this was an unaccustomed activity for her, she paused several times during the exercise, sighing deeply and loudly at the wickedness of the common folk. Finally she was done, and then she found herself unable to resist the need to show the finished product to the correspondence clerk to hear his opinion of it. The letter was addressed to the mother of the treacherous maid and read:

Respected madam!
A letter has reached me from the hand of your daughter, my former

housemaid, and allow me to say right off that this letter is an impertinent and despicable piece of writing. Under the pretext of faithfulness and devotion to an employer, this letter comes out with the crudest possible insults pertaining to a woman who, because she was kind-hearted and forbearing, is now being punished for not having been able to be merciless and hard. Know, respected madam, that this disgraceful daughter of yours stole from me while she was in my employ, and that I could hand her over to the authorities if I so wished, but a woman like myself seeks to avoid such things. Let me be brief: See to it, respected madam, that this good-for-nothing keeps her mouth shut. I know who it is that is spreading wicked and shameless remarks about my person and what the rumors are. It is none other than this same insolent person who herself violated all standards of decorum and virtuous conduct while under my roof, and what is more did so together with the very individual with which this lying gossip is now attempting to place myself, her former mistress, in sordid alliance. This letter has put me in a state of the utmost agitation—you should know this, madam! And now keep an eye on this malicious creature, this is my friendly and sisterly advice to you, for you, as I certainly am happy to assume, are a worthy woman and cannot help it if that utterly outrageous daughter of yours is a wicked hag. Should you fail to do this, I shall be forced to have recourse not to lengthy and good-natured words such as these but rather, as you can no doubt imagine, to criminal law. The high regard in which the world holds a lady cannot prevent her, when necessary, from appearing before the court of public righteousness to see a calumniator of her honor brought to justice.

With this, respectfully yours,
Frau Carl Tobler.

Having glanced over this letter, Joseph said that he found it good, but that it appeared to him somewhat too pompous. Such a style as Frau Tobler had employed was better suited to the Middle Ages than today's world, which was in the process of gradually—if only to the outside observer—blurring and obliterating long-standing social distinctions of rank and birth. For one woman not born into royalty to write so brusquely to another could only produce bad blood and thus fail to achieve the desired effect of the letter as a whole. Affluence, as a rule, did well to not strike too lofty a tone with poverty, rather it appeared to him nothing more than proper and fitting to begin by addressing the maid's mother simply as "Dear madam" so as to make the letter's tone somewhat warmer and at the same time more polite, which certainly couldn't hurt, in his opinion. Frau Tobler, he could see, was not used to writing letters. This was evident from the presence of the many infelicities he had noticed, and if she permitted, he would gladly sit down and correct her charming little essay.

Laughing, he went on to remark that he would also excise the claim that the girl was a thief, although he himself did not for a moment doubt the truth of what Frau Tobler was saying, but it was nonetheless possible that certain inconveniences could result from the assertion and produce more annoyance than satisfaction. Did she have any proof?

Frau Tobler assumed a thoughtful expression, and a moment later said that she wanted to write a second letter. She was less worked up now, she said, and thus hoped to be able to write more calmly and gently. But the letter as a whole had to be written in a vigorous tone, otherwise there was no point to it. Otherwise she would rather not send a letter at all.

As she wrote, unbeknownst to her she was observed by Joseph, who was gazing at her back and nape. Her beautiful, feminine hair was tapping at and touching her slender neck with its curly little locks. How slender she was in general, this lovely woman. There she now sat, immersed in her efforts to pen a letter using her sense and understanding, in accordance with the theories and methods of proper writing, to a woman who perhaps could scarcely read. Joseph now involuntarily regretted, observing her like this, having remonstrated with her on account of her upper-class pride, which in point of fact he found enchanting. He was moved by something about this feminine back, whose garments fell into darling little folds whenever the body beneath them shifted a little. Was this woman beautiful? In the generally accepted sense of the word, surely not—quite the opposite. But even this opposite did not conform to anything generally accepted. Joseph would no doubt have gone on with these and other reflections if the writing woman had not turned around. Their eyes met. Those of the assistant evaded those of the woman, which was more or less the appropriate thing. Joseph felt, and could not help feeling, that it would have been well-nigh cheeky to endure the woman's gaze which, yet again, was filled with that astonishment that so splendidly mirrored the pride which—one could not deny it—was very becoming to her. What were assistants' eyes good for if not for evasion and casting down, and what other expression could be more natural for this other set of eyes than the expression of being amazed and astonished? Accordingly, he bent down over his work again, although work was not, at this moment, his primary concern.

Half an hour later, during coffee hour in the summer house, a rather indelicate scene took place.

Frau Tobler, who appeared to have recovered her composure entirely, suddenly began to sing the praises of Wirsich most vividly, saying how this person, who was unfortunately given to sin, had been so useful, handy and skillful in all other ways, how he had immediately accepted every insignificant assignment, every task he was charged with, without making a fuss about it, and she said several other things of this sort, glancing repeatedly at Joseph with what struck him as a taunting look, and offended him. For this reason he cried out:

"This eternal Wirsich! It's difficult not to come to the conclusion that the man's a peerless genius. Why is it that he is no longer here, given how constantly one hears tell of his virtually divine qualities? Because he got drunk? And is it then just and proper to demand all imaginable excellence from the person of a clerk and then send him away, drive him off into the huge, difficult world just because a single aspect of his character has cast a pall over all his remaining excellent qualities? In truth, this is a bit much. So here we are presented with faithfulness and intelligence, knowledge and assiduous labor, amusing conversation and deference, and all these qualities, along with one or two additional gems, we take into our employment, accepting them serenely and cheerfully since this is what's done, and because we are giving the owner of this large gunny-sack of distinctions a salary, food and lodging in exchange for all these qualities.

And now one day we detect a black stain on this handsome body, and all at once our easygoing satisfaction has vanished and we tell the man to pack his bundle and move on to wherever he pleases, but we'll nonetheless go on speaking for a half meter, or a whole one, and a goodly year long and wide about this man and all his 'good qualities.' Surely one must admit that this is not such a terribly proper sort of conduct, particularly when one insists on rubbing the nose of this person's successor in all these precious and princely attributes, no doubt in order to wound him—just as you, Frau Tobler, have been doing to me, the successor of your Wirsich."

He gave a loud laugh, intentionally in fact, so as to diffuse and disperse somewhat the insubordinate impression left by his rather long speech. He was a little frightened now that he was coming to his senses, and in order to add a note of humor to mask the touchiness of the words he had spoken, he started laughing, but it was a forced laughter that was more of an apology.

Joseph had no cause, Frau Tobler said after a few moments of silence, to speak to her in such a way, she would not permit him to use such a tone with her, and she was astonished to see him adopting this sort of behavior. If he were really so proud and sensitive that he could not bear to hear his predecessor praised, then it would be better for him if he were to build himself a hermit's cottage high up in the forest and make his home among the wildcats and foxes, he needn't seek the company of other human beings. Here in the world, one was not permitted to place everything on so delicately calibrated a scale. By the way, she had no choice but to inform her husband of the contents of the exceedingly peculiar speech he had made, Tobler should know what sort of man this clerk of his was.

She was about to get up and leave when Joseph cried out:

"Don't say anything. I apologize for everything. Please, forgive me!"

Frau Tobler gave the young man a look of contempt. She said: "That's more like it," and went away.

"Just in the nick of time. That's Tobler himself down there," Joseph thought, and indeed, there was the boss on his way home unexpectedly earlier than usual.

A mere quarter of an hour later, Herr Tobler had been informed in meticulous detail of all that had transpired. To Joseph he remarked:

"So you're starting to mistreat my wife, are you?"

This is all he said. When it had seemed as if his wife's complaints would never come to an end, he had shouted at her, "Leave me in peace with this foolishness!"

Indeed, the engineer was now occupied with graver concerns.

That evening, the tower room became once more the quiet, lamplit setting for a soliloquy that was spoken aloud. Joseph, taking off his jacket and vest, addressed himself as follows:

"I've got to pull myself better together, things can't go on like this. What could possibly have possessed me to speak so roughly to Frau Tobler? Do I place so much value and importance in what comes from the lips of such a lady? All this time, poor Herr Tobler is working himself to the bone on his business trips, while his clerk occupies himself with sentimental nonsense in a summer house over cups of coffee. These womanish concerns! What is it to me if Frau Tobler finds this and that characteristic of Wirsich worth praising? It's all so simple. This pale knight with his poor-sinner face left an impression on her feminine mind. Need this alarm me? Why should it? Instead of thinking every hour and half hour about the technical enterprises, I have made it my business to convince a woman of my character. Convince her of what? Aha, character! As if it were necessary for an engineer's clerk to have character. It's just that my head is always brimful with the silliest things when it ought rather to be concentrating on my duty to engage in truly profitable and enterprise-furthering reflection. Is my sense of duty so poorly developed? Here I am eating bread and drinking coffee, and I accompany these pleasant advantages and benefits with a truly inappropriate longing for the most damaging thoughtlessness. And then I hold half-hour-long speeches before a horrified and astonished woman to make it clear to her she has aroused my wrath. What use is this to Herr Tobler? Will it make his difficult financial situation any easier? Has it caused the transactions that need to be carried out to recover from the paralysis with which they have been stricken? Here I am occupying one of the most beautifully situated rooms in all the world, with one of the best views. Lake and mountains and meadow landscape have been laid before my eyes and feet as an extra bonus, and how am I justifying such utterly wasteful generosity? With an utter absence of wits! What are Wirsich and his nocturnal visitors to me? There is something far more important that concerns me far more greatly, namely the firm whose insignia is emblazoned on my brow and whose interests I should bear in my head and my heart. In my heart? Why not? One's fingers and thoughts can hardly work as they should if one's heart isn't in it. There's a reason people speak of certain matters as being 'close to one's heart.'"

He racked his brains for some time longer over the question of what could be done to help get the Advertising Clock back firmly on its feet—"business reflections" over which at last he fell asleep.

In the middle of the night, he suddenly awoke. He sat up in his pillows: Ah, that was Silvi screaming! He got up, went to the door, opened it and listened, and then he heard the sounds of a repugnant scene. It was Pauline's voice now, shouting:

"So you were too lazy to get up and sit on the chamber pot, were you, you hideous creature?" Silvi whimpered and tried to justify herself, speaking in a stammer, but in this she had no hope of succeeding, for in response to her miserable protests the maid was slapping her so hard it sounded like wet laundry.

Joseph got dressed, went downstairs to the children's bedroom and gently reproached Pauline. She, however, shouted that he should mind his own business—she knew what her duty was—and he should get out of her sight at once, whereupon she yanked Silvi by the hair, as if to demonstrate what authority she enjoyed in the nursery, and ordered her to get back into bed—into the wet bed, for that was part of her punishment.

The assistant withdrew, to all appearances meekly acknowledging the sovereignty of this martinet. "Tomorrow, or the day after, or whenever it will be," he thought, lying back down in his bed, "I shall have to make yet another speech before Frau Tobler. Even if it's ridiculous. I wonder whether she has a heart. As an employee of the Tobler household, I am obligated to put in a word for Silvi, for Silvi too is a member of this household whose interests I am supposed to represent."

The next day he hurried by train to the capital, having received, as usual, his allowance of five marks. It was beautiful warm weather, and the train tracks ran along the shoreline of the gleaming-blue lake. He had scarcely gotten off the train when he was struck by how unfamiliar this city he once had known so well now appeared to him. His relatively short absence had so transfigured and tinted this place; he would never have thought it possible. Everything appeared to him so small. Along the quay beside the lake, many people were strolling in the glaring noonday sun. What utterly unfamiliar faces! And all these people looked so poor. To be sure, these were people from the underprivileged, working classes, not gentlemen and ladies—but a web of misery that had nothing to do with the wretchedness of poverty in the economic sense had wrapped itself around this entire bright perambulatory scene. It was nothing other than the strangeness, the unfamiliarity casting its glare into his eyes, and feeling this, he said to himself that when a person had lived for weeks at the Villa Tobler, there was no need for him to be surprised at the sight of an urban setting and his own estrangement from it. Faces were plumper and redder out where the Toblers lived, hands grasped more firmly, and people walked with more of a swagger than you saw here in the rarefied city, whose inhabitants quickly took on a pinched, inconspicuous appearance. After all, Joseph considered, it was natural for the small and narrow to become a large, significant world in its own right for a person who had not experienced anything else for a period of time, while the most significant and far-reaching things could appear at first modest and shabby, just because they were so breezy, diffuse, and expansive. In the Tobler household, a certain modest plumpness and thickness had prevailed from the outset, and these qualities had some weight to them, giving them an obvious appeal; whereas wide panoramic vistas of freedom and prolixity might easily leave a person cold, for they appeared so insubstantial. The most comforting things, Joseph felt, always looked so modest, though to be sure the world of a Tobler or tyrant might also display a certain coziness or human warmth emanating enticingly and invitingly from tower rooms and the like. At times the state of being fettered and bound to a particular place could be warmer and richer, more filled with tender secrets, than outright freedom, which left all the world's doors and windows standing wide open. In freedom's bright spaces, people all too often found themselves beset by bitter cold or oppressive heat; but as for this other sort of freedom that he, Joseph, was thinking of—well, goodness, freedom of this sort was, in the end, the most fitting and loveliest sort, possessed of an undying magic.

Yet soon the image of urban Sunday leisure stopped looking so strange to him, so perfunctory and rough-shod, and the further he walked, the more familiar everything appeared to his eyes and heart. He sent his eyes off strolling among the many people strolling before him, and with his nose, which was accustomed to Tobler cuisine, he inhaled the scents of the city and city life. His legs were now marching quite jauntily again upon city streets, as if they had never once set foot upon country soil.

How brightly the sun was shining, and how modestly people were walking to and fro. How lovely it was that one could lose oneself amid all this bustling, standing, strolling and swinging. How high up the sky was, and how the sunlight was making itself at home upon all the objects, bodies and movements, and how lightly and gaily shadows were slipping in between. The waves of the lake were striking not at all tempestuously against the stone barriers. Everything was so gentle, so overcast, so light and lovely—it all became just as large as it was small, just as near-at-hand as distant, just as extensive as minute and just as dainty as significant. Soon everything Joseph beheld appeared to have become a natural, quiet, benevolent dream, not such a terribly beautiful one, no: a modest dream, and yet it was so beautiful.

Beneath the trees of a small park or common, people were resting upon benches. How often Joseph as well had availed himself of one or the other of these benches, back when he had been living in the city. He took a seat this time, too, beside a good-looking girl. The conversation then initiated by the assistant revealed her to be a native of Munich who was hoping to find work in this city that was utterly foreign to her. She seemed to be poor and unhappy, but he'd so often encountered poor and melancholy individuals on these benches and spoken with them. The two of them exchanged a few more words, then the girl from Munich abruptly got up to go. Joseph inquired whether he could come to her aid with a small sum of money. Oh no, she said, but then did accept something and took her leave of him.

You found such different sorts of people sitting upon public benches like these. Joseph began to observe each of them in turn. That young man sitting on his own over there tracing figures in the sand with his walking stick, what might he be, what of all things in the world, if not a bookstore employee? Perhaps this classification was in error, well, in that case he was surely one of those numerous department store clerks who always had "plans" of some sort on Sundays. And that girl over there across from him, was she a coquette or a respectable lady, or perhaps simply a prim, well-mannered little ornamental plant? Or a doll disinclined to accept the experiences the world was holding out to all mankind with its rich, warm arms like a magnificent bouquet? Or might she belong to two, even three different categories at once? This was certainly possible, for such things were known to occur. Life did not so readily allow itself to be sorted into boxes and systems. And that old, decaying man over there with the unkempt beard, what was he, where had he just come from, to what profession and walk of life could we presume him to belong? Was he a beggar? Was he one of those indefinable individuals who spent their weeks sitting in the marvelous Copyists Bureau for the Unemployed, where they earn a couple of marks as a daily or weekly wage? What had he been before that? Had he worn an elegant suit once, along with a ditto walking stick and gloves? Ah, life may have made him bitter, but it could also make you merry and profoundly humble, and grateful for the little you had, for the bit of sweet open air that was there for the breathing. And what about that refined—even genteel, it appeared—pair of lovebirds or bridal couple? Was it a pair of English or American travelers savoring on the fly the entire existing world? The lady was wearing a delicate feather on her little hat that looked as if it had just sailed up and landed on her head, and the gentleman was laughing, he looked very happy—no, both of them did! How the two of them kept laughing the whole time, it was so lovely to laugh and be glad.

This lovely, dear, long summer! Joseph got to his feet and slowly went on walking, making his way down an affluent and elegant but deserted street. On Sundays, yes, that's just when wealthy people remain at home, they scarcely show themselves at all; perhaps going out on the street on this day struck them as unrefined. All the shops were closed. Isolated, scattered individuals swayed and tottered along, often decidedly unattractive men and women. What humility lay in such a scattered portrait of persons out for a stroll. In what bitterly impoverished a guise a human Sunday could appear. "Becoming humble," the assistant thought, "isn't this where so many find their final refuge in this life?"

Little by little, he passed through new and different streets.

So many streets! They reached far out into the landscape, building after building, even extending up the hill and along the canals, an endless progression of larger and smaller blocks of stone, with apartments carved into them for both the wealthy and the indigent. Now and again came a church—a rigid, smooth new one, or else a stately, tranquil older one with ivy on its crumbling walls. Joseph went past a police building, from whose premises he had once heard, years before, the screams of a mistreated person whom they had bound and were trying to subdue by beating him with a stick.

Now his path led him across a bridge, gradually the streets were becoming less regular and restricted, and the region he was walking through took on a village-like character. Cats were lying before the doors of the houses, and the houses were encircled by little gardens. The evening sun was laying itself yellowish-red upon the upper walls of the buildings and the trees in the gardens and on the faces and hands of people. He had reached the suburbs.

Joseph walked into one of the newer buildings that made such a curious appearance in this still almost rural region, climbed the stairs to the fourth floor, and remained standing there, waiting for politeness' sake until he'd caught his breath, then he brushed the dust from his clothes and rang the bell. The door opened, and the woman who appeared behind it gave a quiet little shriek of astonishment when she caught sight of him:

"Joseph, is it really you? It is? Come inside!"

The woman gave him her hand and pulled Joseph into her room. There she gazed for a rather long time into his eyes, took the hat from the head of the one standing there somewhat stiffly, smiled and said:

"How long it's been since we've seen each other. Sit down."

A moment later she said:

"Come, Joseph, come. Come sit here, beside the window. And then tell me everything. Tell me how you were able to go on living for so long without writing me a single solitary word, and without ever coming to see me. Will you have something to drink? Don't be shy, I've got some wine left in the bottle."

She drew him to her side at the window, and he began to tell her about the elastic factory, the English pound, his military service and Tobler's business. Below them, in the meadows on the outskirts of town, a number of children were playing and making noise in the evening sunshine. Now and then a nearby locomotive sounded its whistle, or you could hear a drunkard singing and jeering, one of those fellows who were in the habit of spending their Sunday evenings howling out riotous and flaming red notes, as it were, to give the evening its character.

The name and the story of the woman who now sat listening to her young acquaintance are quite simple.

Her name was Klara, and she was a carpenter's daughter. By coincidence, she came from the same region as Tobler and was therefore acquainted with the circumstances of his youth. Her upbringing had been strictly Catholic, but as soon as she went off into the world, her views changed dramatically, and she devoted herself to reading free-thinkers like Heine and Börne. She worked in a photography studio, first as a retoucher, then as receptionist and bookkeeper; the owner of the business fell in love with her, and she gave herself to him—not without considering the consequences of this unconventional arrangement: indeed, she awaited these consequences with a firm, liberated brow, feeling quite happy. She still was living in her father's home, a younger sister had meanwhile died of consumption. She traveled to work each day and then back home, by train, a journey of an hour and a quarter. At around this time she received her first visits from Joseph. She took pleasure in this young man, who then was scarcely twenty years old, and loved listening to the outpourings of his imagination, which were youthfully and naturally unripe.

What a strange world and age that had been. Under the label "socialism," a notion at once disconcerting and enticing had cast its tendrils, like those of a luxuriant vine, into the minds and about the bodies of even the old and experienced, so that anyone who fancied himself a writer or poet, anyone who was young, quick to take action and seize a resolve, was preoccupied with the idea. Journals of this character and slant came shooting like flame-colored, enchantingly fragrant blossoms from the dark interiors of enterprising spirits into the public sphere, where they elicited both surprise and delight. Workers and their interests were in general, at the time, received with more élan than gravity. There were frequent parades, led sometimes by women waving blood-red or black banners high up in the air. All who had ever felt displeased with the circumstances and regimes governing the world now united, filled with hope and contentment, in this passionate movement of hearts and minds, and what was achieved, thanks to the adventurousness of rabble-rousers, incendiaries and windbags of a certain stripe—raising this movement to vainglorious heights on the one hand, and dragging it down into the gutter of everyday existence on the other—was noted by the enemies of this "no-

134

tion" with a self-satisfied sneer. All the world, including Europe and the other continents, these young and only half-ripe enthusiasts insisted, was being joined and united by this idea into a joyous assembly of all mankind, but only he who worked had the right . . . —and so forth.

At the time, both Joseph and Klara were utterly captivated by this perhaps noble and lovely blaze which, in their opinion, could not be extinguished by either water or defamatory speech, and which extended across the entire round, rolling earth like a red-hued sky. Both of them, as was the fashion in those days, were in love with "all mankind."

Often they sat for hours until deep into the night in the room where Klara lived in her father's small house, speaking about the sciences and matters of the heart, whereby Joseph, shy as he generally was when interacting with others, always did most of the talking, which after all was appropriate, as his friend seemed to him like a revered teacher before whom he was to express his thoughts like school exercises learned more or less by rote for recitation. How lovely these evenings were. Whenever he went home afterward, the woman—who at the time was still a girl—would light his way down the stairs and say goodbye and adieu to him in her gentle voice. How her eyes gleamed when he turned back to catch one final glimpse of her.

Then Klara had a baby and became a "free woman," that is to say she found herself betrayed in the most callous manner by her gentleman friend, the photographer, who filled her with such profound disgust, that one day—she herself was living in the direst poverty—she simply showed him the door, saying only a single, short, peremptory word: "Go!" He was unworthy of her! She had to keep saying that to herself bravely, or else she would have succumbed to despair. But from then on she ceased to love "mankind" and instead worshiped her child.

Somehow she got by, she was courageous and had always been accustomed to putting her shoulder to the wheel. Soon she had acquired a camera of her own and set up her own darkroom, and while she was experiencing all the splendors of raising and caring for a small child—the difficulties, the joys and all the worries—she was turning out picture postcards and negotiating with shopkeepers and wholesalers like the sharpest of businessmen. She established a joint household together with a childhood friend who had suffered a fate similar to her own: the two of them shared a single apartment. This was one Frau Wenger, an intelligent but uneducated woman—a "brick," as Klara called her. The husband of this woman was a member or soldier of the Salvation Army, although he was certainly a well-put-together individual in terms of sanity and temperament and by no means a religious zealot. He had joined forces with the zealots for purely practical reasons. "Just go on and join, Hans," his own wife had said to him, "that's the best place for you to get over your drinking." Her Hans, you see, was a "drinker."

Joseph was a frequent and welcome visitor in this two-woman apartment. There was always bound to be something to eat or drink there, a cup of milk or a glass of tea, and time spent there was always filled with merriment, though it was impossible not to be conscious of the delicate boundaries always drawn around women with life experience. They would laugh, clearly of the opinion that laughter was a splendid activity now that they had put a bit of worldly life behind them. Klara's little boy and his qualities would be discussed. Oh, they had experienced all sorts of things. Joseph, too, had stopped talking about "mankind." Those days were long past. The more difficult a person found it to become "a proper human being," the less inclined he was to resort to grandiose words, and it certainly was difficult to be "proper," they felt this more clearly with each passing day.

Bit by bit, Joseph's visits became less frequent, and then it happened that he went an entire year without showing his face. One day, Klara received an oddly brief letter in which he asked permission to visit her again. She encouraged him to do so, and this was repeated several times more, always after lengthy absences.

And now here he was sitting beside the window, and she was listening to all he had to tell.

Klara, too, related various things, including that she would soon enter into married wedlock. The child must have a father, and she herself was in need of a man's support, as these days she was often indisposed and incapable of enduring the life of commercial activity she had been leading for so long. She'd become too weak to go on living all alone and unloved, and was longing to have the weariness that had taken hold of her entire spirit stroked and caressed by a human hand and a gentle, accepting will. She was only a woman, only a woman filled with hopes. The man she had chosen had simply allowed himself to be moved, won over, and chosen by her—the whole business was far too simple to require being narrated at length. "He" loved her, she said, and all his wishes and desires revolved around making her happy. Wasn't that the simplest thing in the world? And what did Joseph, whom she had known so many years, have to say to all this? Better he should hold his tongue, for she knew he was merely intending to utter some polite remark, she knew him and that was enough.

With a smile, she reached for his hand and pressed it.

All these things now in the past, she went on, all the lovely past things! How good they were, all these things that had occurred, how "proper." And all the various mistakes: how right and proper. And the thoughtlessness, how necessary it was! Youth must err, must speak and act without depth of thought for progress to occur. There would still be thoughts and feelings aplenty after one had begun to accumulate experiences, and eventually, in the course of a long life, youth would be extinguished.

And the two of them now spoke of the past, each seizing the words and exclamations directly from the other's lips, praising and repeating them.

Reunions of this sort are characterized by the complete absence of discord, such a thing simply cannot arise. Each person thoughtfully and warmly repeats the memories being related by the other, the two sets of lips speak at once, and the words they utter are met with echoes and admiration, never with objections. If arguments occur, it is only, one would like to think, in the musical sense.

Yes, the past came over them and rustled about their ears, making them gaze at the world backwards, as if looking downstairs from above. They didn't have to force their memories to cooperate, either, for the memories were already sending their delicate arms and tendrils curling off in search of memorable items so as to fetch and carry them perceptibly closer to where the two were sitting.

"How often I was moody and ungenerous," Joseph said regretfully. And Klara replied that he was the only one who always came back again to see her:

"A long time may pass between your visits, but you always come back. You are fond of making yourself scarce, yet meanwhile a person cannot help but feel that you are thinking of her. And then one day you return, and one feels surprised at how little you have changed, how wonderfully you've managed to remain just the same as ever. And one speaks with you as if you'd just run out to the corner bakery rather than putting a yearlong hole in a friendship, the way it always is with you, the eternal fugitive, it's as if you'd never left. Other men, Joseph, can stay away forever, life thrusts them in new directions, and they never again return to the site of their old friendships. But life has neglected you a little, you see, and this is why you have such a lovely ability to remain true to your own inclinations. I wish neither to wound you nor praise you, neither would be sincere, and a more direct approach has always worked well for both of us, hasn't it? Let's remain what we've always been to one another: you to me and I to you!"

Night had fallen during this conversation. They took leave of one another.

"Will you come again soon?"

Putting on his hat, Joseph remarked that it was, after all, a matter of indifference—seeing as he always managed to remain just the same as ever—whether he came again decades later or four days from now.

Because of these words, they parted coldly.

And now, Mr. Clerk, or however you prefer to be addressed, you are back in the Villa Tobler, make no mistake, and, in the guise of a bird beating its wings above your apparently rather poetically-minded head, the Advertising Clock is hurtling back and forth. Sunday, that softest of days, is over now, and the hard, rugged workday has just grabbed hold of you; you'll have to puff yourself up to full height to have any chance to withstand its powerful waves. Just go on being "the same as ever," as your friend Klara has put it—this will do less harm than if you suddenly resolve to turn over a new leaf. It isn't really possible to turn over a new leaf just like that, from one day to the next: make a note of this, if you will. But when "life has neglected you," to quote yet another of those feminine maxims—one which would appear to be quite appropriate—then you have no choice but to struggle against this neglect, which is in fact unworthy, are you listening, and not just sit about in the brightest-broadest daylight and then on evenings full of melancholy sunsets chat with old ladyfriends about "days gone by." All such activities should be avoided in future. On the contrary, you have to remind yourself of your duties, for it happens to be the case that Sundays and Sunday outings do not go on forever, and you will surely concede that duty has heretofore been a tiny bit "neglected" by a certain assistant, just as life itself has neglected the gentleman in question. And as for the absence or lack of wits—can this problem now be eliminated for good? Filling up a head can't be done overnight, it requires steady labor. Simply refuse to tolerate indolence in yourself and in this way, one would like to believe, things will gradually begin to accumulate in your head.

The Advertising Clock is sprawled on the ground in defeat, wailing for a bit of solvent capital. Go to it and give it your support so that it may gradually, one limb at a time, rise up again and successfully imprint itself on people's opinions and judgments once and for all—a task that is worthy, if you will, of your mental abilities, and useful to boot. See to it as well that bullets soon come flying out of the Marksman's Vending Machine, don't hesitate so long, just give the handle a good yank, and the machine so ingeniously conceived and constructed by your master, Herr Tobler, will soon enough spring into motion. No feelings now. You can't always be going out for a stroll, you must also accomplish things, and you'll also have to take a closer look at that drill one of these days, not weeks from now but rather as swiftly as possible, so that you'll be possessed of the requisite knowledge pertaining to all aspects of the Tobler enterprises.

All too modest a responsibility for the same young man who is permitted to assist Frau Tobler—a circumstance he holds in high regard—in hanging out the wash in the garden. One must also consider those things that lie hidden, for they are crucial in an engineering bureau. Stringing up clotheslines, my dear sir, my dear sprinkler and hoser-down of the garden, is not what you were summoned to the top of this green hill to perform. You are certainly quite fond of watering the garden, aren't you? Shame on you! And have you given even the slightest thought to the patented invalid chair? No? Good Lord above, what a clerk. You deserve to be "neglected by life."

These were approximately Joseph's own thoughts when he awoke in his bed on Monday morning. He got up and was about to swap his nightshirt for a day shirt, but then became immersed in contemplating his legs for a solid minute. After the legs had been inspected, his bare arms became the subject of study. Joseph stood before the mirror and found it most interesting to turn this way and that, observing his body. A good proper body, and healthy, capable of enduring exertions and deprivations. It was surely an outright sin for a person equipped with such a torso to remain lying in bed longer than was needed to take his rest. Someone who pushed a heavy wheelbarrow all day long couldn't have more healthy, more solidly constructed limbs than these. He got dressed.

And did so quite slowly. After all, there was plenty of time, a few minutes wouldn't make much difference. To be sure, Tobler's opinion on this matter diverged from his, as Joseph had already had occasion to experience, but Tobler himself was Mondaying today. Mondaying meant stretching out in bed longer than usual, letting oneself go and indulging oneself a bit more than on any other workday, and Tobler was a real champion in Monday lounging, he wouldn't be putting in an appearance down in the realm of technical solutions and problems until half past ten.

This morning Joseph's hair appeared extraordinarily difficult to brush and comb. His toothbrush recalled bygone days. The soap with which he wanted to wash his hands slipped from his grasp and shot beneath the bed, and he had to bend down and retrieve it from the farthest corner. His collar was too high and too tight, although it had fit perfectly the day before. What marvels. And how tedious this all was.

In some other place and at some other hour, all this would perhaps have struck him as agreeable, instructive, nice, fine, amusing, even enchanting. Joseph recalled certain times in his life when buying a new necktie or a stiff English hat had sent him into a frenzy. Half a year before, he had experienced just such a hat scenario. It had been a quite good normal hat of moderate height, the sort that "better" gentlemen are in the habit of wearing. Joseph, however, felt nothing but distrust for this hat. A thousand times he placed it upon his head, standing before the mirror, only to set it back on the table. Then he moved three steps away from this charming eyesore and observed it the way an outpost observes the enemy. Nothing about it was in any way objectionable. Hereupon he hung the hat up on its nail, and there too it appeared quite innocuous. He tried putting it on his head again—oh horror! It seemed bent on trying to split him in two from top to bottom. He felt as if his very personality had become a bleary, caustic, bisected version of itself. He went out onto the street, and found himself reeling like a despicable drunkard—he felt lost. Stepping into a place of refreshment, he took off his hat: saved! Yes, that had been the hat scenario. He had also experienced collar scenarios in his lifetime, as well as coat and shoe scenarios.

He betook himself downstairs to breakfast, where he ate without restraint, all but indecently. No one else, incidentally, was in the room, but even so! All the more reason! Even when one was all alone, there was no cause to disregard the propriety of table manners. How in the world had he worked up such an appetite? Because it was Monday? No, he was simply deficient in character, that was all. He took such childish pleasure in slicing himself a piece of bread, and yet it was Tobler's bread, not his, and then it so filled him with delight to dish out the fried potatoes, and whose fried potatoes were these if not Tobler's? He found it so astonishingly agreeable to eat a bit more than his hunger required, and whom was he harming by doing so? After he had finished, he ought by rights to have gotten up so as to begin work, but what's to be done when one finds oneself stuck and unable to arise from the dining table? Then Pauline arrived and chased him off with her disagreeable appearance.

Down in the office. The first thing was to pace back and forth a little, after all that was standard procedure, that's how a person always begins when he's resolved to get to work. Was Joseph one of those individuals who always begin some piece of work by first taking a breather and only afterward, when they have finished work, that is, half-finished it, do they begin to display some energy, which suggests perhaps that the impetus behind this energy is merely the wish to indulge in some cheap amusement? In a leisurely fashion, he lit one of the familiar cheroots, which always sweetened the thought of getting down to work, and soon he was puffing away like a member of a smoking club.

And then he sat down at his desk again and began to make himself useful.

At around ten o'clock Tobler arrived, in fine spirits, as Joseph noticed at once. Therefore it was permissible to infuse a certain buoyancy into his "Good morning, Herr Tobler" and re-light his cheroot. And indeed the figure of his superior and the head of the firm was radiating a conspicuous delight. He appeared to have done some proper boozing the night before. Each of his gestures at this moment was saying: "All right, now I know what the snag is. From now on things will be taking a different turn in my business endeavors."

In the friendliest tone of voice, he inquired as to the direction Joseph's Sunday amusements had taken, and as soon as Joseph said where he had been, he exclaimed:

"Is that so? You went to the city? And how did you like it there after such a long absence? Not bad, eh? Oh yes, cities offer a great many things, but in the end one is always happy to come back home again. Am I right or am I not? But what I wanted to say to you was that you no longer—forgive me, but I couldn't help noticing, ha, ha—you no longer have such terribly nice clothes on. So why don't you go to my wife today and have her give you a suit of mine that still looks as good as new. Tell her the gray suit, and she'll know which one you mean. There's no need for you to be at all embarrassed, this is a suit I no longer wear anyhow. And surely we can come up with a couple of colored shirts with matching dickeys and cuffs, certainly a perfect fit for you. Don't you think?"

"I really have no need for any of these things," Joseph replied.

"Why no need? You can see for yourself how bitterly in need of them you are. Don't make such a fuss when I give you something. Just accept it, and that's that."

Tobler was indignant. Suddenly something occurred to him. He sat down on a chair beneath the mechanism for the sample Marksman's Vending Machine and after half a minute said: "I know perfectly well what you are thinking. It is true, Marti, you have still not received any salary, and no doubt you're thinking you will never receive any. Be patient. Others are having to be patient just now as well. Moreover, I hope you will not find it necessary to walk around with a sullen look on your face because of this. I for one certainly won't tolerate any such behavior. A person who eats as well as you do here, and enjoys such splendid air as the air you're breathing up here, has a long way to go before he arrives at grounds for complaint. You are alive! Just remember the state you were in when I hired you down in the city. You look like a prince. And surely you have reason to feel grateful to me."

Joseph replied (and it was later incomprehensible to him where he had found the cheek to express himself in such a way):

"All well and good, Herr Tobler! But permit your subordinate to say to you that I find it highly disconcerting to be always reminded of the good food, the magnificent air, the pillows and the bed in which I sleep. Such remarks can spoil the air, the sleep and the food for a person almost entirely. What makes you consider yourself justified to constantly reproach me for enjoying my sojourn here and the amenities that are quite naturally connected with it? Am I a beggar or a worker? Please remain calm, Herr Tobler. Please, I am not making a scene here, I am quite simply explaining something for the sake of our mutual and necessary understanding. I would like to establish three things. First, I am grateful to you for all the things you have been 'offering' me; second, you know this perfectly well, for you've had every opportunity to observe this in my behavior; and third, I've been doing real work here, the proof of this claim being that neither my conscience nor your calculations have suggested our parting ways. As for the gift of clothing you have so kindly proposed, I have just this moment thought better of my refusal and would like to accept it with appropriate thanks. In all honesty, I could use some clothes and linens. You'll have to forgive the tone of this speech, or else you'll have no choice but to eject me from your household. This speech and this tone were necessary, for I feel the most sincere need to demonstrate to you that I am most certainly able to defend myself against—how shall I put it—unworthy treatment."

"Heaven and earth! Where did you get such a mouth? How utterly absurd. Have you taken leave of your senses, Joseph Marti?"

Tobler found that the most practical thing to do at this point was burst into loud laughter. But the very next moment his forehead was drawn into deep folds:

"So then show me, devil take it, that you are genuinely capable of accomplishing real work. Up till now I have seen only scant proof of this—a quick tongue is no accomplishment to speak of, do you understand? Where are the letters that still need to be answered?"

"Here!" Joseph said meekly. He had once more become utterly timid. The letters were in the wrong place. Tobler picked up the entire letter-basket and hurled it to the floor in a wild gesture of fury, shouting:

"And this is the one who keeps trying to rebel! Why don't you stop being so sensitive and pay attention instead. Write this down."

And he dictated the following:

To Herr Martin Grünen in Frauenberg.

Your letter, in which you give notice of the termination of the loan of five thousand marks allocated to me for the realization of my Advertising Clock effective the first of the coming month, has reached me here, and in response to it—have you got all that?—I would like to point out the following:

1. My current financial situation is such that it is utterly impossible for me to repay the sum in question on the day indicated by you.

2. You are gravely mistaken if you believe you have a legal right to insist on so unexpectedly swift a repayment, as

3. According to the arrangement made between us when the loan was finalized, as far as I recall, and as I can demonstrate if necessary in black and white—are you keeping up?—a repayment of the amount owed was to occur only after the enterprises involving the Advertising Clock had attained a certain profitable objective:

4. This is not yet the case.

5. The loan allocated to me cannot be viewed except in the particular context of the Advertising Clock undertaking, and accordingly the repayment of the former cannot be separated from the success of the latter.

6. One might wonder to begin with whether a demand for repayment on such short notice is permissible in a case such as ours. The main point is that the borrowed funds are tied up in the aforementioned enterprise and subject to the risks entailed in it.

Esteemed sir, it is my hope, now that I have explained my position to you, that you will seriously reconsider this matter. Please consider the predicament in which I find myself, and you will surely not have the heart to wish ruin upon a businessman who is struggling and resisting with all the strength at his disposal against sinking into the depths that loom beneath him. If you wish to get your money back, do not pressure me. The Advertising Clock shall prove its worth! In the hope of having sufficiently convinced you, I remain yours respectfully—

"Give it to me!" And Tobler signed his name, whereby he remained lost in the apparently absent-minded contemplation of the signed letter for a full minute.

Meanwhile the assistant was devoting himself to thoughts of his own. He thought: That's just what he's like, this Herr Tobler. First he assumes an arrogant, threatening position, and then suddenly starts to cower and beg that one "reconsider" etc. Herr Grünen will not "have the heart," Herr Tobler thinks. But what if he does? This letter is composed in a manner which suggests that its author is on the brink of despair. At first it sounds supercilious, then significant, then weighty, then boastful, then bitingly scornful, then all at once timid, then furious, then entreating, then suddenly gruff, then puffed up for one more attempt at an arrogant tone: the clock *shall* prove its worth! Who's going to demonstrate that? Oh, a sharp creditor like this Grünen from Frauenberg will only sneer when he reads this maudlin letter.

He ventured to suggest meekly to his superior that the letter's tone struck him as not quite right. This was a spark in the tinderbox.

Tobler leapt abruptly to his feet: Was it Joseph's business to stand there talking rot? If he couldn't restrain himself from making comments, he should not first wait half an hour after a matter was concluded to open his mouth—and then he should see to it that his remarks were not as idiotic as the one he had just allowed himself to utter.

"Idiotic!" Tobler shouted, seized his hat and walked out the door.

Joseph copied the letter with the copy press, folded it up, placed it in an envelope that had already been addressed, sealed it and put a stamp on it.

A few hundred circulars had just arrived from the printing shop. Joseph began to fold these circulars precisely to fit the size of their envelopes so that they could be sent out in all directions. This leaflet contained, along with a price list, in an attractive typeface and adorned with illustrative plates, the precise description of a small steam apparatus, another of Tobler's inventions. It was of crucial importance that this steam-holding tank be advertised to all the many factories and mechanical workshops scattered about the countryside in the vicinity of Bärenswil as well as elsewhere in the region; this, one hoped, would result in a lovely profit.

The assistant went on folding these papers until noon— work that he found to have something downright festive and thought-provoking about it—and then he went to lunch. During the meal, everyone was silent, with the exception of Dora, who was unable to hold her charming tongue. The boys displayed some naughty behavior. Frau Tobler bemoaned the long school holidays, which she clearly saw as the cause of this general running-wild on the part of young people everywhere, declaring how happy she was that the new school year was about to begin, since now, thank God, a new phase was in the offing for these scallywags. The teacher's authority and cane would perhaps succeed in achieving what had proven impossible for their mother: instilling in her sons courteous and considerate behavior. How very good it was that autumn was approaching. During these long beautiful summer days, young people suffered such boredom that they no longer knew where to find even one more opportunity to get up to something bad and foolish.

The word "autumn" pierced Joseph's soul. Beautiful autumn! A moment later, having finished his lunch, he got up and told Frau Tobler that he needed money to buy stamps. His request appeared to make a disagreeable impression on her, for she replied that she supposed that now she was to be responsible for such matters as well. She heaved a sigh and gave the assistant what he asked for with a rather peevish expression (though she was also, it appeared, somewhat flattered). So it was she, the wife, to whom people had to come to obtain and receive money for stamps. Joseph in turn was acting slightly insulted.

After all, he was the employee of a man, not the assistant of a woman. How irksome it was, having to beg from a skirt two-mark coins. Observing his inappropriate wrath, Frau Tobler contented herself with glancing at him condescendingly.

He started off to the post office. In the garden, several workers and laborers were occupied with shoveling up the dirt and piling it in an enormous heap. The earth was wet, it had rained not long before.

"And now an underground fairy grotto on top of everything else! What is Tobler thinking?" grumbled Joseph as he reached the main road. The sharp odor of schnapps was streaming out the open door of the Rose Tavern, which lay nearby. It was here that Wirsich had drunk up what he had saved from his salary and wages. From here he had gone reeling off into "another world," leaving the best part of himself behind at the Rose, lying beneath the table. When the assistant reached the village, he dropped in—a newly acquired habit of his—at the Sailing Ship restaurant, and who was sitting there at the round regulars' table? Tobler!

So there they were, the two of them, master and servant— and where? In a public house.

Certainly it is customary for a person filled with rage to down a quick drink so as to cool and extinguish the hot temper burning in his breast, and of course equally natural is the thirst of a subordinate who's had to "beg" for postage money, leaving him in a fairly foul humor. Disgruntlement can be alleviated by "tipping one back." And certainly one has to—and is allowed to—do just this, but it was all the same a rather curious feeling that came over both men upon finding their liquid intentions thus exposed there in the Sailing Ship, and the two exchanged a brief but meaningful glance.

"Well, it looks as if you're feeling thirsty, too," Herr Tobler said in a friendly but grave tone to the one who had just entered. The latter replied:

"Yes I am, and why not?"

Herr Tobler always waited at the Sailing Ship for trains that were arriving and departing. Today, too, he was "just waiting for his train." The restaurant was right next to the train station. But Tobler missed his trains rather often nonetheless; one might, if one were an innkeeper, almost suspect him of missing them on purpose. Whenever this happened, he was in the habit of grumbling: "Now that idiotic train has left without me yet again."

Joseph finished his drink and left. His employer shouted after him, in such a way that all the other guests could hear: "Write to the clockmaker, what's his name again, and tell him to get started assembling the clocks for the Utzwil-Staefener Railroad right away. The letter has to go out today. The rest I assume you know."

Joseph felt a little bit ashamed of his "loquacious superior," as he secretly referred to him; he nodded and slipped out the door.

He went to the bookbinder's and the stationer's and had each of them give him a large number of useful objects for the office and drawing table—all to be placed "on the tab."

Such a sweet little accounts book, no end of things could be written down in it. One simply took possession of the goods and allowed the tab to grow.

The owner of the stationery shop made so bold as to inquire when and if he would be able to collect a certain sum.

"Oh, some time soon," Joseph casually remarked.

"It is quite proper, the way I am acting," he thought, "you

have to speak to people in a casual tone of voice, and then they will be utterly trusting. When you give no sign of taking a matter particularly seriously, it appears that seriousness is not yet called for. If I had replied to this man's question in earnest, he would have begun to feel suspicious, and tomorrow morning we would have found him standing in the office with his receipts in his hands. I serve my master's interests when I continue to divert gentle stirrings of suspicion from his person."

While entertaining this train of thought, he seemed to be unhurriedly inspecting a collection of picture postcards. Leaving the shop now, he gave a friendly smile and was smiled at in just as friendly a manner by the shop owner.

When he arrived home, he once more busied himself with folding the circulars. For each individual circular, he employed four hand motions. He daydreamed as he worked. This task practically demanded that one engage in the most leisurely reflections. From time to time, he took an intoxicating drag on the stem of his cheroot. Right in front of the desk and office window, Frau Tobler was seated on a bench that had been placed there; she was sewing and holding a conversation in a singsong voice with her beloved Dora. Joseph thought:

"How good this child has it!"

"Are you intending to mail off this entire mountain of circulars?" Frau Tobler asked. She added: "By the way, it's time for coffee. Come outside. The coffee is on the table already."

In the summer house during this snack, the employee felt compelled by the friendliness with which Frau Tobler was treating him to volunteer that he regretted having behaved so impudently toward her.

What did he mean? she wanted to know, adding that she didn't understand.

"Well, I mean, what I said about Wirsich!"

She replied that she had long since forgotten the entire incident. Her memory in such matters was inexact, thank goodness. Had there been anything more to it? Surely nothing important. But in any case she was happy to hear Joseph confessing that he was sorry to have offended her. He should be easy in his mind, she said, but above all he must always make an effort to do his best in all matters related to her husband's business, that was the main thing.

Ah, sometimes she wished, these days more than ever, that she herself was endowed with good business sense, so that she could help her husband. The very thought of having to move away, having to leave behind the house she'd become so fond of, hav — ing — to . . .

There were tears in her eyes.

"I shall make an effort!" He almost shouted these words.

"Then all's well," she said and tried to smile.

"You can't just give up hope like that—"

She wasn't giving up hope, she said. She was levelheaded enough when it came to all these worrisome things. Yesterday Tobler reproached her bitterly—and, it appeared to her, unjustly—for taking his entire difficult situation too lightly; she found it necessary to respond to these accusations with silence. What could a weak and unpracticed woman do in these circumstances? Ought she perhaps to spend the livelong day wailing with a despondent face? What would be the use? To any reasonably sensible woman such a thing wouldn't even occur—and it wouldn't befit her, she'd deem such conduct more dangerous than fitting. Frau Tobler, on the contrary, was always of good cheer: she even went so far as to praise herself secretly for her comportment. Yes, that's what she did, even if there wasn't a single creature anywhere in the world capable of recognizing this accomplishment. As for the rest, she knew who she was, and felt obliged, even if just for her own private reason alone, not to let the joyous and dignified courage with which she looked life in the face begin to ebb. At the same time, she was quite aware of what a difficult time her husband was going through.

Her gaiety had returned.

"As for you, Joseph," she continued, gazing at the assistant with her enormous eyes, "I know perfectly well how seriously you go about your work. And it would be wrong to expect all solutions and all splendid accomplishments to come all at once from a single man. It's just that you're a bit hard on people sometimes, really you are."

"You are humiliating me, but I deserve it," Joseph said.

Both of them laughed.

"You are a peculiar person," Frau Tobler remarked, bringing their conversation to a close. She got up. Joseph ran after her to ask if she would be so kind as to identify the clothes Herr Tobler had just given him and have them brought to his room, he wanted to try them on this very day. She agreed, saying that she would take the garments in question out of the wardrobe at once.

Approximately one hour later, he watered the garden. He found it so agreeable to watch the thin, silvery stream of water slice through the air and to hear the water strike the leaves of the trees. The excavators soon tossed aside their shovels and pickaxes and called it a day. "A peculiar person," the one occupying himself with the hose mused, and almost fell into a gloomy frame of mind: "Why *peculiar?*"

Doctor Specker and his wife came to call that evening, and Tobler turned up as well, huffily and against his will. He had just been settling down for a cozy evening at the Sailing Ship when he had been reached by telephone and informed of the visitors who had arrived up at the villa.

"Do they have to come again so soon?" he had said to his wife on the telephone, but he couldn't very well send them packing, and so he sacrificed the nice game of Jass he could have had at the inn to instead play cards at home, which to his mind was a bit "infantile." Indeed, the sort of Jass played by true devotees of the game was far more serious and masculine in nature—and above all much quieter; Tobler had come to all but hate the game's chatty, innocent, domestic form.

Joseph excused himself, saying he had a headache and wanted to go out for a little walk in the fresh air. "So he is shirking his duty while I am forced to stay right here," Tobler's face appeared to be saying when he heard Joseph's alibi.

Joseph fled "into nature." The moonlight was delicately, expansively illuminating the whole region. From somewhere or other came the sound of lapping water. He walked up the mountainside between the meadows he knew so well. The large stones beside the path shone white beneath the moon. The thickets of trees were full of a whispering, sighing susurration. Everything had been dipped in a fragrant, wistful haze. From the nearby forest he heard the hooting of owls. A few isolated houses, a few tentative sounds, and suddenly a light here or there, one in motion, grasped in the hand of some late wanderer, or else a steady one, a lamp behind a half-curtained window. What stillness there was in the dark, what vastness in the invisible, what distance! Joseph surrendered himself entirely to his sensations.

Suddenly he thought again of the "peculiar person" he was. What about him was so terribly peculiar? Well, strolling around alone at night—this, to be sure, was curious enough, this sort of pleasure might well be dubbed "peculiar." But what else? Was that all? No, the main thing was his life, his entire life, the life he had been leading until now and the future life one might assume was in store for him—this is what was peculiar, and Frau Tobler was quite right to remark . . .

These women, how well they understood how to read the hearts and characters of others. What a talent to be able to send so right and fitting an utterance directly into the middle of one's astonished soul. A peculiar fellow. But she'd spoken in jest, hadn't she?

Grieving over so very many things, he went home.

The Bärenswilers or Bärensweilers are a good-natured but at the same time somewhat treacherous race—they might best be described as slyboots or tricksters. They are all more or less shifty and crafty, and every last one of them—the one more, the other less—has something secretive or hidden about him, and for this reason they all tend to look a bit artful and wily. They are honest and moral and not without pride; for centuries they have enjoyed wholesome civil and political liberties. But they are wont to combine this honesty with worldly ways and a certain sense of cunning, and they like to give the impression of being sharp as tacks. They are all a little ashamed of their hearty, natural straightforwardness, and each one of them would rather be seen as a "scoundrelly dog" than as a blockhead and donkey who is easily duped. Duping a Bärenswiler is no easy matter—anyone who wishes to attempt such a feat should be strenuously forewarned. They are good-hearted when treated with respect, and have a good dose of honor in them, since for centuries they have enjoyed . . . etc. But they are ashamed of their own kindness, as they are of nearly every expression of sentiment. They laugh using their back teeth where other people and nations laugh only with their lips, they make conversation more with their pricked-up ears than with their unabashed mouths, they are lovers of silence, but sometimes they will set about boasting like proper sailors, as if all of them had been born with mouths destined for use in public houses. Later they will hold their tongues for four weeks without pause. In general, they know themselves quite well, they're able to calculate where their strengths and where their failings lie, and they are always more likely to put their flaws on display than their positive qualities, so as not to let anyone know just how capable they are. This ruse proves much to their advantage in business affairs. In the surrounding region, they have a reputation for being uncouth devils, and this is not entirely without cause, but it is always only a few among them who are disagreeable boors, and thanks to these few exceptions the Bärenswilers have to put up with many an impudent and unjust epithet. They have a great deal of imagination, coupled with the desire to put it to use; those among them who are lacking in taste therefore tend to do more boasting than is right and proper, for which they are held in ill repute elsewhere in the land. But above all else, Herr Tobler, they are down-to-earth and sober, a race apparently made to conduct business in a modest but safe manner and reap profits accordingly. The homes they live in are as clean as they are, the streets they build are a bit bumpy, just like them, and the electric lanterns that light up the streets of their village at night are practical, once more just exactly like them. And this is the sort of people among whom Herr Tobler had to come to live.

Engineer Tobler!

Time made an invisible leap forward. Even in the region around Bärenswil, the seasons don't stand still, but rather they naturally had to do just what they were compelled to in other places as well: they were changing, in spite of Herr Tobler, who might well have wished to see time stop in its tracks. A man like him, whose business was going poorly, was unconsciously the enemy of all that was moving calmly and steadily forward. A day or a week is always either too short or too long to suit such a person—too short because the approaching crisis is already in view, and too long because the sight of the sluggish course his own enterprises are taking can only fill him with tedium. When time appeared to be rapidly advancing, Tobler would murmur that it had been days since he'd been able to sit down to any real work, and when it appeared to be taking slow, unhurried steps, he wished he could be transported far off into a future decade so as not to have to look any longer at all these things surrounding him.

Autumn was arriving, everything appeared to be sitting down, somewhere something was coming to a standstill, nature seemed at times to be rubbing its eyes. The breezes were blowing differently, at least it often seemed that way, shadows slipped past the windows, and the sun became a different sun. When it was warm out, a few people, true Bärenswilers, would say: just look how warm it is still. They were grateful for the mild weather, as just a day before, standing at the threshold, one would have had to say: Good heavens, it's starting to rumble!

Now and again the sky furrowed its beautiful, pure brow, or even went so far as to knit it together in folds and veils of grief. Thereupon the entire hill and lake region would be wrapped in gray damp cloths. Rain fell heavily upon the trees, which didn't keep one from running down to the post office if one happened to be a clerk in the House of Tobler. Herr Martin Grünen appeared similarly unaffected by the beautiful, gentle change of seasons, otherwise he would hardly have been able to write that none of the reasons Tobler had specified in explanation of his refusal to pay were of any concern to him and that he insisted on the immediate termination of the loan in question.

And when the beautiful weather then returned, how happy it could make you! There were above all three colors to be observed in nature: a white, a blue and a gold, fog, blue sky, and sunshine, three quite, quite refined, even elegant colors. You could go on taking meals out in the garden, you stood there leaning up against the trellis and pondering whether you might ever have seen such a sight before, perhaps in your youth. The warmth and colors had melted into one. Yes, you tell yourself, colors like this produce warmth! The region appeared to be smiling, the sky seemed to have been made happy by its own appearance, it appeared to be the scent and the substance and the dear meaning of this smiling of land and lake. How all these things could just lie there, radiant and still. If you gazed out over the surface of the lake, you felt—and you didn't even have to be an assistant for this—as if you were being addressed with friendly, agreeable words. If you gazed into the yellow realm of the trees, a tender melancholy stirred in your breast. If you looked at the house, you felt compelled to laugh, although despotic Pauline was just brushing out rugs at the kitchen window. The world seemed to be full of music. Above the crowns of the trees, the dazzling-gauzy-white outlines of the Alps appeared like notes of music fading into the distance. Looking at all these things, you were suddenly struck by how unreal it all looked. Then another time things were different. Other vistas, other feelings! The region itself appeared to be sentient and to be experiencing different feelings. And what was being felt vanished each time in the all-encompassing blue. Yes, everything had assumed a blue-tinged shade and hue. And then this briskness, this rustling from the trees, which always contained a faint, cool motion. Could a person work in such surroundings, prove himself useful? Yes, by stringing up the clothesline and helping the washerwoman carry a basket of wet laundry up from the cellar into the golden-blue light of the earth. Such activity was perfectly fitting on such a beautiful and, as it were, bright-burnished day whose every corner was flashing with colors and notes. And there was a whole series of these days on which you could only get out of bed, lean out the window and say several times in a row: how splendid!

 Yes, the summer land had become an autumn land.

But the marching pace of Tobler's enterprises had taken no new turn—there was no about-face, not a step out of line. Worry marched in lock-step with disappointment, advancing like two exhausted but disciplined soldiers, not permitting themselves the slightest deviation. On the whole, even taking into account the various failures and futilities, they made up a most orderly procession marching slowly but steadily forward, eyes fixed on what lay ahead.

Tobler was now taking more and more business trips, as if the sight of his charming home were painful to him, a reproach. He was in possession of a rail pass permitting unlimited travel for a full quarter of a year, which after all, since he had made the investment, must be put to use. What would have been the common sense in it otherwise? Travel in and of itself appeared to give him pleasure. He was just the man for it. Waiting for his train at the Sailing Ship, then perhaps missing the train the first time around, only to board the very next one, a weighty briefcase clamped beneath his arm, and then to ride off over hill and dale, striking up a conversation with his fellow travelers, presenting one or the other of them with a cigar or a good cheroot, and at last getting out of the train in some unfamiliar region,

spending time among gay, mirth-loving people, conducting negotiations until deep into the night in first-class restaurants,
etc.: this was just the thing for Tobler, it suited both him and his
character, kept unworthy thoughts from entering his head, and
helped him feel like himself again for a little while—in his suit
that fit him so admirably.

Why should he stay home when he had his clerk, whom he
was obliged to "maintain." It would have been ridiculous. If he
took up sedentary ways, it would utterly destroy his last remaining scrap of enterprising spirit. From there, it wouldn't
take much before he'd have to "shut up shop" altogether. And
that would be the last straw: sitting at home surrounded by
sneering Bärenswil faces. No, he'd rather put a bullet in his
head, that would be preferable.

And so he kept traveling.

At home, meanwhile, concern over the necessities of everyday life had begun to rap lightly at the windowpanes, to pluck at
a curtain so as to gaze cozily into the Tobler family's interior,
and to stand in the doorway to evoke for anyone who happened
past a sense of uncertainty. This concern was taking a bit more
interest now than it had in the summer. It was just standing
there for the time being, inspecting the terrain, without otherwise attracting notice. If its presence was sensed now and again,
that was enough; it displayed courtesy and caution. A threshold, a windowsill, a snug little corner of the roof or under the
dining table—such places seemed to satisfy it. In no way did it
assert its importance, though, to be sure, it did from time to
time touch the heart of Frau Tobler with its cold breath, causing

her to spin around in broad daylight as if there were someone standing behind her, as if she meant to ask: "Who's that standing there?"

The small sums of money that the technical enterprises brought in were immediately—as per her husband's instructions—appropriated by the lady of the house. Bread, milk and meat had to be paid for on a daily basis. The family went on living and eating just as they always had, in no way did they economize on any of these things. Better not to be alive at all than to live poorly. Pauline's salary was paid out to her regularly; the assistant, on the other hand, was expected to have sufficient tact and understanding to grasp the situation without a word and act accordingly. Joseph was a man, and Pauline a capricious child of the lower classes. A man could be called on to make sacrifices where a working-class girl could not—the clerk grasped this distinction.

The boys were going to school again, a great relief for their mother, who was now able to go out on the veranda to enjoy the mild autumn sunshine and recline in a gently rocking chair. Lying there like that, she would sometimes be visited by a dream that in the loveliest hues invited her to bask in life as a fine lady, one of the noblest and best—a charming illusion in which she couldn't help luxuriate for a brief quarter of an hour, though not without a sense of profound melancholy.

One day she called the assistant out to the veranda, she wanted to ask him something. This was shortly after lunch, Tobler was off on some journey, and the two little girls were playing in the living room.

What beautiful weather they were having yet again, Joseph remarked as he stepped outside. The woman nodded, but said there was something quite different on her mind.

"What is it?"

Well, various things. Above all, she had been constantly pre-occupied these last few days, wondering whether it wouldn't be far more sensible simply to sell the house at once, just as it was, and move away voluntarily—the humiliation of having to leave under duress, she felt, was slowly approaching. All her husband's enterprises would come to nothing, this she now felt she knew for certain.

"Why now?"

She made a dismissive gesture and asked Joseph to give her his candid opinion of the Advertising Clock.

"I am firmly convinced," he replied, "that it's on the right track. We just have to be patient a short while longer. Establishing relationships with further capitalists—"

Oh! she said passionately, he should hold his tongue! She could tell perfectly well just by looking at him that he was speaking in bad faith, telling her things he didn't believe himself. That wasn't particularly nice. What possibly could make him consider her incapable of withstanding the full force of the truth? If he insisted on lying, then he was a faithless and disloyal employee, and there was no longer any point in retaining him. She had asked to hear his opinion of the matter in question, and now she was ordering him to speak his mind openly. Above all, to begin with, she wished to learn whether her husband's clerk was capable of independent thought. All he had to do was sit there and provide answers to her questions, assuming that as a man he had sufficient honor to possess his own opinion.

Joseph was silent.

What was she to think of this behavior, she wondered aloud. She believed she was still within her rights if she permitted herself to give him an order. Had his mouth tumbled down to the soles of his shoes? There was certainly plenty of room, given how many holes there were. Why such pride when the honor he put on public display was so paltry? Tobler's clothes suited him extremely well. Yes, they did. And now, she said, he should go away, she didn't care where he went, just so it was out of her sight.

In fact, Joseph had already left. He walked around the perimeter of the house, spoke a few words to Leo, the dog, then went into the office and sat down at his desk. He almost forgot to light himself a cheroot, but soon he recalled the pleasure to be had in this way and held a match to one of these ever-available combustibles. Feeling strangely comforted, he began to work.

A short while later, Frau Tobler appeared at the office door and said calmly:

"Your conduct provoked me, Marti, but you were right. Forget what just happened. Come down for coffee soon."

Shutting the door quietly behind her, she departed. The clerk was trembling violently. It was impossible for him to hold the pen in his hand. Life itself was dancing before his eyes. Windows, tables and chairs seemed to become living creatures. He put on his hat and went swimming. "Just a quick dip before coffee hour," he thought. And this was the woman he had wanted to scold on account of Silvi—what foolishness!

Happiness and health themselves do not plunge into the waves of life with any more delight than that with which he now immersed himself in the lake. The tranquil but already cold surface of the water was steaming; it lay there like oil, so immobile, so firm. The coolness of the element made the naked body move more vigorously and briskly. The attendant stationed beside the changing rooms called out to him: "Don't swim out so far, you out there. Hey! Don't you hear me?" But Joseph calmly went on swimming, he was not in the least concerned that he might get a cramp in his limbs. With broad strokes of his arms, he sliced and carved out a wet, beautiful path. From the depths of the lake, he felt ice-cold streams rising to touch him: how lovely that was, and he lay on his back, raising his eyes toward the wonderfully blue sky. When he swam back to land, he saw before him the whole countryside, which was drunk with autumnal hues, the shoreline, the houses. Everything was enveloped in a blissful flurry of colors and scents. He climbed out of the water and put on his clothes. As he was leaving the bathing establishment, the attendant who had become fearful on his behalf said that he ought to have obeyed him and swum back when he'd shouted to him; if some mishap were to occur, it was he, the attendant, who would be held responsible. Joseph laughed.

Frau Tobler looked shaken when he told her he hadn't been able to resist taking one last swim this year.

They were sitting in the summer house. Joseph found the taste of the brown liquid incomparably delicious after his swim. Frau Tobler offered that one really ought to take advantage of the few warm days remaining to them. She began to chat about her marriage, and the apartment where she had previously lived.

To have a house of one's own like this where one could come and go as one pleased, she said, was really a charming and peaceful thing. It might be a while before they were able to find something like that again—

Joseph interrupted her. Politely he said:

"Frau Tobler, you are about to get worked up again. Why do you have to think of this all the time? Allow me to remind you that I am your humble servant. But why all these conflicts? I am going to get up from the table now and await your permission to be seated again."

He had risen to his feet. She said he should sit down again. He did as she instructed.

For a while they were silent, and then suddenly she was seized by the whim to sit on the swing, and she asked the assistant to give her a push and then tug on the ropes that would keep her in motion. Flying high up into the air on her wooden board and then back down again, she cried out that she was enjoying herself and that they really did have to take advantage of the garden as long as it lasted. Soon winter would come and command them all too imperiously: Sit indoors!

But soon he had to stop her, for she was in danger of becoming dizzy. As he did so, he couldn't help but inhale the perfume of her body, around which he had thrown his arms for just one moment. Her hair touched his cheek. These full, long arms! He forced himself to look away. The thought of kissing her neck instantly shot through him, but he restrained himself. One minute later he was filled with horror at the thought of this simple possibility and was very glad he had let it slip by.

Again they sat across from one another. She was chattering away unrestrainedly, telling him how, in the building where she and her husband used to live, a young man had courted her, such a foolishly infatuated fellow—no, she couldn't help laughing aloud even to think, much less speak of it. One night this young man, who, incidentally, belonged to the upper crust, had slipped into her bedroom—she was already lying in bed—and had thrown himself on his knees before her and confessed his passionate longing. In vain she had shouted at him indignantly that he should remove himself at once. The young man got to his feet, but instead of taking his leave, he'd embraced her. Even now, recalling this horrific moment, she could feel the pressure of the hands clutching her. Naturally she cried out for help, and by chance—and now came the funny part of the story—her husband was just coming up the stairs. Hearing her cries, he burst into the room and set upon the young man with a vengeance. He brought his stick down so hard upon the lad's head and shoulders that it broke in two, and it was a thick one, and in the end she, the cause of this beating, had to implore Tobler to go easy on his opponent who, it seemed, was no match for him at all. Her husband had then thrown him down the stairs.

"I will have to be careful, then," Joseph said.

"You?" Never was a face more uncomprehending than the one Frau Tobler displayed to the assistant as she spoke that word.

She began to occupy herself with Dora. Then suddenly

turned to Joseph and asked whether she might ask a favor of him. There was a rather large parcel for her at the post office containing her new dress. She really would love to try it on today. Would it be asking too much if she were to request that he go and fetch it? Perhaps it was too burdensome a task, and it might well be that Joseph had more important matters to attend to.

Not at all, Joseph replied, he would go and fetch it at once. He was quite happy to have a reason to make the trip to the post office again.

He ran off at once, and half an hour later brought the package into the living room of the Villa Tobler. The woman was raptness personified as she opened this long-awaited parcel. She went up to her bedroom to try on the dress, Pauline had to assist her. It was good that the master of the house was not at home. With what scoffing and scolding he would have greeted this display of ecstatic womanly excitement.

A few minutes later she returned to the living room wearing the highly modern ensemble. It suited her splendidly. She asked Joseph to tell her how she looked. Silvi, the little messenger, had to run down to the office to summon him. The assistant was astonished to see Frau Tobler looking so beautiful.

"Exactly like a baroness," he said, laughing.

"No," she said, "seriously, how do I look?" She looked magnificent, he confessed, and allowed himself to add: "Your figure is shown off to excellent advantage. Actually you don't really look like Frau Tobler any longer, but more like a mermaid just emerged from the lake. For the eyes of the Bärenswilers, this dress might in fact be almost too beautiful. But in the end, even they deserve to learn and discover what feats can be accomplished by the seamstresses of the capital. The material and form of this garment are such that one supposes the material itself provided the idea for the form, and conversely that the form itself appears to have chosen this lovely material."

These remarks filled Frau Tobler with delight. Perhaps she was somewhat unsure of herself in matters of taste. Smiling, she replied that she wouldn't dream of appearing in such a get-up on the streets of Bärenswil, she intended to wear the dress only when she had occasion to go to town.

Unpaid bills and obligations. The bank was becoming incredulous. The tone of voice in which the teller at the Bärenswiler Bank conversed with Joseph when he had business there no longer expressed merely astonishment, but now condescending pity as well. "Things must be rough up there on your hilltop," this tone of voice said. Warnings and notices demanding immediate payment arrived by mail at the Evening Star on a daily basis. Nothing had been paid for, not even the cigars that were going up in smoke.

The grotto in the garden had now been completed as well, except for a few minor details that Tobler intended to have taken care of later, as soon as things were looking up. The contractors submitted their bill, which ran to approximately one thousand five hundred marks, a sum that had not been seen in the Villa Tobler in quite some time. Where would they get it? Could they dig it up from beneath the earth? Should they set Leo on some retiree out for a nocturnal stroll, knock him down and rob him? Alas, it was the twentieth century, the age of moonlit robberies was over.

And now the time had come to at least throw a little party once more. Cards were sent out to seven well-respected men in the village, and three accepted the invitation to attend the nocturnal grotto celebration, while the other four were—as regrets are so commonly phrased—unfortunately unable to attend. Which, by the way, was of no consequence. The fewer participants in attendance, the more each of them would get to drink. There were still a few bottles of excellent Neuenburger wine in the cellar. Their moment had come. A worthier occasion would not so soon present itself.

The three men—the owner of a grocery and general store, the innkeeper from the Sailing Ship and an insurance agent—arrived one stormy evening at the appointed hour. At once they proceeded to the fairy grotto, a cave-like, cement-lined, wallpapered thing, oblong in shape like the inside of a stove, and somewhat too low, causing the visitors to strike their heads on more than one occasion. A table was placed in this grotto along with a few chairs which the assistant and Pauline dragged in. A lamp provided the illumination.

Soon the wine arrived as well, a noble fiery beverage that flowed into the glasses and then went leaping across the savoring and tasting and smacking lips and down throats. As long as he still had such a splendid little wine on hand—Tobler broke off mid-speech, reminded of the need to display discretion and prudence by a glance flashed from the eyes of his wife. Yes, he had been about to say something stupid in front of three

Bärenswil slyboots. As for him, he was an open book.

The conversation grew ever gayer, ever more unconstrained. Crude jokes that in fact were quite unsuitable in the presence of three ladies (the parquet factory ladies were there as well), flew from mouth to mouth, received in each case with loudly laughing approbation. Joseph alone was not laughing much. Was he out of sorts, Tobler wanted to know. He should have some more wine, then his spirits would improve. Worries lay at the bottom of the glass; one had to make short work of them and just swallow them down. Where was Pauline? She should come try the Neuenburger as well. Frau Tobler declared this unnecessary, but the engineer insisted on it.

Stories of the most salacious sort were now being exchanged. The three Bärenswilers proved to be masters in the comical presentation of such tales. If Tobler had received a hundred-mark banknote for each burst of laughter that erupted on this evening, he would have become in fact a regally wealthy man overnight, affluent enough a hundred times over to eradicate all his debts at a single blow. But the laughter brought no profit, it faded out against the walls of the stone grotto—amusing but not enriching.

"To the success of your enterprises, Tobler!" the innkeeper from the Sailing Ship cried, raising up his full glass. Both moved and hurt by this, Herr Tobler summoned all his strength and made the following speech:

I should certainly hope so!

When a healthy man stakes all he has on his ideas, there will always be idle chatter in the wider circles of humanity, slandering and belittling the work of this man. This man, however, stands high above these suspicions. He is an entrepreneur and as such is obligated to venture not just some of what he has but all of it. His risk-taking, gentlemen, may appear bold, but it may often look boastful and ridiculous as well, for its sole and never-ending task consists in not shying away from anyone's judgment. What could such daring accomplish in a garret or laboratory, in a notebook or on a drawing table? A venture comes into existence in these places, but if it were to remain where it began its existence, then it would be nothing but a luxurious daydream. It must go out into the light of the world. It must show itself, must triumph over the danger of being thought ridiculous or useless, or else it must be crushed by that danger. What use to the world are clever minds if they live out their lives in hiding, what use are the inventions themselves? An invention is work, but it is not a risk—a mere noble thought rattles the edifice of the world not in the slightest. Ideas must be put into practice, thoughts aspire to be embodied. This requires a bold and intrepid man, a healthy, strong arm and a firm and true hand. Requires a foot that, once it at last, after many adversities, succeeds in gaining a foothold, will not so quickly give up the ground it has gained. A heart that can withstand storms—in a word, a manly soul. This is not to say that such a man will be happy as soon as his enterprises are crowned with fragrant and resounding success, it is not personal power he aspires to, he has merely achieved what—had he failed to achieve it—would have smothered him. It is his idea that wishes to achieve something, not he himself; but what his idea wishes to achieve is everything. An idea either dies or is victorious. This is all I have to say.

The quiet, canny Bärenswil gentlemen smiled, their lips pressed tightly together, after hearing this speech with its rather romantic overtones. Frau Tobler had become exceedingly anxious. The young neighbor lady appeared to be embodying the entire ear-pricking, eavesdropping environs: that's how very open-mouthed she was sitting there. The older lady understood not a word. Joseph shared the sentiments of Frau Tobler, and like her, he was glad when Tobler took his seat again to down yet another full glass of Neuenburger. His speech had exhausted him even more than the wine. But soon everyone was laughing again. The sense of solemnity that had mistakenly wandered into the grotto for a moment flew off again. It was decided they would play a game of Jass. Tobler's eyes were once more gleaming just as feverishly as they had that long-ago summer night when the firecrackers had flown into the air by the dozens. "Yes, for celebrations of every sort he is exceptionally well-suited," Joseph thought.

The next morning, there were a number of corks floating about in the pond, along with a few yellow leaves that had been blown there by the storm the day before. It was raining. The entire property looked doleful and abandoned. Joseph was standing in the garden: what a sight! But he refused to allow himself to indulge the mood that was attempting to seize hold of him and forced his thoughts to take a practical-quotidian turn.

There were fewer and fewer business matters in the affirmative, profitable sense to attend to. The main order of business no longer consisted in anything other than fending off the creditors who were beginning to exert pressure from all sides and ever more brusquely, as well as prolonging and postponing the necessity of having to fork out cash. Cash—cash which had to be procured by all the means at their disposal, but the means and measures by which this could be achieved were becoming ever more rare, and the few measures remaining to them were highly dubious and uncertain. One of these still possible methods for obtaining cash consisted in vile, shameful and secretive sponging of a quite personal nature. On his travels, for instance, Tobler might encounter a relation or acquaintance, and to this person he either confessed the naked, unfriendly truth or else lied to him, telling a tale of some momentary quandary, and in this way he managed now and again to come up with something, insignificant sums to be sure. This money was then, as a rule, posted to the private or household account.

In principle, Joseph was to maintain his regular hours in the office, but in truth there was scarcely anything serious to be done there, anything that might further Tobler's affairs; it was simply a matter of being present. One morning, the assistant left the office door standing open out of forgetfulness when he went down to the post office. When he returned, there was a scene: Tobler said testily that there was no need for disorder to descend upon them just because there was no money left. He would not stand for it. Even if there was no cash to be stolen, someone— the postman or someone else—might come in unannounced through the open door without anyone in the house being any the wiser and rummage about in their books and papers.

Joseph replied that it must have been Pauline who'd left the door standing open. He himself would never do such a thing, maintaining order was a matter of the highest priority for him.

It was Pauline, his superior now blustered, who had brought Tobler's attention to Joseph's negligence which he was now, with astonishing impudence, attempting to blame on her. He always blamed everything on Pauline.

What business did she have tattling like that, said the one caught in the snare, the chatterbox. Tobler bid him hold his tongue.

What days these were, wet and stormy, and yet there was still something magical about them. All at once the living room became so melancholy and cozy. The damp and cold out of doors made the rooms more hospitable. They had already begun lighting the heating stoves. The yellow and red leaves burned and gleamed feverishly through the foggy gray of the landscape. The red of the cherry tree's leaves had something incandescent and aching and raw about it, but at the same time it was beautiful and brought peace and cheer to those who saw it. Often the entire countryside of meadows and trees appeared to be wrapped in veils and damp cloths, above and below and in the distance and close at hand everything was gray and wet. You strode through all of this as if through a gloomy dream. And yet even this weather and this particular sort of world expressed a secret gaiety. You could smell the trees you were walking beneath, and hear ripe fruit dropping in the meadows and on the path. Everything seemed to have become doubly and triply quiet. All the sounds seemed to be sleeping, or afraid to ring out. Early in the morning and late in the evening, the slow exhalations of foghorns could be heard across the lake, exchanging warning signals off in the distance and announcing the presence of boats. They sounded like the plaintive cries of helpless animals. Yes, fog was present in abundance. And then, now and again, there would be yet another beautiful day. And there were days, truly autumnal days, neither beautiful nor desolate, neither particularly agreeable nor particularly gloomy, days that were neither sunny nor dark but rather remained consistently light and dark from morning to dusk, so that four in the afternoon presented just the same vision of the world as eleven in the morning, everything was quiet and pale gold and faintly mournful, the colors withdrew into themselves as if dreaming worried dreams. How Joseph adored days like this. Everything appeared to him beautiful, light and familiar. This slight sadness on the part of nature banished all his cares, even his thoughts. Many things then appeared to him no longer dire, no longer burdensome, though they had seemed so burdensome and troublesome not long before. An agreeable forgetfulness sent him drifting through the pretty streets of the village on days like this. The world looked so peaceful, so calm and good and pensive. You could go anywhere you liked, it was always the same pale, full image, the same face, and this face was gazing at you earnestly and with tenderness.

Around this time, a new advertisement bearing the invisible heading "Give us money!" was placed in the newspapers: *Factory Investment Sought*. The owners of several small businesses in the village had tried to collect their money and had been sent away with a promise of later payment. As a result, it was soon public knowledge that Tobler wasn't paying his bills. Frau Tobler scarcely dared show her face any longer in the village proper, she was afraid of being insulted. The seamstress from the city sent a letter requesting payment for the dress she'd made. The requested sum was an even hundred marks, a round figure that impressed itself all too well upon a feminine memory.

"Write to her," Frau Tobler said to the assistant. A barrel of young wine, so-called Sauser, had just been delivered. Even now there was no tightening of belts in the household, such measures were forbidden by the natural good cheer that was just now beginning to assert itself once more. Let the people in the village say and think whatever they pleased, even Doctor Specker and his wife, who had stopped visiting them three weeks ago.

Joseph wrote to the seamstress—one Frau Berta Gindroz, a Frenchwoman—requesting that she be so kind as to have a bit more patience. At the moment it was simply not possible for the account to be settled. Frau Tobler was moreover not so completely satisfied with her work as on earlier occasions: the bodice had come out too tight and pinched at the armpit. But in any case Frau Gindroz should not worry as far as the payment of her bill was concerned. It was just that this was a particularly bad moment to approach Frau Tobler's husband in this matter, Herr Tobler being overburdened at present with business affairs and other concerns. Should the dress not first be altered? A response to this query would be appreciated. Please accept, Madame, the assurance, etc.

Frau Tobler signed this letter in the manner of a businessman signing numerous pieces of correspondence.

The entire garden was filled with leaves that had fallen there or been deposited by gusts of wind. One afternoon the assistant took it upon himself to begin gathering up this foliage, raking and heaping into piles as much as he was able. The day was cold and dark. Large indefinable clouds lay somber upon the sky. The Tobler house appeared to be shivering and yearning for the noble, merry days of summer. Throughout the region, all the trees had grown quite bare, their branches black and wet. Then the signalman from the train station showed up. He lived quite nearby, a friendly, modest man given to acts of gratitude, and now he came into the garden and helped Joseph gather up the leaves, saying that whatever was fitting in good and better days was surely no less than proper when times were hard. Herr Tobler had done him many a good turn. He had, for example, given him cigars on many an occasion, and many a fine gratuity, and so he did not see why things should go on like this—he, in any case, was one of those Bärenswilers who meant well by Engineer Tobler, who had always been so generous to him.

Soon the entire garden was cleared. "Yet another task brought to completion," the signalman said, laughing. "That's right, young man, there are many different sorts of occupations, and everything one performs with an honest effort brings with it a certain honor. If you would be so kind as to give me a few of Herr Tobler's cheroots to smoke, I wouldn't be disinclined to accept them. In weather like this, something nice to puff on can be just the thing."

Frau Tobler sent him down half a liter of Sauser.

*

Overtures were made to the Bärenswil Joint-Stock Brewery with regard to the allocation of a number of the Advertising Clock's fields or wings. The firm declined the offer: perhaps some other time! This was a new, humiliating disappointment and prompted Tobler to hurl the lion-shaped paperweight to the floor, where it flew into bits that were later cleared away by the assistant. At the same time, a new piece of request-for-payment artillery was being fired at the technical workroom, and while this cannonball produced no casualties, it was nonetheless vexing, an annoyance, and increased Tobler's agitation.

In fact it was none other than Tobler's erstwhile agent and traveling salesman, one Herr Sutter, who had come trotting up via registered mail to demand payment of his back wages and commissions pertaining to the acquisition of licenses for the Advertising Clock. Tobler would have liked best to respond to this individual by inviting him to apply his lips to his posterior, preferably in the environs of Genoa, the fool; but reason dictated that he acknowledge this new demand for payment, unpleasant as it was, and he wrote to the man: "I am unable to pay you!"

Patience! Herr Tobler was finding himself obliged to ask for patience from of all his associates, his suppliers and his fellow men, more or less as follows: Be patient, for I, Tobler, have honest and upright intentions. I was so rash as to throw all my liquid funds into my enterprises. Do not force me to extreme measures. I am organizing my obligations, I can still inherit additional sums, I am entitled to an inheritance on my mother's side. In addition, I have placed a new advertisement, *Assets Sought,* in the most influential newspapers. Admittedly, my head is spinning, but, etc. . . .

Concerning the expected inheritance, Tobler was in negotiation with his lawyer, to whom letters and postcards were dispatched on a daily basis.

The first model Marksman's Vending Machine had meanwhile been completed, and indeed it functioned gloriously and occasioned the gayest hopes. This apparatus, its inventor believed, would quite possibly succeed in redeeming both the Advertising Clock and the capital that had been thrown into it. One day the machinist invited Joseph to inspect the finished product, an invitation the latter was quite happy to accept, all the more so as it was a beautiful, mild autumn day. He set out on foot, strolling agreeably toward the neighboring village, a good hour's foot journey distant. He was accompanied on the right by woods that shot straight up toward the sky, and on the left by the placid lake, making his walk along this country lane the most agreeable sort of "business trip." When he arrived in the village, he inquired after the mechanical workshop, which he found after a great deal of searching through narrow streets that had been kneaded and built into knots, and now he stood before the Marksman's Vending Machine, which had been elegantly adorned with decorative paints. The manufacturer of this item, demonstrating for Joseph how smoothly and noiselessly the apparatus functioned, grumbled that now it was time for Herr Tobler to provide appropriate remuneration, at least it was reasonable to expect compensation after having done—though Tobler was unwilling to admit this—the lion's share of the work. Jumping about, giving orders and traveling did not, in fact, contribute much to the progress of such an undertaking. Progress required hands performing actual work. Yes, Joseph should let his employer know how matters appeared from the perspective of the mechanical workshop, it couldn't hurt for him to know this.

Joseph listened in silence to all these grievances and soon thereafter set out for home.

Back at the villa, he was met by shouts informing him that a gentleman was waiting down in the office to speak with Mr. Joseph Marti.

It was the man who ran the Employment Referral Office in the city, the man to whom the assistant owed his position: an oddly disheveled-looking gentleman who, however, appeared to be possessed of the humblest and gentlest of dispositions. The two men greeted one another in a friendly, almost brotherly manner, though they were separated by a significant age difference. The as it were tousled and tattered face of the supervisor recalled to Joseph hardships he'd long since put behind him. A shabby room filled with copyists appeared in his mind's eye, and he beheld himself sitting there at a desk, then he saw Herr Tobler walking in, saw the man in charge get up from his chair to look about the room in search of the individual who would best serve Herr Tobler's needs. How long ago all of that was!

Joseph asked what had brought the supervisor to Bärenswil.

The older man, glancing about the office in all directions, said that above all he had come merely out of interest; he wanted to have a look at the place that, it would appear, had won Joseph's favor. It was a sleepy day at the copyists' office, not a single commission, and so he'd simply decided to catch a train and permit himself this modest outing. But in truth he had not come exclusively to satisfy his curiosity, he was fond of combining pleasure with utility and necessity, and so he would like to allow himself a question: why was it that to this day, despite repeated reminders, he had not yet been paid the sum that was his quite customary referral fee? Had the letters and bills he'd sent failed to arrive?

"Oh yes, they arrived," Joseph responded, "but you see, sir, there isn't any money."

"No money? Not even for such a trifling sum?"

"None at all!"

With a thoughtful expression, the supervisor asked whether he might speak to Herr Tobler. Joseph replied:

"For many days now, Herr Tobler has been absolutely unavailable to speak with any person desiring to collect money from him. This is the task of his clerk, that is, myself. Won't you please sit down for a moment, sir? You will rest for ten minutes and then depart again. Despite all the esteem I have for you, I am forced to tell you that here in the Tobler household those to whom we owe money are anything but welcome. Both Frau and Herr Tobler have given me strict orders to make short work of individuals belonging to this category, and under no circumstances to engage them in conversation, but rather to dismiss them coldly. You yourself, sir, once admonished me, when I was saying goodbye to you three and a half months ago in the copyists' office, to prove myself a faithful, obedient and diligent employee so that I would be of use and would not be sent packing after half a day's unsatisfactory trial. As you see, I am still here, and so it would seem I have proven my worth. I have made my peace with the peculiar conditions here, and find that I've adapted well to them."

"Is your salary being paid?" the visitor inquired.

"No," the assistant said, "and admittedly this is one of the things with which I am not fully satisfied. Often I have wanted to discuss this with Herr Tobler, but each time I am about to open my mouth to remind my superior of this matter which, as I have had occasion to perceive, is not exactly the most agreeable to him, the courage to speak deserts me, and so each time I tell myself: Put it off! And I'm still alive today, even without a salary."

"What is your life like here? Are you fed well?"

"Excellently!"

The administrator then said, his voice filled with concern, that after all they had discussed he had no choice but to take legal action against Herr Tobler.

"Why not," Joseph said. The supervisor reached for his threadbare hat, gave the assistant a paternal look, shook hands with him and left.

Joseph took up a piece of paper and, as he had nothing more important to occupy him, penned the following:

Bad Habits

One such habit is the need to ponder every living thing with which I am confronted. The slightest encounter arouses in me the most peculiar urge to think. Just this moment a man has left me who, on account of the memories I associate with his old, poor figure, is dear and meaningful to me. I felt I had forgotten, lost or simply misplaced something when I looked into his face. A loss immediately impressed itself upon my heart, and an old vision upon my eyes. I am possibly a somewhat high-strung person, but I am also a precise one. I feel even the most trifling losses, in certain matters I am meticulously conscientious, and only occasionally am I obliged, for better or worse, to command myself: Forget this! A single word can thrust me into the most monstrous and tempestuous confusion, and then I find myself utterly possessed by thoughts of this apparently miniscule and insignificant thing, while the present in all its glory has become incomprehensible to me. These moments constitute a bad habit. Even this is a bad habit, what I am doing right now, making memos of my thoughts. I'm going off to find Frau Tobler now. Perhaps she has some sort of household work for me.

He threw what he had written into the wastepaper basket and left the office. And indeed there was work of a household nature awaiting him: carrying the storm windows intended for winter use from the attic down to the cellar, where they were to be cleaned off and washed. He removed his jacket straightaway and began to lug the windows downstairs. Frau Tobler was astonished to witness such ardent zeal, and the washerwoman who had meanwhile begun to clean them said he appeared to be one of those fellows who could make themselves useful in all sorts of ways. She attached to this praise a moral lesson, noting in her rough voice that nowadays, with the world becoming ever more uncertain and changeful, it was almost a necessity for young people to learn to reconcile themselves to whatever might come along. In any case, it certainly did a young man no harm to be able to handle even despised, lowly things.

After the windows had been washed, they had to be carried into the rooms and hung up neatly in the window openings to which they belonged. Frau Tobler exhorted the assistant to be careful, and stood there watching, somewhat anxiously, his hanging-up motions, some of which struck her as too forceful. "How becoming it is to this woman to look a bit worried," the window-hanger thought and felt quite pleased with himself.

This was perhaps yet another bad habit of his, that he always felt pleased, indeed happy, when he was granted the privilege of performing physical labor. Was he really so unwilling to exert his mind, the better half of a human being? Was he destined to become a wood-cutter or a coachman? Ought he to live in primeval forests, or as a sailor upon the high seas? What a shame that there were no log cabins to be built in the environs of Bärenswil.

No, he was perhaps by no means unintelligent—a deficit, by the way, which persons born healthy are unlikely to suffer. But there was something about him that favored the physical. In school, as he often recalled quite vividly, he had been a good gymnast. He loved walking through the countryside, clambering up mountains, washing dishes at the kitchen sink. He had performed this latter task at home as a boy, regaling his mother with stories as he worked. Moving his arms and legs struck him as highly enjoyable. He preferred swimming in cold water to pondering lofty things. He liked to sweat, which was possibly quite revealing. Was he destined to tote bricks about a building site? Should he be hitched to a cart? In any case, though, he was no Hercules.

Yes, he was possessed of intellect when he wished to be, but he liked to take breaks from thinking. One day he saw a man carrying sacks in the middle of the village and immediately thought that he would do the same as soon as Tobler sent him away. This was at the height of summer. And now it was late autumn and time to hang the storm windows.

At the conclusion of these labors, there was young wine to drink. Besides, night had fallen and it was time for supper. The conversation at table was animated, and everyone remained sitting there long after they had finished eating. The washerwoman's husband, a simple factory worker, turned up. Frau Tobler invited him to join them for a glass of Sauser; he sat right down at the table and soon was singing a jolly song. His glass was refilled again and again, and the others drank a good deal as well. To bed with you, children! Frau Tobler cried after an hour. Pauline carried Dora in her arms from one person to the next so she could say good-night. The washerwoman made it clear to all present that her tongue was both witty and swift: she reeled off a whole series of village tales, love stories and tales of horror. The man resumed his singing. His wife tried to make him stop, as he was taking certain liberties in his choice of songs, but Frau Tobler said he should sing whatever he pleased, the children had gone to bed, and as for the rest of them, a word uttered in exuberance would do no harm, she herself was perfectly happy to listen to such things now and again. The wine cast its spell, placing the most fantastical rhymes upon the lips of this blackish-looking, one-eyed fellow. Everyone was over-come with uncontrollable laughter, above all Frau Tobler, who seemed to wish to "take advantage" of the opportunity, seeing as she had been, to her distress, largely deprived of social inter-course in the past few weeks. And if the people keeping her company this evening were not exactly refined, they were merry all the same. Poor folk, but people of honest sensibilities. Besides which, she was feeling—she herself could scarcely say why—the need to be a bit exuberant for once, and so she took pleasure in filling the glasses ever anew until midnight arrived. Joseph was drunk, he was babbling and was nearly on the point of sinking under the table. The others were holding up better. Frau Tobler had indulged more in the pleasures of conversation and laughter than in the wine. But the factory worker seemed able to tolerate an tremendous quantity of drink. Joseph was just staggering upstairs on the way to his room when Tobler ap-peared, crossly demanding to know why it was that the veranda light had once again not been left burning for him. It was pitch black out in the garden, a person could break an arm or a leg. He saw what was going on in the living room. The woman and man from the neighborhood had risen to their feet. Shortly af-terward, they said their timid good-nights and departed. Tobler asked his wife what in the world she was thinking. She could only laugh, and pointed at the clerk, who was struggling with the simple difficulty of making his way up the stairs. Tobler was tired so he didn't say much. It had been a Sauser evening, a bit unseemly perhaps, but not a crime.

The next morning Joseph arose somewhat earlier than

usual and worked with extra diligence; he was feeling pricks of conscience and dreaded seeing his master. But neither was one of his ears torn off nor were there objects flying about his head. Tobler was friendlier and more casual than ever, indeed, he even told jokes.

In the course of the day, the assistant confessed to Frau Tobler that he had been frightened. Gazing at him in surprise, as if there were something about him she couldn't fathom, she said:

"You are a curious mix of cowardice and boldness, Joseph. You can balance on narrow window ledges and swim far out into the lake late in autumn without the slightest thought of fear. You can even insult a woman without losing your composure. But when it is time to take responsibility for a perfectly innocent failing before your lord and master, you're frightened. You truly force a person to conclude that either you are utterly devoted to your master, or you secretly hate him. Which should one believe? What can it mean for a man to harbor such unmistakable respect for another? Especially at this particular moment, when Tobler's position in the world appears so precarious, how could one not be surprised to witness such affectionate esteem? I can't make heads or tails of you. Are you magnanimous? Or mean-spirited? Go back to work. I have to keep my emotions in check, but in your presence I cannot. And in the future do not fear my husband, he hasn't bitten anyone's head off yet."

These words were spoken in the living room. Somewhat later Joseph surprised Frau Tobler upstairs at the door to her bedroom wearing a negligee, by chance she'd left the door standing open. Thinking nothing in particular, she stood with bare arms beside the washstand and was occupied with putting her hair in order. When she heard and saw Joseph, she gave a shriek and slammed the door shut. What splendid arms! the assistant thought, and continued on his way upstairs. He meant to look for something in the attic rubbish. Instead of what he was looking for, he found an old pair of Tobler's high-shafted boots that were apparently no longer in use. He gazed at these tall boots for an unreasonably long time, then burst into laughter at his own absent-mindedness.

Then Silvi appeared, she was carrying some laundry in her hands that she had been instructed to hang up in the attic to dry. She remained standing there before Joseph, looking at him as if she had never before laid eyes on him. What a child! Then she spread out her things, but instead of going back downstairs, she poked about—senselessly, it appeared—in an open crate, addressing all manner of incomprehensible questions to the young man observing her. He soon found the sight of Silvi unbearable and went downstairs.

In the office: "Frau Tobler is surprised at my behavior. Yet I am all but astonished at hers. How can she take it upon herself to speak such words to me, she, the anything but independent woman, Silvi's mother? I am on the point of telling her to her face what a neglectful parent she is, what a mother raven. To be sure, I am only a clerk in the Tobler household. But since this house is swaying on its foundations, my own post might as well rock a little as well."

At the door to the living room, Frau Tobler stood speaking

into the telephone with great agitation. Apparently there was once more some disagreeable matter to be dealt with. Her back was trembling, and her shoulders rose and fell violently. She spoke severely, imperiously. Could the person on the other end be an impertinent creditor? Her voice sounded so high it was threatening to burst its own sounds and chords. At last she was finished. She turned a face to Joseph that was as proud as it was pain-filled. She had been weeping as she spoke.

"Who was that?" he asked.

"Oh," she said, "the contractor, the one who built the grotto. He wants money. But, as you no doubt heard, I put him in his place."

What place that was she didn't say. But whether or not she could have said this, the assistant no longer had the courage to accuse her of being a bad mother.

He could very well have answered the telephone himself, she went on. Hadn't he heard it ringing? No? Then he should always leave the door to the office slightly ajar, then he'd hear it all right.

Joseph had heard it ringing perfectly well, but had been too indolent and had thought to himself: "Let her answer the phone herself for once, that might do her haughtiness some good."

Walter came and reported that Edi, his brother, had stuck out his tongue and thumbed his nose at a man in Bärenswil. Edi had snuck into the man's garden to get some pears, but he'd been surprised there and had his ears boxed. From a distance, Edi had then shouted all sorts of bad words at the man.

Frau Tobler said she'd have to inform her husband.

"In your shoes, Frau Tobler," Joseph interjected, "I would

punish the boy myself—severely, if you like—but I would never go and 'inform my husband.' To begin with, Herr Tobler, as you yourself know better than anyone, is sufficiently occupied with other matters, and secondly you are, after all, Edi's mother and in just as good a position to gauge the severity with which the rascal deserves to be punished. If Herr Tobler comes home tonight only to hear—as he so often does—complaints of this sort from your lips, he might easily fly into a rage, and the punishment could all too quickly become more cruel than just. Please consider, my lady, the fury provoked in your husband when you annoy him with matters of this sort, which indeed are not terribly important, just at a moment when he's hoping to rest for a while in the bosom of his family from all his undertakings and schemes for raising money, and you will have no choice but to admit, inclined as you might be to suspect me of insulting you, that I am right. Forgive me. I have spoken in the interests of the Tobler household, I cherish this home, and my one wish is to be of use here. Are you angry with me, Frau Tobler?"

She smiled and said nothing, apparently finding it unnecessary to utter a single word in response. She went out to the kitchen, and he downstairs to the office.

Herr Tobler came home for dinner, a rare occurrence. In a dark, choked voice, he asked how things were at home; he was in a foul humor. Joseph immediately felt uneasy upon hearing this voice. How the voice impressed itself upon him! Did Tobler have to come home in time for supper just to see how his assistant was enjoying his meal? Joseph nearly lost his appetite, and he resolved to run down to the post office immediately after

supper. Tobler had taken off his overcoat with effort. It occurred to Joseph that perhaps it would've been good had he
leapt from his chair to help his master out of his coat. Possibly
this would have caused a significant improvement in Tobler's
mood, the wretchedness of which was plain to see. Why this
absence of courtesy? Would such an act have harmed his sense
of masculine honor? How honorable was it just to sit there,
anxiously hoping there would not be a scene? Tobler's demeanor always made Joseph fear a scene. Yes, there was something about this man that appeared just barely held in check,
something piled up in a thick red heap, something clattering
and faintly crackling within him. It looked as if there might be
an explosion at any moment. Under circumstances such as
these, it was truly inappropriate to think of injuries to one's
honor—rather, the main thing was to do what was good, necessary and likely to avert an outburst of rage. One took hold of an
overcoat, and the entire family evening might be saved. Tobler
could be so enchantingly affable when he was in good spirits,
generous even. But Joseph had been ashamed to be so polite,
and there was something else as well: the woman now opened
her mouth, just as if it were on springs and had been mechani-
cally activated, and in an infuriating tone of voice recounted the
story of Edi's transgression.

Tobler walked up to his son and gave him such a blow on his
little head that a strong man might have been knocked down by
it, much less a little mite of a thing like Edi. Everyone in the
room was trembling. Frau Tobler cast her eyes down, shamefaced. She now regretted having spoken. Tobler drove Edi into

the dark next-door room, slapping him and thrusting him before him. Walter, the little snitch, had turned deathly pale. Dora was clutching her mother's arm. The mother had the courage to say that it was enough, Tobler should calm himself. Tobler was moaning.

"An incomprehensible woman," Joseph murmured to himself.

So now this had to happen, at a time when every voice and every mouth in the entire village was speaking against him, Tobler said, sitting down at the table. Such mischief-makers! So that anyone who pleased could now point a finger at him, the father who was raising these brats, and say they were just imitating their old man. He couldn't so much as set foot in the house without being confronted with some unpleasantness or other. With things like this, how was a person supposed to have the courage to imagine that a change for the better might still be possible? Having such children was a punishment in itself. All this had only come about because he'd thought it his duty to maintain them, clothe them and feed them properly, devil take it. He'd send them to school barefoot, the rascals, and give them dry bread to eat instead of meat. He'd beat time for them quite differently than what they were used to. But in fact he didn't have to do any of these things, these changes would come about of their own accord. Soon enough there would be nothing left to eat, and then he'd see how differently this brood of his would act.

To talk like that was a sin, Frau Tobler said: he had said enough.

*

Tobler did not institute a new regimen in his household, the baton beating time and the key remained unchanged at the Evening Star. The conductor had too many other things on his mind, and the assistant conductor was too modest a soul, too easily contented. One didn't even have to pay him his long-overdue salary. He was satisfied with the idyllic surroundings, with what was there. Clouds and breezes were still drifting about the Tobler residence, and as long as these entities were of a mind to remain there, the assistant too was unencumbered by thoughts of departure.

One day it snowed. First snow of the year, how thick with memories you are to look upon! Past experiences fling themselves to the earth along with you. The faces of one's father and mother and siblings emerge distinctly and meaningfully from your wet, white veils. One cannot help but be in grave and merry spirits when you arrive with your countless flakes. One might take you for a child, for a brother or a sweet, timid sister. One holds out one's hand to catch you, not all of you, just little bits of you. The bucket that wants to catch you would have to be as wide and immense as the earth. Dear first snow, come snowing down. It looks so splendid, this soft thing you're spreading quiet as can be across Tobler's house and garden.

"It's snowing!" Frau Tobler exclaimed in astonishment. The children came running into the warm room with shouts and with snowflakes on their red faces and bits of snow in their hair. Soon Pauline would have to dig and sweep pathways into the snow so Herr Tobler's feet and shoes would not get too wet.

Tobler wasn't yet sending his sons to school barefoot, either.

There was time enough for such measures. And there was still plenty to eat in the pretty little villa despite the blustering flurries outside, the cold and damp. Joseph put on his overcoat when he went to the post office, it was a hand-me-down, but it kept him warm and looked quite smart on him. Frau Tobler asked the assistant to bring her something to read from the village, reading was beginning to be just the thing for the long nights. One couldn't play Jass after supper every single day. Joseph stopped by the lending library and fetched and ferried home reading matter. The girls went out into the snow wearing small, red, thick coats and carrying sleds so as to ride down the hill, but this didn't go so well, the young snow was too wet and did not yet cling well to the stony earth. Leo, the dog, helped them all cavort about.

How true it is that each of the four seasons has its own particular scent and sound. When you see spring, you always think you've never seen it like this before, never looking so special. In summer, the summery profusion strikes you as new and magical year after year. You never really looked at fall properly before, not until this year, and when winter arrives, the winter too is utterly new, quite quite different from a year or three ago. Indeed, even the years have their own individual personalities and aromas. Having spent the year in such and such a place means having experienced and seen it. Places and years are intimately linked, and what about events and years? Since experiences can color an entire decade, how much more powerfully and swiftly they can color a short year. A short year? Joseph was by no means satisfied with this expression. Just a moment before he had been standing before the villa and, lost in thought, said to himself: "Such a year, how long and full it is."

And this long year hadn't just whizzed by him; only now when he stopped to consider did it seem possessed of wings, feathers and downy-lightness. It was now mid-November, but, thinking back, he felt he had displayed just this mien and just these manners to the world last May already. As his friend Klara said, he changed little.

And the world, was it changing? No. A wintry image could superimpose itself upon the world of summer, winter could give way to spring, but the face of the earth remained the same. It put on masks and took them off again, it wrinkled and cleared its huge, beautiful brow, it smiled or looked angry, but remained always the same. It was a great lover of make-up, it painted its face now more brightly, now in paler hues, now it was glowing, now pallid, never quite what it had been before, constantly it was changing a little, and yet remained always vividly and restlessly the same. It sent lighting bolts flashing from its eyes and rumbled the thunder with its powerful lungs, it wept the rain down in streams and let the clean, glittering snow come smiling from its lips, but in the features and lineaments of its face, little change could be discerned. Only on rare occasions might a shuddering earthquake, a pelting of hail, a deluge or volcanic flare disturb its placid surface, or else it quaked or shuddered inwardly with worldly sentiments and earthly convulsions, but still it remained the same. Regions remained the same; skylines, to be sure, were always waxing and expanding, but a city could never fly off and find somewhere else to live from one hour to the next.

Streams and rivers followed the same courses as they had for millennia, they might peter out in the sand, but they couldn't suddenly leap from their beds into the light open air. Water had to work its way through canals and caves. Streaming and burrowing was its age-old law. And the lakes lay where they had lain for a long, long time. They didn't leap up toward the sun or play ball like children. Sometimes they became indignant and slapped their water in waves together with a great whooshing noise, but they could transform themselves neither into clouds one day nor wild horses one night. Everything in and upon the earth was subject to beautiful, rigorous laws, just like human beings.

Thus winter arrived all around Tobler's house.

About this time there came a Sunday on which Joseph decided for a change to take a train to the capital to amuse himself once more. In the city, he discovered fog in the streets, wet leaves upon the ground, benches in the parks on which one was no longer able or eager to sit, and in the winding little alleyways he found noise and, in the evening, raucous drunkards before the numerous bars. He had spent half an hour with his Frau Weiss in order to explain to her who Tobler and Frau Tobler were, but a secret shame and impatience had prevented him from staying too long in the company of this calm, easy-going woman, he had gone out again into the Sunday-night streets and had visited a few public houses of a dubious sort so as to "amuse" himself. Was he the man to succeed in such a venture? In any case, he had drunk quite a lot of beer, and in the tavern known as the

Winter Garden he had gotten into a quarrel with some young, dandified Italians at the bar. In this very place, he clambered onto the little variety stage before the eyes of all present, to their enormous delight, and began to lecture the juggler who was presenting himself there on the laws of taste and of manual dexterity, until at last he was ejected from the tavern by a handful of waiters.

In the cold night, he sat down on a bench in one of the little parks to let the harsh, imperious weather blow the intoxication from his head and limbs. A proper storm wind was howling and shaking the branches of the park's trees. This, however, appeared a matter of complete indifference to a second person who seemed likewise to be taking a rest here at this nocturnal hour, for he had made himself at home on a bench across from Joseph. What sort of a person might this be, and what had caused him to sit down in this exposed, inconsiderate stormy night like Joseph? Was such a thing done? The assistant, sensing some misfortune or pain, walked over to the resting, dark figure—and saw it was Wirsich.

"You here? How have things been with you, Wirsich?" he asked, astonished. His intoxication had suddenly left him. For a long time, Wirsich gave no answer. Then he said:

"How have things been? Bad. Why else would I be lying here in the rain and cold? I am unemployed and have lost my footing. I'll become a thief, and they'll send me to prison."

He burst into loud, wretched sobs.

Joseph offered his predecessor in Tobler's office a gold coin. Wirsich took it, but then let it fall to the ground. The assistant shouted at him:

"Don't be so hard-headed, man. Take the money. Tobler himself gave it to me today hesitantly enough. Up at the Evening Star it seems we too are now, as it were, out of funds, but we are not by any means ready to lose heart. You, Wirsich, have no right to say you're being forced to turn to stealing. One should smite one's own mouth before saying such a thing. Why stealing? Is there not a copyists' bureau for the unemployed? But you are probably ashamed to go there to see the gentleman who runs this bureau, who is a very, very dear, gentle-minded and experienced individual. We at the Evening Star were one day open-minded enough to visit this very office and there procure for ourselves a young man who was perhaps in fact not entirely capable but at any rate certainly useful and pliant, Joseph Marti by name, for Herr Wirsich was no longer willing to trod the straight and narrow path. Go now and get to work, and everywhere you go tomorrow morning ask if there is work for you, and be convinced: somewhere and somehow you will be given some! What a way to act. Surely you will be sent away disdainfully and coldly in some places, but then you'll just have to keep looking until you find the thing that puts you in a position to become a human being once more. No one should permit himself to think of stealing. Your healthy mind should be and remain your ruler, do not antagonize it until it becomes a scoundrel and a fool. And now in your shoes I would take this money that was given to you not by me but by Tobler and find some sensible bed for the night, for the sleep that will prepare you for all these other things. Tell me, how is your mother?"

"Sick," Wirsich replied more with his hand than with his mouth. Joseph cried out:

"And on account of you, isn't it? I'll hear no retort, I know perfectly well that it's so, just as if I'd been a constant witness to this illness and decline. What mother would not despair at seeing her son go so utterly to seed that he no longer dares meet the eyes of a man diligently occupied with picking up cigar butts on the street? For years on end she felt proud of her splendid son, always looking up to him with eyes filled with love and admiration, she provided and cared for him, and she is still alive—sick, to be sure, but she could easily enjoy good health in the final, fading days of her life if only the object of her care and love were prepared to comport himself in a just and capable manner and be just a tiny bit stalwart. It wouldn't take much to satisfy the old woman, and she would then do her best to rekindle her old battered pride. She would practically worship her child because of his efforts to remain honorable and strong. And on top of everything else, this forgetful and degenerate person is her only son, her first and final chance to stoke the fires of maternal sentiment, yet he is so inept and cruel, clumsily trampling this love and these days and years of joy. You know what, Wirsich? I've a mind to give you a good thrashing."

Together they went in search of lodgings for the night. There were still lights on at the Red House Inn, they went into the tavern. All sorts of craftsmen and journeymen were sitting around a table, one of them was telling tales of the cunning pranks he had apparently carried out in great number, and the rest listened. Joseph ordered a light meal and something to drink. He would, he thought, take the very first train back to Bärenswil in the morning.

There was only a single room left at the inn, so Wirsich and Marti spent the night in one and the same bed. Before falling asleep, they spent a good half hour chatting. Wirsich's spirits were beginning to improve. Joseph suggested that he just go on living in this room at the inn and diligently compose letters of inquiry which, neatly enclosed in envelopes, he could deliver personally to their recipients. One should never feel ashamed to display one's poverty and need openly, Joseph said, but at the same time, one must take care not to assume a self-pitying, mournful expression, which might easily strike those on whose benevolence one was depending as repugnant. Besides which, open displays of misery were tasteless. Personally going to see the business owners one was writing to had the advantage that these generally well-educated and sensible people were as likely as not to present one with a five-mark coin, as it was being made clear to them that the one seeking employment is making an honest effort. Various of Joseph's acquaintances had gone about things in just this way, and they had always been able to report certain modest successes. The names and fates of those pleading for help were generally not of interest to the rich, but these gentlemen did give gifts, as this has long been the gracious and genteel tradition in old families and firms. True poverty did well to pay a visit to true gentility, for this is where poverty is least likely to find itself suffocated and choked, where it is permitted to breathe, show its true nature, and, indeed, let its sufferings be known. If one is already lying on the ground in the grip of deprivation, one has to learn to show decorously and openly that one is asking for help, this will be excused and condoned, it softens hearts a little and will never be deemed offensive to morality, which is flexible by nature. But the person undertaking this must also have poise, he is not permitted to start wailing like a babe-in-arms; rather, he should show by his conduct that he has been cast down by something great and mighty, by misfortune. This, in turn, does him honor and causes even the hardest person to become fleetingly, sweetly, nobly, decorously gentle. Well, now he'd held a long speech, and a fairly stirring one at that, but now, as he fully intended to do, he must get to sleep, for he would have to get up early the next morning.

"You are, I believe, a good fellow, Marti," the other replied. Then they went to sleep. It was already half past three in the morning. At eight o'clock, after three hours of sleep and a train ride at dawn, the assistant was again standing in the engineer's office between drawing board and writing table. Now he went to the living room to have breakfast.

One week later he returned to the city, this time as a prisoner. He had been sentenced to two days' confinement for missing the compulsory military training he was to have completed in the fall. At the appointed hour, he presented himself at the barracks, where his military papers were taken from him; then he was escorted downstairs to his cell. The fifteen or so younger and older men lying there on cots with their coats spread out beneath them all turned to appraise the newcomer. Bad smells of every possible variety suffused the room, whose high barred window gave directly onto the street at ground level. "At least I have something to smoke," Joseph thought, and proceeded to make himself comfortable, insofar as this was possible, on one of the cots. Soon each of the inmates had addressed a few words to him, one colorful figure after the other. Men from all walks of life had sentences similar to his. Every one of them was aggrieved. Perhaps it was a senior officer being reviled for his heinous deeds, or else some state or civil official was being raked over the coals. The faces of all of these fifteen or sixteen individuals displayed boredom, an appetite for freedom of movement, and dissatisfaction with the lethargy that dominated the room. Young men were there who had been serving time for weeks, and one, a milkman, had been there for months.

A paperhanger lay beside a hotel owner's son who'd been to America. A clerical worker lay beside a mason and day-laborer, a wealthy Jewish merchant beside the dairyman and milkman, and a master baker beside an apprentice locksmith. None of these fifteen individuals resembled the others, but all of them resembled one another in the way they inveighed against whatever had brought them here and sought to pass the time. That their number included even well-to-do and educated persons could be explained by the legal impossibility of substituting a fine for one's sentence of confinement, and so an equality of treatment could be observed here such as was scarcely to be found anywhere in the free, unfettered world.

Suddenly a game started up, one which, it seemed to Joseph, was a regular part of daily life here. It was called "Slap the Ham" and involved walloping fairly brutally, using the palm of the hand, the buttocks of a person condemned to make this part of his body accessible to these merciless blows. One of those not participating in the game had to cover the victim's eyes to prevent him from noting the origins of these slaps and blows. But if he nonetheless succeeded in guessing the identity of the person who had struck him, he went free, and the one who had been found out was forced to bend down, willingly or not, in the unpleasant position vacated by the one just released, until he, too—either swiftly or after a long struggle—was fortunate enough to guess correctly.

This game was eagerly pursued for a good hour until everyone's hands were tired from all the slapping. A short while later, food was brought in—goodness—it was prison fare, after all: no beans, carrots or cauliflower, not even a little strip of pork tenderloin, but just soup and a hunk of bread, dry, tedious bread, along with a sip of water. The soup, too, was a sort of water, and the spoon, to add insult to injury, was chained to the soup bowl as if someone might have wished to steal the lead, which would certainly have been uncalled-for. But it was practical, this chain, and military and insulting into the bargain, and it was quite comprehensible that prisoners in confinement were not there to be caressed, stroked and flattered. "Contemptuous behavior shall be met with contemptuous punishment": these words appeared to have been written clearly and disheartingly upon this spoon and bowl.

What a dull, tedious two days!

The milkman or dairyman was the merriest of the bunch.

"They" had carried off this young man—who was really quite handsome to look at—bound hand and foot, because he had taken the liberty of dealing the police corporal arresting him such blows about the head that blood came spurting out of his mouth and nose. For this deed, the milkman was naturally condemned to an additional month's confinement on top of his original sentence, which, however, seemed of little concern to this apparently unflinching individual who was utterly indifferent to matters of honor. On the contrary, he took this humdrum compulsory leisure as a jolly, hilarious joke that had gone on for months, he was highly accomplished at entertaining both himself and others, and the laughter in this basement room never entirely died out or flagged. The milkman never spoke of state or military officials without assuming a tone of childishly blunt arrogance and pride. Never did words marked by bitterness or repressed anger cross his lips. The thousand anecdotes he recounted—some genuine, some invented—were all more or less concerned with making fools and laughingstocks of various persons of rank, whom this handsome, profligate individual seemed accustomed to treating like ridiculous wooden puppets. Robust and clever as he was, one could believe a good half of the tales he told without injury to one's common sense, for indeed he appeared to be just the man for such exploits, a direct descendent of his homeland's proud, fractious ancestors, equipped with a sense of both mischief and pugnacity that had long since vanished from generations of his countrymen and gifted as well with a courage that was all but compelled to feel scorn for the laws and dictates of the public sphere. A curious touch that contributed to the devilment he inflicted on superiors of every stripe was the army cap he wore atop his curls, having saved it after God knows what drill. Along with all his vagabond habits, he seemed at the same time not at all averse to simpler, softer sentiments; at least he could sometimes be heard yodeling and singing, which he did quite beautifully and with a good sense of rhythm. He also told tales tinged with longing of how he had traveled far and wide across Germany in all its immensity, journeying from one manor house to the next. His accounts of his dealings with the gentlemen who owned these manors and estates were—even if they consisted in part of lies or runaway narrative imagination—highly comical and pleasing, even romantic to listen to. This fellow had a mouth whose curve and shape were truly lovely, a face that was nobly, freely and serenely framed, and you couldn't help thinking when you looked at him that in circumstances dominated by peril and the call to arms, he might well have been able to serve his country extraordinarily well. Everything about him spoke of forms of life and of the world no longer extant; especially when he sang—which he did once without warning in the middle of the night during Joseph's time in the "jug"—one seemed to hear the sounds and the magic of vital ancient times. A wonderful evening landscape rose mournfully into the air along with his song, and, listening, one pitied both the singer and the age that found itself compelled to contend with persons of the milkman's disposition in such a petty and faulty way as was in fact the case.

During these two days in prison, the assistant might have

had the most splendid opportunity to think over all sorts of things, for example his life up to then, or the difficult position Tobler occupied in this world, or the future, or the "General Law of Obligations," but he didn't do this: he failed to take advantage of so precious an opportunity and instead contented himself with listening to the jests and songs and dirty jokes told by the dairyman, which appeared to him more interesting than all the pensiveness to be found in both the new and old worlds. Besides which the game "Slap the Ham" was repeated nearly every two hours, providing additional relief from any urge to engage in philosophical reflection; or else the prison guard came in through the rattling door to call for one of the prisoners who was "done," which likewise diverted intellectual attentiveness from higher matters to base and common interests. And what was the point of thinking?

Wasn't it most crucial to foster thoughts of sharing in the lives of others, and experiencing things? And even if the forty-eight hours of confinement might have produced forty-eight thoughts, did not a single, general thought suffice to keep one's life progressing along a good smooth path? What use could these enchanting, respect-inspiring, laboriously pondered forty-eight thoughts be to a young person, as it was foreseeable that he would forget them all tomorrow? A single thought to chart his course by was surely far preferable, but you couldn't just think it, thoughts like these melted into sentiment.

Once Joseph heard the milkman remark that his entire glorious little fatherland was more than welcome, if it wished, to kiss his ass.

How natural and how unjust these words were. To be sure, the fatherland, or at least its legal concepts, was victimizing the milkman, obstructing and shackling him, dictating tedious and limb-shattering terms of imprisonment, boring him and exposing him to unpleasant circumstances, financial losses, and harm to his physical health. And there were thousands whose opinions corresponded exactly to the milkman's. Thousands whom life had not treated quite so equitably, who had not been helped to advance along some path quite the way the obligation to do military service blindly, dryly assumed. Fulfilling one's duty was not quite so convenient for some as for the many others who even managed to turn this obligation into a living and an advantage, allowing the state to support and feed them. Some indeed found that military service ripped an unfortunate hole in their careers, and some were even thrust into the most bitter and brutal dilemmas, as the demands of the military establishment consumed their last laboriously saved-up pennies, whether Rappen, Pfennige or centimes, and by the time they'd completed their duties, their money was all gone. Not everyone could then go running to father and mother asking for support, not everyone would at once be offered renewed employment at the same office, factory or workshop; often a long time might pass before a person belonged once more to the community of working, apprenticing, earning and goal-driven individuals. Under circumstances like these, could a person's love of country still be counted on? What an idea!

"But even so!" Warmed by the feeling contained in this "even so" he'd just thought, the assistant leapt up from his cot to take part in a round of "Slap the Ham." Luck was on his side, he never had to "stick it out" for long. He always guessed at once which hand was striking him. He recognized the apprentice locksmith by the violence of the blow, the paperhanger by his clumsiness, the Jew by his bad aim, the American by the ginger-liness and embarrassment with which he participated in the game, and the milkman by the intentionally tempered and muted force of the blows. The milkman had, from the begin-ning, felt a certain tenderness toward Joseph. Whenever he be-gan one of his stories, he always turned to Joseph because he saw that the assistant was his most attentive listener.

The "prisoners" were forbidden to smoke, but schoolchild-ren came up to the barred window and carried out the sweetest and most charming smuggling operation. One of the inmates climbed onto the shoulders of another and—with the help of a nail attached to a mysterious stick—quickly and skillfully speared the packets of tobacco and cigars and tossed the small change up to the little salesgirls and smugglers through the window, so that the "jug" was always full of smoke. The guard, apparently a good-natured fellow, said nothing.

For Joseph, these two nights in prison were cold, shivering and sleepless. During the second night he was able to sleep a lit-tle, but it was a restless sleep full of feverish dreams.

The milkman's "little fatherland" lay stretched out wide, with all its districts and cantons, before his passionately gazing eyes. From a layer of fog, the ghostly, dazzling Alps towered up. At their feet stretched divinely green, beautiful meadows filled with the ringing of cowbells. A blue river described a luminous and peacefully charcoaled ribbon that curved through the region, gently touching the villages and cities and knights' castles. The entire countryside was like a painting, but this painting was alive; people, occurrences and feelings were moving up and down it like attractive and meaningful patterns upon a large tapestry. Trade and industry seemed to be flourishing wonderfully, and the serious beautiful arts were lying in fountain-plashed corners, dreaming. You could see Poetry seated at a lonely desk, lost in thought, and Painting working victoriously at an easel. All the many factory workers were returning—silent, beautiful and exhausted—from the place of their labors. You could tell by the evening light on the roads that these were roads home. Distant and echoing and poignant bells rang out. This high ringing appeared to be echoing around everything there, thundering about and embracing all of it. After this, you could hear the delicate silvery notes of a goat's little bell, and it seemed as if you were standing high up upon a mountain pasture ringed all around with neighboring mountainsides. From deep below, down in the lowlands, train whistles could be heard, and the clamor of human labor. But all at once these images were sliced into bits, dispersed as if by a breath, and a barracks rose up clearly, proud of its façade. Before the barracks, a company of soldiers stood facing forward at motionless attention. The colonel or captain, seated on horseback, ordered the formation of a square, whereupon the soldiers, led by their officers, carried out this maneuver. Curiously, however, this colonel was none other than the milkman. Joseph recognized him clearly by his mouth and his resonant voice. The milkman now held a brief but fiery speech exhorting this young militia to protect the fatherland. "Despite everything!" Joseph thought, smiling. After all, they were standing at ease, and so it was certainly permitted for one to smile. The day was a Sunday. A young handsome lieutenant walked up to soldier Joseph and said in a friendly tone: "No shave today, eh, Marti?" Whereupon he strode off along the front rank, his saber rattling. Joseph rubbed the underside of his chin in embarrassment: "I haven't even had a shave yet this morning!" How the sun was gleaming. How warm it was! Suddenly there was an abrupt shift in the dream, and an open field appeared with a group of marksmen lying spaced out in a half-circle. Gunshots resounded in the nearby wooded slopes, and the signals rang out. "You're dead, Marti, fall down!" the milkman-colonel cried from atop his horse, where he was surveying the battle. "Aha," Joseph thought, "he's being kind to me. He's letting me rest here on the splendid lawn." He remained lying there on the ground until the skirmish was over, passing the time by pulling blades of grass through his thirsting mouth. What a world, what sunshine! What freedom from cares there was in just lying there like that! But now it was time for him to spring to his feet again and rejoin the formation. But he couldn't, he was pinned to the ground. The blade of grass refused to budge from his mouth, he began to struggle with it, sweat appeared on his brow and fear in his soul, and he woke up to find himself on his cot once more, beside the snoring locksmith's apprentice.

Three hours later the guard called him. He was "done." He took his leave of all of them. Warmly he pressed the hand of the poor milkman, who had another six weeks to serve. He was given his papers back and was free to go out onto the street. His limbs were cold and stiff, his head was still buzzing and ringing and shooting from his dream. An hour later he was once more surrounded by workaday Toblerian projects. The Advertising Clock and Marksman's Vending Machine were beckoning to him in annoyance but also imploringly, and once more Joseph did some writing at his desk.

"Well, you've certainly allowed yourself a nice vacation," the engineer said, "two whole days do not go unnoticed in a business like mine. So now I'll expect you to work twice as hard. I hope my words are making an impression on you. Naturally the purpose of my having an assistant is not to send him off to serve prison terms every week. No one can demand that I pay out a sal—"

He had been about to say "salary," but stopped in midbreath, looking thoughtful. Joseph did not think it necessary to say anything at all in reply.

The invalid chair was now finished. An adorable little model stood upon Tobler's drafting table, and was constantly being admired from every angle while the engineer, apparently delighted, turned it this way and that to enjoy the view from all sides. At once the assistant had to busy himself with writing letters introducing the new product to various domestic and foreign firms of a certain size specializing in furniture for the infirm.

Tobler collapsed the delicate apparatus by a simple turning of screws and shifting of levers, then he had Joseph wrap the thing up in good paper, took his hat and went down to the village to show those infidels, those sarcastic Bärenswilers, what a splendid invention had been completed and once more made viable in his workshop.

Joseph meanwhile was to write to the village magistrate that Tobler would be unable to attend in person the meeting to be held the following morning at nine regarding the litigation brought by Martin Grünen: urgent business prevented him. Therefore he was taking the liberty of presenting the magistrate with the necessary clarifications and compilations of figures, from which he would see that . . . , etc.

"My Herr Tobler is an angel!" The assistant smiled inwardly, feeling a brief twinge of malice. After this document had been prepared, his next task was to compose a similar explanatory note in a tone almost even more brusque than the one before, addressed to the most worthy district court. Once more Joseph marveled at the pithiness of his own epistolary style, as well as at the flowery and polite expressions interwoven here and there amid the forceful statements. "One should never be too coarse," he thought whenever he found himself sidestepping into the realms of respectfulness and modesty. This letter, too, was quickly dispatched, for he had now become fairly handy at such things, a self-satisfied insight which prompted him to light himself, yet again, one of those familiar and infallible cheroots. Just let them come, the Office of the Magistrate and the district courts, as well as all the numerous treacherous official demands for payment—he and Tobler would go right on, calmly and with peace in their hearts, puffing away at their fragrant cheroots and cigars, and would keep this up for quite some time.

The Bärenswilers had gradually—first just whispering it to one another, but now proclaiming it openly on the street, in a wave of insight cresting higher and higher—reached the conviction that up at the Evening Star there would soon be nothing left to "salvage" if the necessary steps allowing at least something to be fished out of the place were not quickly set in motion with the help of the laws for the recovery of debts. And so it had come to pass that Herr Tobler was being illuminated, shadowed and pursued on all sides in accordance with the laws covering bills of exchange, both with respect to the firm and to his household finances. It was like a javelin competition on a public holiday, the way the spears came shooting up from the left and the right, from this way and that, poking the Tobler villa full of holes and ill humor. The court or debt law representative sidled about the house and the entire garden all day long, gloatingly and at the same time cozily, as if he found this locale up here particularly inviting, as if this happened to be his favorite place. It looked as if the man were secretly an admirer of nature and ornamental gardens.

Or had this haggard pointy figure been engaged by a construction syndicate or even a geographical society to take the measurements of the region using merely his eyes and his memory? Hardly! But that's what the fellow looked like. Frau Tobler hated and feared him and hurriedly fled from the windows of the house whenever she caught a glimpse of him, as if this man were the personification of cheerless forebodings and gloom. The woman was right, for any time you ventured to observe the face of this individual, which appeared to be slammed and hammered shut, the sight chilled you to the bone—you couldn't help feeling you'd been touched and stroked by the ice-cold hand of calamity.

This man interacted with Joseph in the most exquisitely idiosyncratic manner. He was skilled, for example, in appearing unexpectedly—as if the dark earth itself had spat him out—before the office door, where he blotted out all light and air. Then he would remain standing there for a full minute, not because he was doing or preparing something, but rather, it appeared, for his own personal delight and pleasure. Then he would open the door, but he didn't yet enter, no, he wasn't even thinking of that; rather, he remained standing there, apparently wishing to see what impression his sinister behavior was making. Fixing his cold eyes firmly upon the unnerved assistant, he then would enter the office, only to pause yet again for the time being. Never did he say "good day" or "good evening." For him, the hours of the day appeared not to exist, nor even the God-given air—the man looked as if he found breathing superfluous. Clamping together the features of his bony face, he now took one or two official forms from a black-leather carrying case, raised them up absurdly high in the air, and allowed them to descend upon the desk of the assistant, his hand as silent, pointy and hooked as the talons of a bird of prey. Having fulfilled his mission, he appeared to be luxuriating in the consciousness no doubt telling him that his presence there had been comfortless and oppressive, for he gave no thought to departing but rather spent several minutes attempting to determine whether he might manage to replace the case in the pocket of his coat. Then he said—or almost said—goodbye, and left. The goodbye uttered by this man was far chillier than had he said nothing at all, it sounded offhand and at the same time intentionally cold and hard. The man then appeared about to leave, but no, first he did that horrifying thing: he stood measuring the surroundings, the house and garden, with his eyes. Then the other door opened, and Frau Tobler appeared all in a dither, her eyes like saucers, crying out anxiously: "Now he's back in the garden again! Look, just look!"

On days when this man appeared, the weather was mostly a gray, cold, silent cross between snow and rain. The outer walls of the house were wet at their base, a piercing wind was blowing off the lake, promising new snow flurries or pelting rain, and the lake lay there so leaden and colorless and sad. Where were its beautiful evening and morning colors now? Sunk beneath the depths of the water? On days like this, morning and evening no longer existed, the hours all had the same bleak look, and the times of day seemed to have grown weary of their designations and the dear, familiar differences in the light. And if now, amid all this dreariness and this disfigurement of nature, the man with the black-leather portfolio were also to appear, it seemed to Frau Tobler and the clerk that the world had suddenly turned inside-out and that they were now gazing at the reverse of all familiar factual life rather than at earthly things. There appeared to be something spectral lingering about the lovely Tobler residence, and the happiness and delicate charm of this home, indeed its very legitimacy, appeared to have been lost in a pallid, weary, lackluster and fathomless dream. When Frau Tobler then looked out the window and beheld her summer lake, which had now become a thing of winter and fog, when she glimpsed and felt the melancholy that had laid itself over all visible objects, she was compelled to press her handkerchief to her eyes and weep into it.

One of the most savage creditors and dunners proved to be none other than the gardener who until then had always managed the work in the garden and had provided and cared for all the plants. This man railed like an entire battalion of railers against Tobler and his whole family, saying he would not permit himself an hour's rest until the day came when he would have the satisfaction of seeing this "arrogant brood" thrown out of the Evening Star and all their worldly goods impounded. These harsh words were brought to Herr Tobler's attention— half in flattery, half secretly to offend—and at once Tobler ordered that all his plants currently being stored in the greenhouses at the nursery be collected there without further ado and transferred to the cellar of his friend, the insurance agent, the one who'd taken part in the grotto celebration. Joseph was entrusted with the swift execution of this order, and he had no cause to delay. And so he set off for the nursery with a one-horse cart, which was loaded with the plants there, among them a splendid silver fir sapling that had already grown rather tall. The cart, now transformed into a garden, drove off through the streets, past a number of astonished villagers, and stopped before the quarters of the house and gentleman indicated to the driver. The insurance agent himself helped unload and carry down to the cellar as many plants as could be accommodated there. The noble young fir tree had to be tied up with ropes so that it could at least lean diagonally in vaults that were too low for its slender, proud growth. The assistant felt very sorry to see the tree housed in such conditions, but what could be done? Tobler wished it, and Tobler's volition remained the sole unconditional guideline for Joseph's actions.

This insurance agent had indeed remained faithful to Tobler. He was a simple but enlightened man to whom it would never have occurred to withdraw his friendship and camaraderie from a person he had come to value just because of difficulties of an external nature. He was now almost the only one left who might come up to the villa on a Sunday so as to help get up a round of Jass. There was still always something to drink at the Toblers', thank God. Just in the past few days, a small barrel filled with excellent Rhenish wine had arrived from Mainz, a delivery that was tardy and thus all the more welcome, no doubt the result of an order placed in earlier, better days. Tobler gaped in surprise at this barrel, he could no longer even remember having commissioned this firm to send him such expensive wine. Joseph now had the additional task of bottling the wine and then sealing these bottles properly with corks, a task at which he displayed quite astonishing adroitness, so that Frau Tobler, observing this swift operation, asked in jest whether he had ever worked for a wine merchant. In this way, certain cheerful hours of diversion were to be had in the household, which contributed not a little to helping its members endure the many difficult hours, a boon that was necessary indeed for all of them and not to be underestimated. But then one day Frau Tobler suddenly fell ill.

She was forced to take to her bed, unwilling as she was to do so at such a time, and they had to send for the doctor, the very

221

same Doctor Specker who for many weeks now had successfully avoided setting foot in a house whose inner supports were crumbling. He responded to the call, though he had every reason to fear he would receive no payment for his ministrations or for the trouble of making a midnight journey though pitch-black streets. Quietly he approached the woman's bedside and in his manner and speech acted as if he had never given up his friendly visits, but rather had continued always to maintain his warm ties to the family. He asked sympathetically about the pain, how long Frau Tobler had felt it, etc., and performed the solemn duties of his profession in as pleasant a manner as he was able. Afterward, despite the fact that it was nearly one in the morning, Tobler showed the doctor the invalid chair, whose first life-sized model had arrived that very day. Now he could give the model its first practical trial by using it on his wife, the inventor said, attempting a humorous tone of voice, but not quite succeeding. "How about a quick glass of wine before you go?" No. The doctor left.

And so now, on top of all the other unlovely things that were occurring, she would have to stay in bed, the woman complained to everyone who appeared at her bedside. It wasn't enough, she lamented, that everything in household and business alike was on the point of collapse—now not even health itself remained. She had to be ill just when a hand to perform labors and an eye to keep watch had become indispensable. And of course illness costs money, and where would they get it? She felt so feeble, and she so wished to be on her feet again, so wished to face the worst. Where was Dora? Dora should be sent to her.

Joseph was not allowed in the sickroom. But since her illness dragged on for days and he once had to ask her something that could not be put off, he made so bold as to enter the room. He did this with the timidity of persons usually coarse in their habits. She looked at him with a smile and offered him her hand, and he managed to wish her a swift recovery. How large her eyes were. And this hand. How terribly pale. Was that a mother raven? She asked how things were looking down in the living room, and how the children were behaving, and said weakly that now he would have to do a bit of child-rearing until she was able to get up again. She so longed to get up. Was Pauline still doing the cooking properly? And what was happening in the office?

He answered her questions and felt very happy about this moment. Was this the woman—a woman who even lying in bed was able to remain a perfect lady, whose beauty was increased rather than lessened by her illness—whom he had wished to scold with a moralistic lecture? How unjust and immature. And yet, how plausible! For Silvi was even now being treated no better than before.

Whenever Silvi was about to cry out during this period, Pauline hissed in her ears: "You keep still!" After all, there was a sick person in the house.

At the soonest appropriate opportunity Tobler set about testing his patented invalid chair on his wife. She was far from satisfied with the properties of this invention and dared to criticize the errors that marred this piece of furniture. Above all else, she said, the chair was too heavy, its weight was oppressive, and then it would have to be made wider, she felt too confined in it.

This was unpleasant news to receive from one's own wife.

223

Tobler, who realized that he had failed to take certain things into account, immediately set about making the necessary adjustments, quickly sketching out a few new parts at the drawing board so that the patterns could be sent to the carpenter's workshop right away. Just a very few changes were required, and then the chair could be put into production all the more vigorously. Already a number of shops and companies had written to him to say they were looking forward to receiving a first complete model.

And the Advertising Clock, how was it faring? Negotiations were in progress with a newly founded commercial enterprise concern, all manner of quotes had been submitted, along with biographical information for the head of the firm, as this had been requested. Now it was time to wait and hope!

Meanwhile the electric lights had been shut off in the entire household by the power company for the same reasons preventing other firms from continuing to provide goods and services to the Evening Star on good faith. The sudden switching off of the electric current made Tobler nearly sick with rage and caused him to write the gentlemen from the electric company a letter that was both impotently fuming and excessively rude, one that, when it had been received and read, made these people, above all the director of the plant, burst into good-natured, derisive laughter. The members of the Tobler household now had no choice but to avail themselves once more of the humble petroleum lamps, to whose light all of them except Tobler quickly adjusted. Tobler could not reconcile himself to the absence, when he came home late at night, of his beloved electric veranda lamp: it had always appeared to him as the beautifully radiant emblem and brightly shining proof of the continued secure existence of his home. The pain he felt at the loss of this brighter light joined in his breast with the other grievous wounds and contributed to the bleakness of his state of mind, with the result that the abrupt changefulness of his moods became daily bread for all of them.

But now, above all else, a sum of money had to be procured by any means possible, at any price. Their most urgent obligations, at the very least, had to be attended to, and so one morning it was decided that a letter would be sent to Tobler's mother, a woman who was wealthy but stubborn and known to be unshakable in her principles. This letter went as follows:

Dear Mother!

You have no doubt heard from my lawyer Bintsch in what wretched circumstances I currently find myself. I am sitting here in my house like a bird trapped by the piercing gaze of the snake—already being killed in advance. I am so surrounded by creditors that if they were friends and benefactors I would be one of the richest and most beloved of men; but alas, these people are utterly ruthless, and I am the most beleaguered of men. Dear mother, you have already helped me extricate myself from a tight spot on more than one occasion, this I know quite well, and I have always been secretly grateful to you for this, and so now I am asking you once more, in the most urgent possible terms, the way people beg for help when the knife of public disgrace is being held to their throats: help me to save myself one time more, and send me by return mail if at all possible for you at least some provisional part of the monies to which I am still entitled to-day by everything that bears the name of law. Do not misunderstand me, Mother, I am not threatening you, I realize that I am entirely dependent upon your good will and that you can thrust me into ruin if you so wish, but why should you wish such a thing? At the moment my wife is also sick, your daughter. She is lying in bed and will not be able to get up again so very soon; indeed, I shall have to count myself fortunate if she is ever able to get up again. You see, this as well! What is a businessman to do when he finds himself so buffeted by slings and arrows? Until now I have always managed somehow to keep my head above water, but today I have indeed arrived at the outer limits of the absolute impossibility of keeping this up any longer. What would you say if one day soon, one fine morning or afternoon, you were to read in the newspaper that your son had taken his own li— ... but no, I am not capable of uttering such a thing in its entirety, for it is to my mother I am speaking. Send me the money at once. This, too, is not a threat, I am merely urging you to do so, urging you desperately. Even in our household budget almost nothing remains, and both my wife and I have long since had to accustom ourselves to the idea that sooner or later there will be nothing left for our children to eat. I am describing to you my circumstances not as they are, but as I am making an effort to see them so as to maintain a certain propriety in what I write. My wife sends her heartfelt greetings and embraces you, as do I, your son

Carl Tobler.

P.S.: Even today I am firmly convinced of the success of my enterprises. The Advertising Clock will prove its worth, you can count on it. And one more thing: My assistant will leave me if his outstanding salary is not *paid out to him now.*

The same.

While Tobler was composing this letter at his desk, the clerk seated at his writing table was leveling the muzzle of his epistolary musket at a brother of Tobler's, a widely respected contractor in government service who was living in a remote region of the country, calling his attention, as his superior had instructed him, to the piteous conditions prevailing at the Evening Star and pointing out that it was high time that..., etc.

"Have you written it? Show me. Let me sign it, or, wait, no— the letter ought to be composed in such a way as if you yourself had written it of your own accord, out of concern for your employer. Write it the other way and then sign it yourself. Do it as if you were writing without my knowledge, do you understand? I am not on good terms with my brother; you, however, are a perfect stranger to him. Hurry up, I've got to read what you're putting down there. And then I've got a train to catch."

Tobler laughed and said:

"These are tricks, my dear Marti, but for the love of God, one has to know how to help oneself. And go ahead and write that other thing to my esteemed brother, the thing about your overdue salary. And then we'll both just have to wait and see where these tactics get us. My mother will no doubt have to comply. If she doesn't . . . and don't forget to write out a nice clean copy of the whole Advertising Clock business in a tidy hand. Have a smoke! At least we still have some cheroots in the house. Now either the devil is going to come for us, or we'll have a breakthrough."

"How caught up he is in all these hopes and 'tricks,'" Joseph thought.

After a few days, Frau Tobler was able to get up again. A good thing, too, for Pauline did in fact require supervision. She was becoming neglectful. The lady of the house appeared once more in the living room, loosely draped in a dark blue housedress, and quietly began to attend once more to the business and cares of the household. Her manner was quiet and lovely, and she appeared to be smiling silently with her entire being. Her voice had become thinner, her gestures more fleeting and timorous, and her eyes darted about like the inquisitive eyes of children. Her infirmity had cast a beautiful mildness over her entire conduct, she looked as if from now on she would never again be able to fly into a passion, to take sides. She behaved in a more natural way toward her Dora, no longer speaking to her in such a sugary voice—the confectionary shop was no longer doing such brisk business—and she was able now to look at Silvi without her face filling with obvious anger, which had almost always been the case before. In general, she appeared to have cast off certain emotional complexities, she made a nobler, more straightforward impression, you felt this when you looked at her, and she herself felt she had to perceive herself this way, too. Her face expressed sorrow, but also warmth and composure and something almost majestically maternal. "I am more or less healthy again, thank God!" all her smallest gestures appeared to be saying, and the language they spoke had to be a profound and true one, for gestures and manner are not good liars. Her mouth was still a bit feverish, as if the agitated tremor of unlovely past excitations had not yet left it, but in her large peaceful eyes the clear message lay gleaming: "I have become a bit better, more superior and refined. Look at me. It shows, doesn't it?" Her hands reached out cautiously to pick up her needlework or some chinaware or a book, it was as if these hands had been given the gift of thought. They appeared to have lips, which were saying: "We have begun to think about so many, many things far more peacefully and openly. We have become more tender." Yes, all of Frau Tobler had become somewhat more tender, but also paler.

How pleasant she found it in the living room. The room had been thoroughly heated. She looked out through the windowpanes. Outside, everything lay beneath an opaque fog. How beautiful it was that one couldn't see anything at all. How cozy it was inside here. For just an instant, an image of summer fluttered before her contented eyes, in her thoughts she gazed at it peacefully with a "well then!" before it vanished once more. Then she thought of her new dress and of the seamstress in the city, Frau Bertha Gindroz, and she couldn't help laughing softly. She wiped a bit of dust from the furniture, but in fact what she was doing was more just touching the furniture as if she wished to caress it and to say hello. How dear and new everything appeared to her. These few days! And these few days, this one short week, had given everything an exotic, agreeable novelty in her eyes. Everything lay beneath a peculiar shimmer that made all it touched smaller and more delicate; she felt a bit dizzy and sat down.

The dog now spent most of his time indoors. It had long since become too cold for him out in the doghouse. Only at night did he have to lie there.

Up in the tower room, too—which could not be heated—it began to be unpleasantly cold, and Joseph spent his evenings and sometimes half the night down in the living room, most of the time alone with the woman, who scarcely received visitors any longer. The parquet factory women, the old lady and the young one, had quarreled with the Toblers over a legal question. The cause was a tiny bit of land that abutted the property of both neighbors and which both claimed as their own. The matter was too trivial to be taken to court, but it made for bad blood and led to insults and words of abuse, and the old friendly-neighborly interactions had come to an end. Tobler had declared that he didn't want to see that clucking old hen coming over his garden hedge and into his house ever again. And with this, the friendship was cancelled. To be sure, was there anyone of whom Tobler had not said something similar? In the case of most of his acquaintances, or nearly most, Tobler's position was: just let them dare set foot once more upon Tobler terrain, they'll see what sort of welcome they get!

And so the family spent the long evenings alone. Mostly the lamp illuminated two heads, the woman's and that of the assistant, who was keeping her company, along with a card game or book that lay open on the dining table.

Several days passed. Not one hour went by unnoticed.

These days were counted, they were tallied up, for it was not a matter of indifference whether they passed swiftly or slowly— after all, the existence of the Tobler household was now merely a matter of days. The family got out of the habit of thinking in months or years, or else they compressed these thought-months and thought-years and forced their memories to grasp them more quickly, and so they went on living, waiting for whatever signs the day might bring. Any rustling sound was important, for it might be the postman delivering some new, worrisome unpleasantness in the form of a letter or a demand for payment. Ringing sounds were important, for it might be the sound of the doorbell announcing the arrival of some person with distressing intentions. A shout was important, for it might be significant: "Hey there, Herr and Frau Tobler," this voice might cry out, "hurry up, it's time for you to leave behind this loveliest and most familiar of all human habitations. Come now, get a move on. You've been living high on the hog long enough." Any shout they heard might well contain hideous words like these. But colors, too, were important—the day's visage, the features and gestures of these, as it appeared, final days—for they spoke of final hopes and final exertions and the things one must do in order to continue to be filled with hope. How soft-spoken they were, these days. The days were by no means angry with the Tobler household, far from it! Rather, they seemed to wish to shelter it from high up and far away, in the form of clouds and spirits, to smile at and console it. These days almost resembled Frau Tobler a little. Like her, the days appeared to have been ill, and now the days had just as pale and soft a countenance as the woman around whom they were giving way to one another in irreversible succession.

But Frau Tobler was little by little becoming the old Frau Tobler once more. The more she recovered, the more she resembled herself. Well, it would have been exceedingly peculiar, wouldn't it, if she had become another person instead! No, a living human creature is not so quick to leap out of its own nature. Provisions are in place to ensure that a thing like that will never come to pass. If the woman made a gentler impression, it was only because she was still feeling weak.

One evening around this time, the two of them, the woman and the assistant, were sitting beside the lamp in the living room. Her husband was on the road. When wasn't he on the road these days? Upon the table, beside each of the two persons sitting there, stood a half-full glass of red wine. They were playing cards. Frau Tobler was winning, therefore her expression was gay. She was in the habit of laughing whenever she was winning at cards, and this is what she was doing now. She allowed naively gleeful laughter to leap out of her mouth, laughter that might at some other time have annoyed her partner. But Joseph just took a sip of wine to accompany his loss, and the two of them went on with their game; Frau Tobler shuffled the cards. After approximately one hour, she said she would like to read a little in the book the assistant had brought her from the village that day. The game was interrupted, the woman at once began to read, while Joseph, feeling no desire to pick up a newspaper or book himself, sat down on the daybed and began to observe the reading woman. She appeared to have immersed herself completely in the story contained in the book she was reading. From time to time she passed one hand carefully across her apparently highly pensive brow, while her mouth began to move silently but uneasily, as if it wished to comment on the events she was reading about. Once she even gave a faint but mournful sigh, her audible breaths making her breast fly up and down. How strange this was to silently observe! Joseph became more and more immersed in his observation of the reading woman, and it seemed to him as if he, too, were reading a large, mysteriously suspenseful book, indeed, it seemed as if he were reading virtually the very same book as Frau Tobler, whose brow, which he was diligently watching, seemed in an odd way to be communicating the book's contents and explaining them to him.

"How quietly she is reading," he thought, still gazing at her. Suddenly she looked up from the book, glancing over at the assistant with a look of surprise, as if she and her thought-eyes had been off in some far-distant realm and her eyes were now having difficulty making sense of what they saw. She said:

"It seems you have been looking at me the entire time I was reading, and I didn't even notice. Do you enjoy this? Aren't you bored?"

"No, not at all," he replied.

"How a book can draw you in," she said and went on reading.

After a while she seemed to have grown tired. Perhaps her eyes were hurting a little. In any case, she stopped reading, but did not yet shut the book, as if she were still considering whether or not to continue.

"Frau Tobler!" Joseph said softly.

"What?" she asked.

She shut her book and looked over at the clerk, who, it appeared, had something special to say to her. But an entire minute of silence passed. Finally Joseph said hesitantly that he was being incautious. He had wished to say something quite specific. He had noticed that she appeared to have just finished reading, and that, as he even now beheld, the expression on her face was good-natured. Suddenly it had occurred to him that he might seize this opportunity, which he had been awaiting for such a long time, and speak to her, and now he found himself once more lacking the courage to speak those words he'd been intending to utter. Now he himself realized something that Frau Tobler had already said to him many weeks ago, namely that he was a peculiar individual. What he had wanted to say was foolish and not even worthy of being heard. She should permit him to hold his tongue.

The woman furrowed her brow and asked the assistant to come sit closer beside her and speak. She wished to know what it was he'd wished to tell her. One couldn't just start talking to people and make them curious about things that then did not come. Such behavior was cowardly, or thoughtless. She was listening.

Joseph had taken a seat at the table as she'd instructed him and said that what he had to report concerned Silvi.

The woman was silent and looked down. He continued:

"Allow me, Frau Tobler, to tell you frankly how repugnant I find the treatment reserved for this child. You say nothing. Very well, I will take this to mean that your kindness is bidding me continue. You are doing this tiny creature a huge injustice. What is to become of her some day? Will she ever have the courage and the requisite desire to display any sort of human behavior to others? After all, she will remember, and be compelled to remember, that in her own youth she was raised in a most inhuman fashion. What sort of child-rearing is this, delivering a child into the hands of a coarse and stupid maidservant, a hussy, a Pauline? Cleverness must forbid such a thing, even if lovelessness allows it. I am speaking in such a way because this has been occupying me, because on many a day I have witnessed things that have quite honestly caused me pain, and because I feel within me the urge to serve you, Frau Tobler, in every way I can. I'm being rude, aren't I. Well, that's the way peculiar persons behave at times. But no. I would like to speak to you quite differently. This is not appropriate. I have already said too much, and not a single word more shall cross my lips today."

For several minutes silence prevailed; finally Frau Tobler said that the thought had long since crossed her mind that they had cause to reproach themselves on Silvi's account. All of this, by the way, appeared terribly strange to her. But the assistant need not be afraid, she forgave him for the words he had just spoken, she could see he meant well. Once more she was silent. A bit later she said, "The thing is, I don't love her."

"Why not?" Joseph asked.

Why not? This question appeared to her foolish, ill-considered. She simply did not love Silvi and in fact couldn't abide her. Could one force oneself to feel love and goodwill? What sort of feeling would this be that one forced and gagged out of oneself?

Could she help it if she felt she was being driven away from Silvi with iron blows and hammers the moment she laid eyes on her even at a distance? Why was it that Dora appeared so sweet to her? This she didn't know and had no desire to understand. Even if she wished to learn these things: would the fitting answers to these, as it appeared to her, superfluous and hopeless questions ever be hers to know? How difficult it all was. Yes, she knew quite well that she was in the wrong. Even when Silvi was a tiny child she had, strangely enough, begun to hate her. Yes, hate, that was the right word, it perfectly described the feeling she associated with this child. She would make an effort in the next few days to see whether it was possible for her to cultivate an attachment to the child once more, but she had no high hopes for such experiments, love could not be learned: one either had and felt love, or one did not. Not having it meant, she believed, that one would never have it. But she would try, and now she wished to go to bed, she felt quite tired.

She got up and went to the door. At the threshold she turned around and said:

"I almost forgot—good night, Joseph. How distracted I am. Put out the lamp before you go up to your room. It will be quite some time yet before Tobler returns. You have made my heart a little heavier this evening, but I am not angry with you."

"I wish I had kept my peace," Joseph said.

"Think nothing of it."

With these words, she went upstairs.

The assistant remained standing in the middle of the room. A short while later, Tobler appeared. The other said:

"Good evening, Herr Tobler, hmm, what I wanted to take the liberty of saying is that half an hour ago I committed the incautiousness of saying rude things to your wife yet again. I wish to confess this to you in advance. Frau Tobler will no doubt be inclined to complain about me. I assure you it was nothing but foolish trifles, things of absolutely no importance or weight. I would ask you most politely not to look at me with such big eyes, I believe that neither are your eyes a mouth nor am I some edible object—there is nothing about my person that can be eaten. As for the tone of this speech, it can be explained by the fact that it is being dictated by a mind filled with ravings. Would it not be better if you were now finally to drive your most peculiar clerk out of the house? Your wife mistreats Silvi all year round undisturbed. Have you no eyes in your head? Are you a father or merely an entrepreneur? Good night, good night, I suppose there is no longer any need for me to wait and hear what you might have to say in response to this strange performance. I shall assume I am being relieved of my duties."

"Are you drunk? Eh?"

Tobler was shouting in vain. The assistant had already ascended the stairs. Before the door to the tower room he suddenly stopped short. "Have I lost my mind?" And he ran downstairs again as fast as he was able. Herr Tobler was still sitting in the living room. Joseph remained standing at the threshold, as the woman had done shortly before, and said that he was sorry he had behaved in such an unseemly and senseless fashion, he regretted this, but he also saw that he—had not yet been let go. If Herr Tobler had any business matter he wished to discuss with him, Joseph was at his disposal.

Tobler shouted at the top of his lungs:

"My wife is a goose, and you are a lunatic. These damn books!"

He picked up the lending library book and hurled it to the floor. He was searching his memory for insulting words, but couldn't find any. In part, the words he found said too little; in part, too much. "Robber" was on the tip of his tongue, but how could this word be an insult? Because of his confusion, his fury knew no bounds. He would have liked to say "cur," but this word would have served to make mincemeat of all reason. He kept silent, for he found he would be unable to trounce his opponent in a respectable way. Finally he laughed—no, brayed:

"Get back up to that lair of yours at once!"

Joseph deemed it advisable to withdraw. When he had reached his room, he remained standing there for a long time, unable to think even the tiniest thought. There was only the one notion flickering before his consciousness like a will-o'-the-wisp: he still hadn't received his salary and nonetheless had had the audacity . . . such foolhardiness. What would happen tomorrow? He resolved to throw himself at the woman's feet. What nonsense! Tormented by the impossibility of thinking, he went out onto the balcony. It was a dry, cold night. The sky was gleaming and glittering and frozen full of stars. It was as if the stars were radiating all the cold everywhere down at the earth. There was still one person walking on the dark road. His shoes made a metallic clacking sound upon the paving-stones. Everything out there appeared to be made either of steel or of stone. The night's very silence seemed to be ringing out and jangling. Joseph thought of ice skates, then of iron ore, then suddenly of Wirsich. How might he be faring? He felt a faint sensation of friendship toward this person. Surely he would encounter him again one day. But where? He went back to his room and undressed.

At this moment, a cry of Silvi's rang out.

"The poor little thing is being dragged out of bed yet again," he thought. "Brrrr, how cold it is!" He went on listening for a while, sitting up in bed, but he heard nothing more and soon fell asleep.

The next morning he crept fainthearted and trembling down to the office. He thought: "Will I be sent packing? What? Could I leave this house?"

Yes, he felt how dear it had become to him, and in his thoughts he went on:

"Could it be possible for me to live without doing stupid things? And in this household I do them so splendidly. What will things be like in this regard elsewhere? And how can I think of existing without drinking Tobler's coffee? Who else will feed me till I've had my fill? And so hospitably, and with such variety? In other places, the food is so bland, so utterly the opposite of lavish! And in whose neatly covered and turned-down beds do I intend to go to sleep afterward? No doubt beneath the arches of some cozy bridge! But perhaps I am being too hasty. Oh, Lord, can things already have come to such a pass? And how can I go on breathing without being present in this picturesque landscape so enchanting even in winter? And how will I entertain myself in the evenings, as I have been doing with dear, magnificent Frau Tobler? To whom will I say rude things? Not all people have such a special, personal, lovely way of receiving such boorishness. How sad. How I love this house! And where will a lamp be so tenderly burning as Tobler's lamps, where will there be a living room so homey, so full of heart, as Tobler's living room? How despondent all of this makes me. And how will my thoughts get by without everyday objects such as the Advertising Clock, Marksman's Vending Machine, Invalid Chair and Deep Hole Drilling Machine? Yes, all this will make me unhappy, I realize that. I have ties here, I live here. How strangely devoted I am! And Tobler's deep rumbling voice, how bitterly I shall miss the sound of it. Why hasn't he yet come downstairs? I would like to know where I stand. Yes, all these things. What? Where will a summer like this ever again press me with its voluptuous green arms to its blossoming, fragrant bosom like the summer I had the privilege to experience and savor up here? Where, in what region of the world, are such tower rooms to be found? And such a Pauline? Though I have quarreled with her on many an occasion, she too, in the end, is part of this beautiful whole. How wretched I feel. Here my lack of "wits" was tolerated, at least to a certain degree. I would like to know in what other places in the civilized world this would have been permitted. And the garden I watered so often, and the grotto? Where will I be given such things? Persons such as I are generally never permitted to enjoy the pleasantness and magic of gardens. Am I lost? How wretched I feel, I think I'll have to smoke a cheroot now. That, too, I shall miss. So be it."

And when he thought now of the flag from the previous summer, he found himself compelled to grin so as not to have to start crying like a weakling. Then Herr Tobler came into the office, just the same as always, with a proper "Good morning." Not a word about throwing anyone out.

Nothing of the sort!

Joseph put on his humblest and most assiduous face, he was indescribably happy that it had not yet "come to that." He set about performing the various business-related tasks of the day with a veritable passion, and every few moments he turned about on his chair to see what Tobler was doing at his desk. Tobler was doing the same things he always did.

"What sort of fit was it you were having yesterday?" the boss inquired in an incredibly friendly tone of voice.

"Yes, that was stupid," the assistant said meekly, with a shamefaced smile.

He needn't worry, Tobler grumbled. He was going to get his pay.

"Oh, I don't even want any pay. I don't deserve it."

"What rubbish," Tobler replied. "Aside from a few foolish incidents which have regrettably occurred, I am satisfied with you. And if I get the factory I've applied for a share in, then with any luck we'll be able to remain together. In such a case, a book-keeper will be necessary as well."

Later the boss left.

Dora had taken ill on this day, not seriously. It was only a minor head cold, but this sufficed to cause the girl to be tended to as though her final day had come. She was lying on the sofa in the living room, and when Joseph happened to mention he would be going down to the post office—it was getting on toward evening—he had to promise to bring Dora a couple of oranges from the specialty foods shop, which he did.

During the evening meal, Frau Tobler constantly addressed words to the charming, indisposed little creature, directing these comments toward the daybed. Silvi was gaping a little with her mouth wide open, as though pondering how it could happen that a person could be ill so charmingly. Why was it that Silvi herself was never sick? Was this simply not for her? Did Nature have to refuse her this attractive condition? Was she too unimportant to be permitted to catch a little head cold? She would so love to be treated a bit more tenderly than usual, just once to be treated a bit more warmly and gently. Dora! No. Silvi gazed at her sister, sorrowful and marveling, as though she were simply incapable of explaining to herself how Dora could be lying there so beautifully ill.

"Take the spoon out of your mouth, Silvi. I can't stand looking at it!" Frau Tobler said. Her face appeared at this moment to have taken on two expressions at once, a sweet smooth one for Dora, and, hidden beneath it, a furrowed severe one for Silvi. At the same time, the woman glanced at the clerk as if examining his face to see what he might think or say about this. But Joseph's face was smiling over at Dora.

This was certainly no wonder: human beings simply prefer to direct their eyes to where the beautiful and well-formed can be seen, not to where a teaspoon is being poked about unappetizingly in an expressionless mouth.

Dora's round face peered out prettily from amid the snow-white pillows; scattered about them, and pressing hollows into the down, lay the oranges Joseph had brought back with him. This charming, voluptuous, childish mouth. These small but already almost self-consciously lovely and graceful gestures. This suppliant, dear, light voice, this trustingness! Yes, Dora, you were permitted to be trusting, constantly you saw kindness streaming from your mother's face in your direction.

How impoverished Silvi was. Would it ever have occurred to this little girl to ask someone to bring her oranges from the specialty foods shop in the village? Absolutely not. She knew all too well how inclined everyone would be to deny her request. Her requests were not even requests at all, but rather just stammered-forth envy. She asked for something only long after Dora was already in possession of the desired object. Never did Silvi think of a wish that was all her own. Silvi's wishes were all copies of wishes, her ideas were never truly ideas, but rather only imitations of ideas that Dora had had first. Only a true child's heart can produce fresh ideas, never a heart that has been beaten and despised. A true request is always first and never second rate, just like a true work of art. Silvi, as it seemed, was first and foremost just second, third, perhaps even seventh rate. Everything she said was forged and baked in a false tone, and everything she did seemed somehow passé. How old Silvi was despite her blossom-young years. What injustice!

Joseph had considered these things for a moment while gazing at Dora. Looking at her, one could form a clear image of her counterpart, and so it wasn't really necessary to cast one's scrutinizing and comparing eyes upon Silvi for very long.

How sad this was. These two unequal children! Joseph would have liked to heave an audible sigh from the very bottom of his contemplations. When it was time for Dora to be carried upstairs to her proper bedroom, he went up to her and was so struck by the sight of her pert, innocent face that he couldn't help kissing her little hand. With this kiss of homage, his intention was to caress both types at once, the Dora-type and also the Silvi-type. But how could he have actually paid homage to this second type? Impossible! And so he tried to say, at least in thought, something consoling and respectful to that young bitterness and shunted-off-to-the-side-ness, by using his mouth to press these unsaid words upon the hand of sisterly love and natural graciousness.

Frau Tobler observed this. His behavior met with her approval. "A peculiar individual, this Marti!" she thought. "Just yesterday he was scolding me on Silvi's behalf, and now I find him half in love with Dora!" She smiled graciously and said to Dora that in future she should keep her hands cleaner if she wished to go on receiving kisses of this sort, and she laughed.

To Silvi she said goodnight with a grimace, adding that she should pull herself together and stop giving her mother cause to be harsh with her; then she, too, would be treated lovingly. It was a terrible shame the way she forced people to be stern with her and punish her over and over. Her mother was now expecting some real improvement from her. After all, Silvi was getting older. And now off with her, march!

At first the tone of this brief speech had been trying to

sound affectionate, but then, as if this gentleness struck it as inappropriate and impossible, it had gradually, one degree at a time, switched over to severity, until finally it concluded with that imperious "March!"

When the four children had left, a game of Jass was begun. The assistant had now achieved a fairly significant level of skill in this game, which he demonstrated by winning rather consistently; this gave him cause to choose his words with particular care, for he was quite well acquainted with the irritability that losing provoked in the woman. They played for an hour, from time to time sipping at their glasses of red wine, just as on the evening before. Suddenly Frau Tobler, interrupting their game, said:

"Did you know, Marti, that my husband is sending me to see my mother-in-law? Yes, it's true, and tomorrow morning I shall catch the train to go visit her. After all, we must have the money now, otherwise we are lost, and she has not sent a penny. She is extremely stingy or at least keeps a tight grasp on her money. I'm sure you can imagine how unpleasant it is for me to be making such a journey now, but there is no help for it. I shall have to plead—yes, Marti, plead—with this woman whom I have not seen in so many years, whom I hardly know. And she will receive me coldly, condescendingly, this I can feel all too clearly. It will be só easy for her to offend me, to hurt me, for after all one hardly treats a beggar with kid gloves. And she's always had something against me, just a little, I've always felt that. As if I'd always brought nothing but misfortune to her son, my husband. And that's just the way she'll treat me now: like a sinner.

She will reproach me for the clothes I am wearing, their unnecessary elegance, the utterly superfluous good tailoring. No, I certainly won't be putting on my new dress. There wouldn't be any point. Someone who comes begging should come dressed in black, I shall put on my old black silk dress, that should make a very subservient impression. Yes, Joseph, as you see, other people as well are having to force themselves and endure and struggle their way to modesty. That's just how it is, and we don't even know where all of this has come from, and how, and why so quickly. What a world!"

"Let us hope you are successful," the assistant remarked. She continued:

"That's why Tobler is sending me in the first place, he thinks that at such a difficult and awkward juncture as this, seeing me will be more pleasing to his mother than seeing him. If it weren't for that, I don't see why he couldn't be making this journey himself. There might also be a certain degree of laziness on his part. Men are happy to take upon themselves all sorts of dry, dispassionate labors. But the moment it's a question of some sort of personal or inner sacrifice, a duty and task involving the heart or anything emotionally strenuous, then they prefer to send their women to the front in their stead, saying: 'You go! You'll do better than I would!'—which one is then almost forced to take as a sort of favor, a caress."

Both of them laughed. Frau Tobler went on:

"Yes, you are laughing! Not that I would command you not to. Go on and laugh. I'm laughing as well, though in fact both of us ought to be in a more sober frame of mind. Yes, let's hope I'll be successful. But then what am I saying! I for my part gave up all hopes offering the promise of success for Tobler's enterprises a long time ago. This is how things now stand with me: my faith in my husband's aptitude for business has begun to falter decisively. I believe I am now convinced that he is not sufficiently callous and sly to be able to carry out profitable business ventures. It is my opinion that during all this time he has taken on only the tone of voice of clever cunning people, their public behavior, their mannerisms, but not their abilities. Of course, a person who is successful in business need not necessarily be a blood-sucker and villain. This is not at all what I wish to say. But my husband is too volatile, too hasty, too good and too natural in his sentiments. He is also too easily duped. I'm sure you must be surprised to hear me speaking in such a way, but believe me, we women, who are constantly chained to the narrow confines and limitations of our households, do quite a lot of thinking about things, and we also see things and feel things. It is given to us to guess at things a little, since the correct sciences are our sworn enemies. We have a knack for reading glances and behavior. Oddly enough, we never say anything, we keep silent, since we express ourselves so poorly as a rule, and always so inappropriately. Our words generally just annoy our overburdened men without convincing them. And so we women just go on living, declaring ourselves satisfied with most everything that is happening around us, we speak of trivial matters, which makes us ever more vulnerable to the suspicion that we are intellectually small and subordinate, and yet we are always content, at least I think so. No, my husband's ship is never going to come scraping into port, my little finger tells me so, and the shoe on my foot, and my own nose. He is too fond of living in high style, and that is something which entrepreneurs cannot allow themselves, at least at the outset. He is too wild, and that makes things tricky. He loves his own schemes too much, and this undermines them. He is far too sunny a person and takes things too literally, too abruptly, and thus far too simply. He has such a beautiful, full character, and such individuals never, or almost never, succeed in undertakings of this sort. Goodness, Marti, the way I'm talking today!"

He remained silent and allowed himself an imperceptible smile. She had already recommenced speaking:

"People fear my Carl, and at the same time they hoodwink him and laugh at him behind his back, for some reason they take special pleasure in misfortunes that happen to befall him in particular, and I think this is because he has displayed his affluence and his possessions too openly and with too little modesty, in a way that forces one to take notice. He has always been naïve enough to assume that others would take pleasure in the pleasure he himself takes in life and delight in his delights: obviously a standpoint diametrically opposed to a correct view of matters. He has always been overly generous, this is a weakness, one that in my eyes is excusable, but it has proven inexcusable in the judgment of those who enjoyed just these acts of wasteful benevolence, in other words who profited from him. He has his own particular way of being a bit brusque and loud, and now that he has fallen into unfortunate circumstances, people are calling that braggadocio. If he were successful, then this very same habit would be called flair! Yes. No, my husband would have done much better if he had never struck out on his own, had never set himself up independently, but rather had gone on quietly in his modest position as technical assistant. We were all doing so well back then. Admittedly we didn't have a house of our own, but what need is there of such a thing, since such a house just fills up with worries? When he came home from work, we would take our quiet, pretty walk around the hill. It was too beautiful to just throw it away willfully like that, but one day it did in fact get thrown away."

"Everything might still take a turn for the better, Frau To-bler," Joseph said. These words struck her in the face as if they were on fire. She cried out:

"Don't say that! Words like that are reprehensible. This is not the way one speaks to the wife of a businessman into whose books one is able to peer day after day. One should not wish to be gentle in such a manner, which piles weights upon the heart of a weak woman. How could things take a turn for the better? Why don't you try using this execrable expression on the people besieging my husband? Once more you have made me unhappy. I shall go now and try to forget this."

She ran out of the room.

The assistant thought: "So what was it this time? Does there have to be some sort of tempestuous scene every single evening or nearly? Now it is I who am annoyed, now she, now both of us, and now there is yet another explosion of Toblerian spleen. Now Silvi is screaming, now Leo is barking, now Dora is ill again. All that is lacking is for all of us to keel over backward one fine day, at noon or in the evening. Then good night, beautiful Tobler villa! But things have not yet come to this. Let us first await the arrival of the maternal money and then pay down at least a portion of our debts. The dressings-down I have received in this household are unrivaled by anything in my previous experience. Perhaps there is some good in it. By the way! Could it be that I am feeling frightened once more? Am I agitated? No, thank God, I am not. Tobler is no doubt planning to spend the night at the Sailing Ship again. This is apparently one of my professional duties: keeping his wife company here in the meantime. The poor thing! Why has she no better companion?"

He put out the lamp and went to bed.

The next day—the weather was once again more wet than cold, and the air hung down heavily—Frau Tobler could be seen descending the garden hill dressed in black silk, heading toward the train station. Tobler accompanied her part of the way, telling her to keep her spirits up and make sure not to catch a cold again in the drafty railroad car, and more things of that nature. From above, one could see a smile on the woman's face and her handkerchief waving; this was meant for Dora, who was waving at her mother as well. How wet everything was. At this stage of winter, it really might have been drier and colder, one thought, and then the eyes following the movements of Frau Tobler lost sight of her: these were the eyes of Joseph, Pauline, Silvi, Dora, the boys and Leo. The dog was barking sadly to see his mistress go off like that.

The entire scene resembled—if a person had wished to indulge his romantic imagination—the departure of a queen. Joseph, the vassal, would have had to weep bitterly at this point if he'd been one of those loyal subjects from days of yore sending a greeting to us moderns, while Pauline, the lady-in-waiting, would have let out a cry of sorrow had she been one of those women who in ancient times, as stories instruct us, served beautiful noble queens. And the dog would perhaps have been a dragon, and the children princes and princesses, and Herr Tobler one of those doughty knights who used always to be in attendance for this sort of sad farewell, back when there were still castles, fortresses, walled cities and tears of loyalty. But no. Here things were quite different.

What was being embarked on here was not everlasting exile on some rocky desert isle, but rather a mere daytrip by rail and a practical and somewhat disagreeable visit. Nor was there a queen present, unless one chose to see Frau Tobler as the sorrowful queen of the House of the Evening Star, which after all wouldn't have been so terribly fanciful and odd. Nor was the figure of the melancholy hero represented; rather, it was only the engineer Tobler, modern in both his garb and sensibilities, escorting the lady on the first bit of her journey, not to comfort her exactly, but to share with her a few sensible words. And there was as little question of there being a particularly gloomy knave and vassal in attendance upon this scene as of an even more dumbfounded lady-in-waiting. Joseph and Pauline—it was these two persons standing there and none other, except for the children, of course, and they were the offspring neither of kings nor of princes but rather ordinary citizens, children such as could be found in any better household. Leo was no dragon. He might even have responded somewhat currishly to such outrageous Medieval assumptions. All in all, it was a twentieth-century tableau.

It would soon be seen what they would have to reckon with, Herr Tobler opined as he returned to the office. As for himself, he would and must persevere. Any other thought was ridiculous. He would continue to maintain what he had always maintained, in fact now more than ever.

And he busied himself with the Deep Hole Drilling Machine. The commerce department wrote a letter to the civil engineer Joël, who, it appeared, took a "massive" interest in this project. The children were playing and roughhousing in the office. Tobler chased them out. Later, he himself left the technical workroom and went down to the village on some errand concerning the vending machine.

A bit later, the assistant, too, left and set off for the post office. While he was on his way there, two agricultural laborers shouted words of abuse at him. These farmhands addressed to the assistant the words they would have bellowed at his employer if they'd had the courage. Joseph reached the village without further incident and was walking down the wider road there when he encountered someone he would have more expected to find at the Red House Inn: Wirsich.

"So you're back again?"

They shook hands. Wirsich was positively beaming, he looked as if something highly agreeable had just happened to him. He told Joseph that he had just been offered employment at the colonial merchants Bachmann & Co. He had done just as the assistant had advised: set out with a pocket full of nicely written letters of application in envelopes, going from business to business, and in fact he had been treated in a most hospitable way almost everywhere he went, but no one had had an opening for him until at last he'd inquired at Bachmann & Co., whereupon everything had been settled to his complete satisfaction. And now, for the first time in quite a long while, he felt he could once more see himself as an upstanding individual. In any case, he was in a position to say: "Hello there, friend, you can see that all is well with me." Wouldn't it be nice for the two of them to pop into the first public house they came to and quench their thirst?

"Certainly, I'd love to. But listen, Wirsich, tell me, can you tolerate it?"

"Naturally!" the other assured him. And so the two of them went into the nearby Restaurant Central, where each of them ordered a Schoppen, a glass of beer.

"Because if you couldn't, I'd rather not. It would be a shame, given your new position," Joseph thought fitting to add.

Wirsich, amused, made a dismissive gesture. He wouldn't dream of drinking irrationally the way he used to, he said. He had now, he believed, broken that habit for good, and after all he wasn't such a dissolute sort. And how were the Toblers?

"Things are bad," the assistant said and briefly described to him the waning fortunes of the House of Tobler. But Wirsich, he added, must take care not to divulge anything of what he'd told him, these were professional secrets and nobody's business.

Wirsich said:

"So in fact I was right when I prophesied to that big-britches Tobler that he would be turned out of that swanky house and garden of his one of these days. He heard it from me that night, and now what I said is coming true. What he has done to others is now being done to him, and it serves him right. Are people of our sort not people too? Did we clerks come into the world lacking all trace of human feelings? One evening we simply find ourselves cast out of our home and livelihood, and meanwhile the person doing this believes he is acting righteously and mercifully. Forgive me, Marti, you are my successor and it is on account of my downfall that you enjoy what you yourself have said is an agreeable sojourn. Of course you cannot help it that you replaced me. What am I saying: it is through you that I was able to find my new position. Please pardon me. It's just that anger can run away with a person who's found himself thrust into the most desperate confusion and degradation for so long. And because of what? Because of some mistake? Thunderation, I'm going to have to have another. Hey there, innkeeper, or better yet you, kind hostess, bring me another one of these Schoppen. You, Marti, will most assuredly take another as well."

"All right, but I would ask," Joseph said, "that you stop these attacks on my employer. And that you lower your voice, if I may. My current superior is no big-britches. You must take back this indiscreet expression which, as I will readily admit, was only spoken in anger. Do it right now, otherwise we shall have to part ways. I did not provide you with confidential information regarding Tobler's circumstances only to listen to this man being insulted afterward. As for the rest: Cheers! I am glad that things are going well for you."

"Indeed, it was spoken in anger," Wirsich said by way of apology.

Their disagreement, then, was over, Joseph remarked. The two of them then drank one more glass each, a "layer" to which a fourth was added. They would have continued in this way if the door had not just then flown open and Herr Tobler himself had not walked into the restaurant. He surveyed the two swillpot clerks with a censorious look that told them all they needed to know.

As soon as Tobler had made his appearance, Joseph had immediately removed his hat, which before he had, in rather cavalier fashion, left sitting on his head. The laws of courtesy required this, and the look Tobler was giving him was no less exacting. He soon got to his feet, in any case, as his conversation with Wirsich had come to an end; he called to the innkeeper to prepare his bill and began to make his way toward the exit. A nod from the engineer, however, prompted him to approach his employer, who asked:

"What's that lout Wirsich doing here?"

Joseph replied: "Oh, he's found a job. It's very close to here, at Bachmann & Co. Starting today. He's very happy about it." "Is he? And he's still fond of drinking, too, eh? He'll no doubt last a long time in his new job, that one! Very well. Have you gone to the post office yet?"

"No, I'll go now. Please forgive me, I was detained by my predecessor. I'll go right away, and if you'd like me to bring the mail to you here . . ."

Tobler declined this offer, and the assistant went on his way.

Wirsich too had now gotten up, he paid his tab and marched hesitantly forward, uncertain whether or not he should greet his former employer, but then he did, and did so with a deep humble gesture and, in the process, bumped into a table, which nearly caused him to fall over. His respectful greeting received not the slightest hint of a response. Tobler wished to have "nothing more to do with this individual." In the doorway, Wirsich stumbled a second time. Was this an ominous sign?

Frau Tobler came home on the late-night express train. Herr Tobler, Pauline and Joseph were waiting for her at the station. The train arrived with a great snorting and clattering. All sorts of people crowded about the long, black, magnificent-looking monster. The woman got out, Joseph and Pauline leapt forward to relieve her of baskets and packages. Mother Tobler had laden her daughter-in-law with various gifts, they had been expecting this, which is why all three of them had gone to the station. Two baskets were filled partly with nuts, partly with apples. The packages held things for the woman herself and for the children.

It could be read in the face of the woman alighting from the train that things had gone neither very well nor very poorly. Her face expressed weariness and calm. It looked as if one half of her face might have been smiling just a little. On the whole, she appeared to have given her husband, who had eagerly pelted her with questions, answers that pleased and satisfied him, for Tobler seemed inclined to head to the Sailing Ship for a bit. His wife said that she could tell where it was he was hankering to go, and these few words simultaneously granted him permission. He shouted to the departing group that he would be back at the Evening Star in an hour at the most, and then he vanished into the pub where he was a regular.

The rest of them went home. The assistant found it an agreeable duty to carry the baskets, heavy as they were. At least this was "physical" work for a change. He walked with light steps behind the two women, the maid and the woman, utterly empty-headed. This was because of the baskets. "I was born to be an errand boy," he thought.

At home, they were besieged with questions that sprang from childish curiosity. And the packages and fruit baskets were set upon. Three children wanted to know what messages their grandmother had given their mother for them. Only the fourth was silent. Silvi remained sleepy and indifferent. Even the presents left her indifferent. "None of this is meant for me," her expression said. Well, all the more reason for these things to have been meant for the other three. Soon, however, all of them, along with all their demands, questions and curiosity, were packed off to bed.

"How tired I am," Frau Tobler said.

Pauline knelt on the floor at her feet and took her shoes off. She was sitting on the sofa. Joseph, who was standing beside them, thought: "I must admit I would have found it not at all disagreeable if it had been me to whom she'd said: Take my shoes off! I believe I would have bent down with great pleasure."

A glove fell from her grasp; at once he leapt to her side and picked it up for her. Smiling wanly, she thanked him and said:

"How attentive you are! You weren't always like this. Do you think my husband will be home soon? How are you, Joseph?"

"Quite, quite well," he replied. Pauline had left the room.

He was still so young, that's why he spoke like this and no doubt had to speak this way, the woman said. She felt so heavy-hearted.

"Was it very trying?" he asked.

"In part," she replied. But this minor vexation had taken little toll on her. Today she found herself drawn to entertain many different trains of thought. What would Joseph say to a round of Jass? Yes? That was nice of him. Just now she had such an indescribable urge to play cards. It might make her feel better.

The two of them sat down at the table and began to play. Pauline brought Frau Tobler something to eat and then left. "Perhaps this woman is inclined to feel light-headed and heavy-hearted all at once. That may well be," the assistant thought. "Besides, what an idiot I am!"

"She doesn't really want to give me anything, the old woman," Frau Tobler announced in the middle of their game.

"Who? Oh yes, Mother Tobler! I can imagine. But she will have to!"

"Precisely!" she replied. The two of them laughed. "How light-headed this all sounds," thought the bookkeeper and chief correspondent of the C. Tobler Technical Office. The business! After all, he was in fact a mature, sedate individual. There the two of them were, once more sitting one beside the other: she, the "incomprehensible woman," and he, the "peculiar individual." Joseph couldn't help laughing aloud. She asked what was the matter.

"Oh, nothing. Foolishness."

She remarked, sounding more serious now, that she hoped he wasn't allowing himself jokes at her expense. To this he replied that he was the commercial clerk of the House of Tobler, whereupon she said that she indeed hoped he most distinctly felt himself to be just that. He threw the cards he'd been holding in his hand down on the table, trembling, and declared that a serious and respectable clerk was not in the habit of playing cards all night long. Having risen to his feet, he now made for the door, expecting she would call him back. She let him go.

Instead of going up to his room, he went down to the office, lit the lamp that was to be found there, sat down at his table and wrote to the head of the Municipal Employment Referral Office as follows:

Dear Sir!

I should like to request as politely as possible that you kindly keep me in mind as an applicant for any appropriate position that should happen to come available. I am not inclined to take a chance on possibly winding up back on the street. The state of affairs up here, sir, is becoming ever more precarious. Just in case! Sending you my most respectful regards,

Your genuinely devoted servant, Joseph Marti.

He had scarcely finished enclosing this letter in its envelope and addressing it when he heard footsteps coming from the garden.

Half a minute later, Herr Tobler and two other gentlemen, apparently regulars from the Sailing Ship, came into the office, speaking loudly and laughing, and, it appeared, filled with drunken high spirits.

What was Joseph doing working at such an hour of the night? Tobler asked in an unsteady voice. At least he had, it seemed, a truly industrious and self-sacrificing assistant, he went on to remark, turning with a laugh to his Jass partners. But now Joseph should go on and call it a night, for tomorrow morning would be a day as well. Then he went to the door that lead to the interior of the house and shouted at the top of his lungs: Pauline!

"Herr Tobler?" came the answer from up above.

"Bring a couple of bottles of the Rhenish wine down to the office for us. And be quick about it."

There was scarcely any need for Joseph to take leave of the gentlemen; he said a brief goodnight and went upstairs. The others no longer even heard or noticed him, for they now were occupied with quite different matters. They lay sprawled half on the floor, half on the drafting table, not taking particular heed of what they were sitting on. The chairs were being used as footstools, and sleepy, jolly heads were coming into intimate contact with Tobler's hand-drawn sketches. Tobler, lurching back and forth, filled his pipe, and when at last the wine arrived, he set about the business of filling the glasses with a great deal of effort and gracelessness, whereupon a drinking commenced that was half mixed with snores and joined with enormous yawns. The engineer now all at once decided to use the small quantity of good sense he still had at his disposal to explain the inventions of the Tobler firm to these gentlemen and comrades, but his explanations met only with laughter and with no understanding whatsoever. The serious nature of the masculine world-view now lay on the floor in a glass of wine that had been dropped and had broken and spilled its contents. Masculine and human rationality was now bawling and jeering and babbling so loudly that the walls of the house were nearly shaking. And now, as the crowning touch to this setting of the stage, Tobler had the not terribly considerate idea of shouting for his wife to come down to the office, so that he could introduce her, as he said, to his good friends from the village. She came downstairs, but only stuck her head through the door she had timidly opened and then vanished again, repelled by—as she herself told her husband the next day—the distasteful and scurrilous scene that had opened before her eyes, and which a Dutch artist specializing in tableaus of debauchery could not have painted any more convincingly or repulsively than what she'd witnessed here in reality and truth. The revelry by no means came to an end with the woman's disappearance; on the contrary, it continued to flame and simmer and burn until early the next morning, with the arrival of that exhaustion, that overwhelming fatigue that in the end always pounces upon the napes of even the most stalwart drinkers so as to bend them over and lay them out cold beneath tables and chairs. This is just what occurred, and this rambunctious party spent the night, hideously snoring, in the technical workshop, until Pauline arrived to light a fire in the stove. Day had come. The good fellows woke up. The two Bärenswilers ambled back down to their hamlet and home, while Herr Tobler went upstairs to his and his wife's room to sleep off the tempest and intoxication.

Pauline now had a brutal task before her: restoring a certain degree of order to the devastated and disfigured office. When Joseph came downstairs at eight o'clock, things still looked utterly awful there, and so he decided to go down to the post office right away. Everything lay in a muddle: chairs, drawings, writing and drawing utensils, glasses and corks, and ink had been spilled, both red and black. There was wine on the floor. One of the bottles had been broken off at the neck. It looked as if it had been bears and not just Bärenswilers wreaking their havoc in the room, which was filled with such a stench that it seemed they would have to leave the windows wide open for a good ten days if the room was ever to be clean, cozy and habitable again.

At the post office, Joseph mailed the letter to the head of the employment bureau. "Just in case," he thought.

The next day, four thousand marks were transferred to the accounts of the Tobler household as part of Herr Tobler's inheritance. It wasn't much, but at least it was something, and it was just barely enough to satisfy the most impatient and importunate dunners. Joseph had long since assembled a list of creditors, and so now the most aggressively fragrant blossoms were selected from this colorful meadow to have their odor blotted out at least for the time being. Among these furious, eye-dazzling plants were, among others, the gardener who had declared he would not rest until he had seen Tobler's worldly goods impounded and the man himself cast out of the village; the electric company that had so scornfully shrugged its shoulders and turned off the pretty electric lights; the metalsmith who lived nearby—that "thankless cur," as Tobler called him—who, it had been decided, would have the money "hurled at his feet"; and the butcher—but from now on "not one more bite of meat from that butcher shop!" The bookbinder, "that old saphead," who should consider himself lucky etc.; the clock manufacturers, "who can't really be blamed for insisting on payment"; the metal goods manufacturer who had built and sent a bill for the copper tower; and a few others who "no doubt deserved" their money.

Half a day sufficed to stop up the mouths of these loudest and most importunate demands, but afterwards the money was gone. What do four thousand matks mean to a household that is up to its ears in debt? A small fraction of this sum was earmarked for household expenses, and an even smaller portion was given to Joseph as an installment of his salary.

It had been a sunny, snowy morning with blue skies and winds and the earth wet with snow when the assistant went from door to door, making payments. He even stopped by the Bureau for the Recovery of Claims. And he could note the speed with which the money was vanishing by his coat pocket, which was becoming ever lighter.

Towards afternoon, a letter arrived from the lawyer Bintsch in which this latter declared that nothing more was to be expected from Tobler's mother. He had done everything in his power to convince her; but, as he was most sorry to report, his efforts had met with no success. Therefore his advice to Tobler was to resign himself to this fruitlessness and its consequences.

As Tobler was reading this letter, his face contorted into a grimace that was painful to look at. He seemed to be struggling to master a nameless fury. Then it broke loose and flung him down upon a chair as if a force many hundredweights in strength had crashed down on him. His strong chest was wheezing and threatened to burst, like a bow stretched too tautly. His face looked up from below as if it had been pressed down from above by heavy fists. His neck appeared burdened with weights that were furiously rocking and whizzing about and pressing down upon him, living weights. His face had turned a bright red color. All around him, the air appeared to have become thick and stony, and an invisible-visible figure now appeared to be rising up close beside him to pat him familiarly but coldly upon his convulsing shoulder. Iron necessity itself seemed to have whispered in his ear: "You there! Give it one last try!"

With leaden motions, Tobler opened his American roll-top desk and, groaning and shifting his back as though he were in pain, took out a pen and sheet of paper to write his mother a letter. But the characters he was setting down danced before his eyes. The desk flew up in the air past his sentiments, which were swirling about madly, the office was spinning, and he was forced to desist. With a rattle in his voice, he said to Joseph:

"Call up Bintsch and ask him to tell you when he can be prepared for a meeting with me. Tell him it is a matter of the utmost urgency."

Joseph immediately set about obeying this order. He was agitated, was perhaps speaking not entirely clearly, it was possible that what he was saying was misunderstood; in short, it was quite some time before he was able to speak with Dr. Bintsch. Tobler had come up the stairs after him and now was standing right behind the assistant, who was made even more disoriented by the presence of his so pathologically incensed lord and master, with the result that when the desired connection had finally been established, he found himself struggling in a stammered conversation with the lawyer, unable to make himself understood.

This was too much for Tobler. With a hideous-sounding cry of rage, he threw the inept speaker to one side so violently he was thrust against the doorframe of the living room, and seized the telephone's handset himself to complete the derailed conversation and acquire the information he required.

His rage had subsided, but his entire body was violently shaking. He developed a fever and had to lie down on the daybed, the same spot that not long before had been occupied by Dora. "Is Father sick?" his little daughter now asked. Frau Tobler, who stood with a worried expression beside the man lying there moaning, said to the girl: "Yes, child, Father is sick. Joseph made him angry," whereupon she flashed a look of surprise and contempt in the assistant's direction that caused him to retreat back down to the office. When he reached his desk, he attempted to go back to work as if nothing had happened, but what he was doing there wasn't work, it was merely a tapping and fumbling about with trembling distracted fingers, an attempt at equanimity, an inability, a something-else, a nothing, something black. His heart was beating as if it might explode.

Later he was called up to coffee. Tobler had meanwhile gone upstairs to his bedroom. After all, the consultation with the lawyer could not possibly take place until the following day, and until then there was evidently and apparently nothing left in all the wide world for the engineer to do. What exertion at this point could have some realistic goal? What plans had not become ridiculous? And sick! It felt so soothing to this harried man to think that he could lie in bed and go on doing so undisturbed until the next morning. He sent word to Joseph that if he went down to the post office he should bring him home a couple of good cigars. "And some oranges for Dora, Joseph," Frau Tobler added. Joseph carried out these commissions.

After the evening meal—the children had already been put to bed—the assistant said to Frau Tobler that he was finding it difficult to remain any longer in a place in which the head of the house was now taking the liberty, after he had insulted Joseph often enough with mere words, to assault him physically as well. This was too much for him, and he thought it would be the best thing if he went up to Tobler's room at once to say to this man how coarse and stupid his behavior was. He was no longer capable of working, this he felt distinctly. A person who was shoved this way and that and thrown against doorframes was surely no longer in a position to bring any profit. Such a person must be a blockhead and good-for-nothing, otherwise it certainly wouldn't be possible for him to be treated in such a way as Joseph had just experienced. The very thought of it was suffocating. In his opinion, even if all he had done in all the time he'd spent up here was squander Tobler's resources, even that would not justify the physical disgrace and dishonor, but was that what he'd done? Hadn't he always made a little bit of an effort? He at least knew that he had now and then devoted himself to his work with all his heart and all the strength he could muster, even if this strength was not always, as he would readily admit, enough to satisfy the righteous demands being made on him. But was this an appropriate way of responding to his efforts to remain efficient and honest?

He was weeping.

Frau Tobler said coldly: "My husband is ill, as you know, and a disturbance will not exactly please him. But if it suits your fancy and if you believe you can suddenly no longer endure remaining here among us any longer, then do not hesitate to go upstairs and tell him what's on your mind. I think you will receive the short and sweet reply that you and your conduct deserve."

The assistant remained seated. Then he got up and said, "I'll just run down to the post office."

"So you aren't going upstairs to see my husband?"

"No," Joseph replied. Herr Tobler was ill, it wouldn't be right to disturb him. Besides, he felt like going out for a little walk.

Outside he was received by a clear cold world. A lofty, vaulty sort of world. It had turned cold. He kept striking his feet against stones and chunks of ice. An ice-cold wind was blowing through the trees. Through their branches, stars were shimmering. His heart was full, he ran as if possessed. No, he didn't want to leave. He was afraid Frau Tobler might have gone and told her husband everything. As a result of this thought, he hastened and hurried his steps. Moreover, he still hadn't received the final installment of his salary. In short, the main thing was to remain in the household at all costs. "How improper it was to complain in such a manner," he cried out into the wintry night. He resolved to fall on his knees before Frau Tobler and kiss her hands.

She was still sitting in the living room when he returned. Still standing at the door—which, however, he carefully shut behind him—he at once began to speak:

"I must tell you, Frau Tobler—how good it is that you are still sitting here—that I feel I am utterly in the wrong for having voiced complaints about my superior. I was too hasty, and I beg you to forgive me. My behavior was harebrained, and Herr Tobler was filled with agitation because of that lawyer's accursed letter. Have you spoken with your husband yet? Have you told him everything?"

"No, I haven't said anything to him yet," the woman replied.

"How glad I am to hear it!" the assistant said, sitting down. He went on: "And I raced to get here, filled with terror at the thought that you might already have told him. I am sorry for everything I said. In the tumult of one's feelings, madam, one can say so many things that ought to go unuttered. I'm so glad you haven't yet said anything."

Frau Tobler remarked how sensible his words were.

"I have resolved to throw myself at your feet and apologize on my knees," the assistant stammered.

"How unnecessary, faugh!" she replied.

For a while the two were silent. The assistant found it so lovely to be sitting there in that room. This was something that resembled a home. And how often, in former times, he had walked the city's lively and deserted streets, his heart filled with the cold, wicked, crushing sensation of having been abandoned. How old he had been in his youth. How the consciousness of not being at home anywhere had paralyzed him, strangled him from within. How beautiful it was to belong to someone, whether in hatred or impatience, displeasure or devotion, melancholy or love. The human magic that resided in a home like this—how dolefully enchanted Joseph had always been when he saw it reflected in some window that had been left standing open, making it visible down where he was standing on the cold street all alone, tossed from one place to another, without a home. How Easter, Christmas or Pentecost or New Year's came streaming fragrantly down from such windows, and how poor he felt when he thought of how he was allowed to enjoy only the paltry, almost imperceptible reflection of this golden, ancient glory. This beautiful privilege of the upper classes. The kindness in their faces. This peaceful doing, the living, and letting live! He said:

"How idiotic it is to be so swift to find oneself insulted."

It was quite right of him to say so, the woman opined, peacefully continuing to knit or crochet an undervest for Dora. She added:

"And am not I, his wife, compelled to endure and acquiesce to all sorts of things? He is the head of the house, that's all there is to it, a position of responsibility which demands forbearance and respect from the other occupants and members of the household. Certainly he ought not to insult others, but is he always in a position to rein himself in? Can he say to his rage: do be reasonable? Rage and bad temper are simply not reasonable entities. And we others, who enjoy the quite obvious advantage of being permitted to obey the orders that cost him so much effort to conceive and plan and to follow his suggestions, the wisdom of which is almost always clear to us—should we not, in times of uneasiness and resentment, simply make it our business to keep out of his way a little? We ought by now to have learned how to treat him, for even a lord and ruler needs to be treated in a quite particular manner. We ought to be skillful and pliant at moments when he is no longer conscious—as he usually is—of his composure and his reliable strengths, at moments when we perceive him to be incapable of restraining himself, as he once could. And when we have been inept and at least comparatively full of error, we needn't feel too terribly piqued when his voice and the enormous burden of his worries and torments come thundering down upon us. Marti! Please believe me, I too have often been filled with fury at this very same man who wronged you today, who supposedly insulted you and subjected you to indignities. Well, under circumstances such as these, one need only temper one's own dignity a little and forgive—for one has an obligation to forgive one's master and superior. What would become of enterprises, households and businesses of all sorts, what would become of homes, indeed, what would become of the world itself if suddenly its laws were no longer allowed to pinch and shove and wound one a little? Has one enjoyed the benefits of obeying and imitating all year round only so that one might, one day or evening, come and puff oneself up and say: Do not insult me!? No, to be sure, a person doesn't exist for the purpose of being insulted, but neither is it his purpose to give cause for anger. If confusion is unable to prevent itself from behaving in a foolish fashion, why should fury be held accountable for its blustering and ranting? And it is always a question of where one is and who one is. I am satisfied with you now, Joseph. Give me your hand. One can talk with you, and now it's time for sleep."

Christmas was approaching. Even in the Tobler household this festive time of year could not help arriving, the holiday season: it was inescapable, traveling on the swiftest wings, a thought that communicated itself to all people and suffused all sensibilities, and so why should this thought make a detour around the Evening Star Villa? Could this even have been possible? When a house was standing there in the world, standing there so prettily and strikingly as that of the Toblers, there was after all no reasonable or natural cause why it should be spared anything that formed part of this so respectable, fragrant world. And then, too, there was the question: would the Toblers have wished to be spared?

On the contrary, they were looking forward to the holiday. Tobler said that even if things were going poorly for him, that was still no reason to let Christmas pass by and through his house uncelebrated. That would really have been the last straw.

The entire surrounding countryside appeared to be looking forward to the lovely festivities in its own way. It peacefully and languorously allowed itself to be covered with thickly falling snow, calmly holding out, as it were, its large, broad, old and wide hand to catch everything that was tumbling down so industriously out of the sky, so that all who saw this nearly said: "Just look, everything's turning white, it will be a white, white world. Quite proper, too—just the thing for Christmas."

Soon the whole lake and mountain landscape lay beneath a thick, firm veil of snow. Heads that were swift to imagine things could already hear the jingling of swiftly advancing sleighs, though there were not yet any sleighs on the roads. The tables soon to be covered with Christmas gifts had already been set out, for the entire countryside resembled a beautifully adorned table beneath a neat white cloth. And the silence and mutedness and warmth of such a landscape! All the sounds could only be half heard, as though the metalworkers had wrapped their hammers, and the carpenters their beams, and the turbines their blades, and the locomotives their shrill whistles in cottonwool or woolen cloths. You could see only what lay near at hand, what could be measured out at ten paces, for the distance was comprised of impenetrable snow flurries, everything was being vigorously painted over in gray and white. Even the human beings stomping up to you were all white, and among any five persons there was always one who was just shaking the snow from his clothes. There was such peacefulness everywhere that you couldn't help perceiving all worldly affairs as settled and contented and at peace.

And now Tobler was having to make a journey through all this snowy magic, traveling by train to the city to have a conversation with the lawyer Bintsch. But at his side, at least, he had his wife, who was making the trip along with him so as to buy a few presents at the capital's large department store for the rapidly approaching holiday.

That evening there was again a train-station scene, but this time it was a snowy and therefore somewhat gayer one. Pauline's laughter and Leo's gleeful barking made dark sound-stains upon the snow, though ordinarily laughter and barking tend to make things brighter, but what could compete in brightness and luster with the snow's own glittering whiteness? This time, too, packages were received, and a lady in furs who had alighted from the train stood there looking like the veritable wealthy and benevolent Mother Christmas herself, and yet it was only Frau Tobler, the wife of a businessman, and a ruined one at that. But she was smiling, and a smile like that can turn even the poorest and most harried woman into half a princess, for a smile always calls to mind something worthy of reverence and respect.

The snow remained on the ground until the day itself—clean and firm, for there were cold nights that made the white blanket freeze to a crust. On Christmas Day, Joseph took a walk up the mountain he knew so well just as evening was approaching. The small paths went snaking pale and yellow through the shimmering white meadows, the limbs of the thousand trees were glittering with frost: such an utterly sweet spectacle! The farmhouses stood there amid all this delicate white branching splendor, like decorative or ornamental houses created only to be looked at and for the innocent understanding of a child. The whole region appeared to be awaiting some regal princess, that's how delicately and neatly it was dressed. It appeared to be a girl, a shy and somewhat sickly girl, one of infinitely delicate leanings. Joseph strode further uphill, and then all at once the gray veils enclosing the earth lower down frayed and were lifted, pierced through by the most fiery sky-blue, and a sun, just as warm as in summertime, made the walker believe it all just a fairy tale. Tall fir trees stood there with a proud, powerful bearing, laden with snow that was melting in the sun and tumbling down from their large branches.

When Joseph came home, arriving just at nightfall, the Christmas tree had already been lit in the guest room, a corner room that was generally never used. Frau Tobler now led the children into the room and showed them their presents. Even Pauline was given a gift, and Joseph received a little crate of cigars with the remark that the gift was not lavish but came from the heart. Tobler was striving to create a cozy, tavern-like atmosphere for this celebration, smoking his familiar pipe and squinting at the fir tree that was filling the room with the loveliest radiance. Frau Tobler smiled and said a few appropriate words, for example, how beautiful such a little tree was. But she was having a hard time getting the words out. In general, it all felt a bit stumbling, and the mood surrounding this handful of people was one not of joyous contemplation but of melancholy. Besides which, it was cold in the guest room, and a place meant to be filled with Christmas cheer ought not to be cold. For this reason, everyone went back into the living room to warm up a little, and then returned to the tree. Every Christmas tree is beautiful and cannot fail to touch those who behold it. Even the Tobler tree was beautiful, it's just that the people standing around it were unable to bring themselves to feel any sustained, profound sentiment or joy.

"You ought to have seen last year, that was a Christmas! Come with me, have a glass of wine," Tobler said to the assistant and made him return to the living room where it was warm. Joseph was looking slightly out of sorts—as if the cigars had displeased him—a circumstance of which he himself was unaware. This year, the woman said, sighing, they just weren't in the right mood to celebrate. Hesitantly, she suggested a round of Jass. Since they'd played this game all year long, they might as well turn to their cards on Christmas as well, perhaps it would lift their spirits a little. And so they all took refuge in their game.

Meanwhile the tree had lost its radiance and lights. The children were allowed to spend another half hour occupied with their presents and then they were sent off to bed. Little by little, the air in the Christmas living room was transformed into that of a pub. The laughter and behavior of the three lonely people sitting there drinking wine, in part smoking cigars, in part eating bonbons as they played cards, lost all signs of that telltale shyness and singularity that might have called to mind the holiday spirit. It was the most ordinary behavior and the most unfestive sort of laughter. The mood that had taken hold of these players, moreover, was not even their usual sense of casual familiarity, for after all it was Christmas, and the more delicate and lovely thoughts that might now and again occur to one or the other reminded them in passing of the sin they were committing by corrupting and invalidating the holiday and its meaning in this way.

Yes, these three people were lonely, and loneliest among them was the assistant, because he felt, as the new arrival in the household, that he had become part of a home that was gradually ceasing to be one at all; because unlike Herr Tobler he could not say he had the right to do and forbid or avoid anything he pleased between his own four walls, as the house did not belong to him; because he had so wanted to experience and celebrate Christmas now that he was for once part of such a household and bourgeois family; because it had seemed to him in recent years that he was missing a great deal by being unable to experience all these things; and because of all the three card-players he was the one in the worst spirits, which he couldn't help finding unjust.

"So is this really Christmas?" he thought.

The woman suddenly remarked, among other things, that it really wasn't right to play cards on Christmas. At home in her parents' house, such a thing would never have occurred. It really wasn't proper the way they were reverting to tavern life tonight.

Thrust into a foul humor by these words, Tobler replied: "Well then, let's stop!"

Throwing his cards on the table, he cried out:

"Most certainly it is not proper to do such a thing on Christmas. But what sort of circle is this here? What are we? The wind might sweep us from this house tomorrow morning. Where there's money, people can be in a mood to celebrate holidays, even the holiest ones. Yes, where there is prosperity, where there is happiness, success and the general pleasures of domestic life. When a person has had to spend three or four months slaving unnaturally to prevent the failure of his life's work, and this without success, is he supposed to then be able suddenly to enter into festive and celebratory spirits? Is such a thing even thinkable? Am I right or not, eh Marti?"

"Not entirely, Herr Tobler," the assistant said.

There was a protracted silence which, the longer it lasted, no one dared to interrupt. Tobler wanted to say something about the Advertising Clock, the woman something about Dora, and Joseph something about Christmas, but each of them suppressed his thoughts. It was as if all their mouths had been sewn shut. Suddenly Tobler shouted:

"So open up your gobs and say something! This is such a bore, a person would do better to just go to the inn."

"I'm going to bed," Joseph said and took his leave. The others, too, soon went upstairs, and Christmas was over.

The week leading up to New Year's passed quietly and with a curious intensity of feeling; the business was in a shambles, and there was little to do apart from receiving a strange person in the office from time to time, the inventor of a power machine. This crackpot, who had a half peasant-like, half worldly air about him, visited the Tobler household almost daily during this week, attempting to persuade the boss to represent the interests of this work of genius whose plans he left behind in the office. They laughed about this man, whose project could not be taken seriously, but once Tobler said to the others over lunch: "Don't laugh like that. The man isn't stupid."

The enthusiasm with which the creator of this power apparatus was defending the child of his imagination, elevating it to nearly sky-high significance, gave them a good deal to talk about and was quite useful in providing the entertainment for a week otherwise filled only with quiet and lethargy. The strange person possessed no precise, elegant education, he spoke on the one hand like a young dreamer and bumpkin, and on the other one might have taken him for a trickster or sideshow impresario, for one day he proposed to Herr Tobler that his perpetual motion machine be exhibited publicly, by paid admission, in cities and metropolises, in places where a great many people were known to gather—an idea over which everyone in the household laughed themselves silly.

And so Tobler was once more in the position of helping an apparently quite talented individual get on his feet so he wouldn't have to suffocate and deteriorate intellectually in some mechanical workshop—but what about him, Tobler, how were things in fact going for him, and where were the helpful people ready to lend him their assistance?

"They all come running to him," Frau Tobler said, "they all think of him when they are in search of someone to lend a hand, they are all eager to exploit him and his sociable personality, and he helps every one of them. That's how he is."

During this week, the assistant undertook various shortish and longish walks through cold but lovely winter landscapes and tableaus. There were ruts left in the road from carts that had passed there, it was easy to catch your foot in them. There were frozen-stiff meadows running up hillsides, and cold red hands that you held before your mouth to blow into them.

Joseph encountered people bundled in coats, and sometimes nightfall surprised him in unfamiliar regions. Or there might be a skating rink upon what had once been a splendid park-encircled pond, covered with skating and falling-down persons of every age and both sexes, along with the sounds that typically characterize and express a place like this. And then suddenly he was standing once more before the Tobler house, gazing up at it from below, and saw how enchanted it appeared in the cold moonlight with the chiaroscuro clouds flying about it like huge mournful but lovely women, apparently intending to draw it upward into the sky where it might beautifully dissolve.

Then at home everything was so weirdly silent, even Silvi could not be heard. The virtues and vices of the Tobler household appeared to have settled their scores and wordlessly forged a bond of friendship. In the living room, Frau Tobler would be sitting in the rocking chair, working or reading, or else she held Dora on her lap and was doing nothing at all.

"How you pushed me in the swing out in the garden last summer, Marti!" she said once. She was pining for the garden, she went on, more than she even knew. How long ago these days now appeared to her. Joseph had been there for half a year already, and to her it felt as if he'd been near her so much longer. A thing like that could enter so vividly into a person's feelings.

She gazed at the lamp. The look in her eyes as she did so appeared to be sighing. She said:

"You, Marti, are in fact quite well off, far better off than my husband and I—but I don't wish to speak of myself. You can go away from here, you can simply pack up your few belongings, get on the train and go wherever you like. You can find employment anywhere, you are young, and when one looks at you, one has the impression that you are a capable individual, and in fact that's just what you are. You needn't take anyone in the world into consideration, no one's needs and idiosyncrasies, and no one is keeping you from wandering off into the unknown distance. Perhaps this often feels bitter, but how beautiful and free it can be as well. When it suits you, and when the few surely not so troublesome circumstances of your life allow, you can go marching off, and when you feel the time for this has come, you can rest again at some given point and location, and who would want and what would want or be able to prevent you? You are perhaps sometimes unhappy, but who isn't? You may sometimes be filled with despair, but whose soul is spared all tribulations? You are bound to nothing permanent, trapped by nothing that might hinder you, chained and fettered by no surfeit of affection. Surely the most ebullient and frolicsome moods must occasionally take hold of you, given the freedom you enjoy to move about at will. And on top of everything else, you are in good health, and your heart is no doubt in the right place—I assume it is, though I have so often seen you behaving uncourageously. Perhaps I am ungrateful. I have been able to converse with you agreeably, peacefully and at length for all this time, and it was perhaps quite a fortunate coincidence that you happened to come flying into this household, and yet often I have treated you badly..."

"Frau Tobler!" Joseph protested. She cut him off and went on speaking:

"Do not interrupt me. Let me take this opportunity to caution you that one day, when you are gone from us—"

"But I'm not going anywhere!"

She went on:

"—when you are gone and the fancy strikes you to go into business on your own, be sure to go about it in a different way than my husband, a quite different way. Above all else, be more cunning."

"I am not cunning," the assistant said.

"Do you wish to spend your entire life as a clerk?"

He replied that he did not know. He never gave much thought to questions of the future. Once more she began to speak:

"In any case, you've been able to see and absorb this and that up here, and surely you learned a few things if you considered it worth the effort to keep your eyes open, and knowing you a little as I do, I would assume you did. You have grown a little richer in experience, knowledge and laws, and these are all things you will quite possibly be able to put to use some day. Certainly it's true that you've been taken to task many a time here, and that you have borne and endured many things. You had to! When I think of . . . oh, to put it bluntly, I have the feeling, Joseph, that you will soon be leaving us, very soon. No, don't say anything. Please don't say a word. Surely we shall still be together a few days longer, won't we? What do you say?"

"Yes," he said. It was impossible for him to say anything more than that.

The next day he mailed the crate of cigars he had received as a Christmas present to his father, enclosing the following letter:

Dear Father, here is a small New Year's gift for you. These cigars were given to me as a Christmas present by my current employer. I'm sure you will enjoy smoking them, they are good cigars, I tried two of them, as you'll see: two of them are missing. The way my thoughts are jumping about today, if I compare these two missing cigars with two flaws pertaining to my character, then I am struck by the realization, firstly, that I never write to you, and secondly, that I am poor, so poor that I am never able to send you any money—two failings that would make me weep if I were able to permit myself to do so. How have you been? I am convinced that I am a bad son, but I am equally overwhelmed by the certain knowledge that I would be the most outstanding of sons if there were any point to writing letters with nothing joyful to report. Life, with which a person honestly believes he must struggle, has to this day not yet permitted me to please you. Goodbye, dear Father. Remain healthy, may your meals always taste good to you, and may you begin the new year well. I shall try to do the same.

Your son Joseph

"He is an old man and still goes to work every day," he thought.

Tobler's personal negotiations with his legal counsel resulted in the latter composing a vigorously worded letter to Mother Tobler, to which, however, the old lady, utterly unruffled, responded that the remainder of the funds to which her son was entitled had long since been exhausted, indeed, that she herself, who was after all an elderly woman, was finding it difficult enough to make ends meet, and that any further payments to Carl Tobler were absolutely out of the question. The only option remaining to this same man—her son, as she almost regretted having to say—was to bear the inevitable consequences of his incautious and ill-considered actions. In the sort of business ventures into which he had chosen to throw his inheritance, she could see nothing that offered any justified promise of a profit or livelihood. The Evening Star, quite simply, should be sold, as it was high time that Tobler learned to accept his fate and adjust to more modest life circumstances, which would force him to do honest work, just as others were compelled to do. The best thing one could do for him was to leave him in the difficult circumstances he had brought upon himself, so that he might learn something from the indignities he was being forced to suffer. From her, his mother, he would receive nothing more.

Tobler, who had received a copy of his mother's letter from the lawyer, flew into a rage when he read it. He behaved like a wild animal, muttering unnatural curses that he addressed to his mother as though she were standing there beside him and then, as had already happened once before, he collapsed in exhaustion.

This took place on the final day of the year, in the technical office that had so often now had to serve as the backdrop for unseemly and unrestrained scenes. Joseph too was once more having to see and hear all this vulgarity and indecorousness. At this moment he would have liked best to flee, but then he thought: "Why hasten something that will come soon enough of its own accord?" He pitied Tobler, he felt contempt for him, and at the same time he feared him. These were three unlovely sentiments, each as natural as the others, but unfair as well. What was prompting him to continue on as this man's employee? The

283

salary outstanding? Yes, among other things. But there was something quite different as well, something more important: he loved this man with all his heart. The pure hue of this one sentiment made the stains of the three others vanish. And it was because of this sentiment that the other three had always been there as well, almost from the very beginning, and with such intensity. For it was inevitable that something a person was fond of, something he felt bound and conjoined to, would cause him distress as well: he would have to struggle with it, there would be much about it that displeased him, and at times he would even hate it because he had always felt so powerfully drawn to it.

The weather on this final day of the year had all at once become wondrously mild. Wintry nature appeared to be melting and weeping, as it were, silent tears of joy, for whatever happened to be ice and snow was now flowing down all the hillsides and slopes as cheerful warm water, flowing to meet the water of the lake. There was a great rustling and steaming, as if a spring day had gotten lost and wound up in the middle of winter. Such sunshine! A veritable day in May. The two sorts of feelings—both the beautiful and painful—that were stirring today with particular poignancy in the assistant's breast were stimulated even further by the splendid weather, which simultaneously calmed and agitated them, so that now, as he ran down to the post office, it seemed to him as if he were walking down this beautiful road for the last time, beneath these familiar good trees, past all these things and faces that had always been equally pleasant to look upon in winter and summer alike.

He walked into Bachmann & Co. and asked for Wirsich,

whom he had not seen for a good ten days now, for it had occurred to him to arrange for them to spend New Year's Eve together in cozy celebration.

Wirsich? He'd been sent away a while ago, Joseph was told. It would have been utterly impossible to keep him on. He'd spent half the day, if not all of it, drunk out of his wits.

Joseph apologized and left the shop. "Can this be?" he thought and walked slowly toward the building that housed the post office. In the post office box he found a postcard from his Frau Weiss, wishing him luck and success. He smiled, shut the box, and set off on his way home, taking the path along the highway. Passing by the Rose Inn, which was on this road, he glimpsed Wirsich sitting at a table, propping his head in the hollow of his hand with a look of horrifying desperation. The face of this unhappy individual was as pale as death itself, his clothing was soiled, and there was no life left in his eyes.

Joseph went up to his predecessor and sat down beside him. Many words were not exchanged between the two of them. The consciousness of calamity is generally at a loss for words. The assistant drank rather heavily, as if to move one soul-step and a bit of understanding closer to his comrade, for he felt that a sober mind and rationality would have been almost inappropriate. Time passed as he listened to Wirsich's account of how he had come to find himself driven out of a good post and livelihood yet again.

"Come with me, Wirsich, let's take a walk," Joseph said then. They paid their bill, the steadier of the two took the arm of the reeling, inconsolable one, it was already afternoon, and now the two of them went walking side by side, first straight ahead for a bit, then uphill, across the welcoming meadows. How mild it all was. How a person might have chattered and joked about had one been in the company of a child, a girl or a beautiful lady. How one, had this been halfway permissible, might have kissed. On some bench high up on a mountaintop, say. Or how one might have spoken, for example with a brother, or how it might have been if Wirsich had been an established, worldly-wise and kind-hearted older gentleman. They would have laughed, and solemn but peaceful words would have been beautifully murmured. But when you looked at Wirsich, you couldn't help secretly feeling a bit cross and resentful toward the circumstances and fates that govern this world, for Wirsich just then was not a pretty sight.

Joseph thought of the Toblers, and his heart began faintly to pound. How had he come to absent himself from house and office for an entire half a day without first asking leave? He reproached himself apprehensively.

Yet he found himself meanwhile in an almost holy mood. The entire landscape appeared to him to be praying, so invitingly, with all its faint, muted earthen hues. The green of the meadows was smiling out from beneath the snow, which the sun had broken into white islands and patches. Evening was just starting to arrive, and at such a moment he would have found it difficult to regret his decision to go out with Wirsich for a walk.

On the contrary, he'd done quite well to do so, of this he was convinced. How could he have turned his back on an unfortunate like this? And now the figure of the drinker appeared to harmonize so beautifully with the landscape and the gathering dusk. Already people in their houses were beginning to light lamps, already the colors were disappearing and one saw only the softer, broader outlines of things, and now the two of them went home; strangely, both of them chose the path leading to Tobler's house without prior discussion.

Tobler was not at home. His wife was sitting all alone in the living room, in the dark—she hadn't yet lit the lamp—and Pauline and the children were still outdoors somewhere. The unexpected arrival of two such crepuscular figures startled her, but she quickly composed herself, put on the light and asked Joseph why he hadn't appeared for lunch that day, Tobler had gotten all worked up about it, he was angry, and she feared there would be some new unpleasantness.

"Good evening, Wirsich," she said to the other man, holding out her hand for him to press. "How are things with you?"

"All right, things are all right," he said. To this Joseph added: "Frau Tobler, would you allow me to play host to my companion in the tower room tonight? He is, I believe, at a loss as to where to spend the night if not at the Rose, but I wish to do everything in my power to prevent his sitting up all night there. Wirsich has just lost his new position and livelihood—through his own fault, as he himself knows quite well. He has squandered all his money on drink. If he were now to throw himself into the lake, he would be committing an act that might well make those who live a life of luxury simply shrug their shoulders, but this would be a terrible thing that could never be undone. He is a drunkard, a person most likely beyond saving—

287

and this is something I will say here, even in your presence, Wirsich, for there is no point in attempting to be tactful with individuals of this sort, for they have long since lost all self-control. But there is no need for him to meet his end today, and as for myself, I feel no compunction about bringing him, my best friend and comrade, into a house where I have been employed as a worker and made to feel at home as a resident. I shall be going out with him again for a little while, for tonight, on New Year's Eve, there is no sense in locking oneself away in some dry, joyless room; on the contrary, it is my intention to spend the night peacefully and respectably—let me come right out and say it—tippling in the company of my predecessor, for this is what is being done today by all people who believe they may permit themselves to do so. Then I shall return here with Wirsich so as to let him share my room with me, regardless of whether or not this meets with Herr Tobler's approval. I wanted to inform you of this in advance, Frau Tobler. Now that I have witnessed my comrade's misfortune, I find my heart is able to embrace many things with the most beautiful and peaceful equanimity that in previous months might have caused it agitation. I feel the courage to look deeply, boldly and warmly into the eyes of my future life. I have genuine faith in my little bit of strength, and this is more than if a person were to possess entire cartloads of strength and hayracks full of ability but at the same time did not trust them or even really know them. Good night, Frau Tobler, I thank you for having had the kindness to hear me out."

Frau Tobler said good night to the two of them. The children returned at just this moment. "Wirsich is here!" they all cried out in merry, gleeful pleasure. He had to shake hands with each of them, and all who witnessed this had the peculiar feeling that Wirsch was once more being integrated into the Tobler household, or that he'd remained a member of it during all this time of absence, as if he'd only just gone into another room and read a somewhat prolix and extravagant book, as if his straying had only lasted for an hour or two, so eloquently did the children's delight at seeing him again speak in his favor.

Hereupon the woman, who had been meaning to put on a severe, cold expression, became jovial and her usual cheerful self again and told the two companions, who had already gone out into the garden, that they should remember to preserve some degree of moderation and not allow their drinking and carousing to get too terribly out of hand. Of course it went without saying that Wirsich, who once had been a member of the Tobler family, could spend the night here. And she would have a word with her husband to ensure that he would not make a scene.

"Good night, Frau Tobler, so long, Dora, so long, Walter!" resounded from Joseph's mouth back in the direction of the house.

Down in his little shack, the signalman was singing a song. His warm, masculine voice seemed to mesh beautifully with the mildness of the night. The song sounded so constant and unvaried that, hearing it, one could easily believe it would keep resounding and ringing out beyond the end of the old year and into the new one.

Joseph Marti and Wirsich slowly proceeded down the road

in the direction of town.

To describe what these two New Year's comrades performed and set about down in the village in the course of this night—which public houses they visited, how many glasses they emptied, in what sorts of conversations they engaged one another—would be to consign things that are important and essential to the realm of the unimportant and insignificant. They spoke of such things as colleagues are wont to speak of, and they behaved the way people tend to on New Year's Eve, in other words, they devoted themselves to the pursuit of a gradual but therefore all the more pleasurable and purposeful inebriation. In one of Bärenswil's numerous restaurants they crossed paths with Tobler, who was sitting at a table with friends and, curiously, speaking about religion. Joseph heard—at least insofar as he was still capable of hearing at all—his employer exclaiming that he was raising his children according to religious principles but that he himself believed in nothing, things like that ceased when one became a man. The engineer paid no heed to either of his employees, neither the current nor the former one, as he was utterly engrossed in this conversation.

At twelve o'clock, the bells began to ring out and resound, announcing the start of the new year with a great pealing and thunderous clamor. On the square beside the dock, the village band was playing, accompanied and then followed by the choirs of the Men's Singing Club. Many people were standing in a circle, their faces lit up by torches, to take in this nocturnal concert. Joseph noticed the insurance agent who was on good terms with Tobler among the spectators and listeners, but he also saw the furious professional gardener, the most bitter enemy of the technical enterprises.

The innkeepers reaped excellent profits on this night, better than they had in weeks. Many a guest drank a bottle of fine wine today who had drunk nothing but beer all year long. Many a one indulged himself by ordering something he would usually have thought of as beyond his means; this produced lovely fat bills, which were paid at once in cash.

Frau Tobler had come, accompanied by Pauline, to hear the midnight music. She looked quiet and self-conscious, quite the opposite of the female villagers sending impertinent glances her way, who apparently were taking particular delight in causing her embarrassment. She was isolated today, neither well-respected nor well-loved, but she endured this.

Late the next morning, two not yet well-rested heads awoke in the tower room. It was broad daylight, already eleven in the morning if not half past eleven, in other words nearly noon. Quickly Marti and Wirsich got dressed to go downstairs. Herr Tobler was already standing in the office. His rage when he caught sight of the latecomer and the unbidden intruder knew no bounds. He was almost on the point of striking Joseph.

"Not only," he shouted, "did you stay out all day yesterday without a single word of apology or even informing me of your intentions and then malingered all night long, now you have the impudence to miss and sleep through an additional half a day. This is outrageous. Admittedly there may not be anything of importance to be done down here today, but someone might come by on business, and what sort of impression will it make if the maid is forced to announce to the arrival that my scoundrel of an assistant is still lying in the hay upstairs? I don't want to hear a word from you. Consider yourself fortunate if I do not box your ears left and right as you deserve. And on top of everything else he has the audacity to arrive in the company of an individual who, if he does not make himself scarce this instant and get out of my sight once and for all as I am commanding him, will have other, more explicit things in store for him. And he shows up in a state of perfect calm such as might befit some gallows bird but certainly not the, let us hope, dutiful employee of the House of Tobler. This house remains a house and my house, and the uncertainty in which it happens to find itself at present doesn't give anyone the right to make a fool and knave of me, least of all my clerk, to whom I pay the salary he lives on. Sit down at your desk and get to work. Write. We are going to try the Advertising Clock one last time. Pick up your pen."

The assistant said with a calm that was the ultimate affront: "Pay me the rest of my salary as I was promised."

He scarcely knew what he was saying, he was just filled with a definitive sense of finality. It would have been impossible for him to pick up his pen, he was trembling so violently, and for this reason he involuntarily said the thing clearly most likely to put an end to all of this.

And indeed Tobler immediately lost all self-control.

"Get out of this house at once! Go! To my enemies with you! I no longer need you."

He began to hurl invectives at Joseph, at first vicious ones, but then these curses grew weaker and weaker until at last the rage in his voice had given way to sounds of lamentation and pain. Joseph was still standing there. It seemed to him as if he ought to feel pity for the entire world—for himself as well, at least a little, but powerful, contemplative pity for everything around him. Wirsich had long since gone out to the garden for the time being. The dog greeted its old acquaintance with a wagging tail. Frau Tobler meanwhile was standing at the living room window, straining her ears to hear through the plaster and stone whatever might make its way to her from below. At the same time, she was observing the movements of the former assistant standing in the garden.

"I'll just finish off these few letters, Herr Tobler, and then I'll go," was heard from the desk.

Tobler asked whether he really intended to leave without having been paid.

The other replied that it was no longer possible for him to remain, whereupon Tobler said he shouldn't take things so dreadfully seriously. The boss took his hat and left. After an hour, the assistant went up to the tower room as unobtrusively as he was able and there began to pack his few things. One after the other, he once again took up each of these small objects which, though they were insignificant, held great significance for him, and placed them neatly but quickly into the suitcase that stood waiting. When he was done packing, he stood at the open window for two minutes and let his grateful heart take one last good look at the region. He even blew a kiss to the huge lake below him, not stopping to consider what he was doing, but rather simply in the spirit of the leave-taking that had suddenly become necessary.

From the balcony onto which he now stepped, he called down to Wirsich: "Wait for me, I'll be down in a moment." Then he went downstairs with his little suitcase in his hand. How his heart was pounding!

"I must say goodbye now, I have to leave," he said to Frau Tobler. She asked:

"Whatever happened? Do you really have to go?"

"Yes," the assistant said.

"Will you think of me a little when you are gone?"

He bent down and kissed both her hands. She said:

"Yes, Joseph, think of Frau Tobler a little, it will do you no harm. She is a woman like many others, a woman of little importance. Stop that! Don't keep kissing my hand. Say goodbye to my children. Walter! Come here. Joseph means to leave us. Come, Dora, shake hands with Joseph. Children, come! That's right."

She remained silent for a moment and then continued:

"Things will surely go well for you—I hope and wish this, and almost know it for a fact. Always be a little bit humble, not too much. You will always have to stand on your own two feet. But never fly off the handle, always let the first words spoken in ill will remain unanswered; hard words can so quickly be followed by modest, gentle ones. Accustom yourself to overcoming wounded feelings in silence. Women are compelled to do this every day, and it is worth considering for men as well. Life in the world, after all, is subject to the same laws as household life, it is just that they are grander and broader. Never be a hot-

294

head! Have you really packed up everything that belongs to you? Are you leaving now with Wirsich? Listen, Marti, never act merely out of compulsion, and always be a little courteous. Then you're certain to better yourself. As for me, I too will soon be leaving this place. This house is lost. We—I and my husband and my children—will go live in the city, no doubt in cheap lodgings somewhere. One can get used to anything, and isn't it true you were a tiny bit happy here with us? No? After all, there were so many nice things. Wouldn't you like me to say goodbye to Tobler for you?"

"With all my heart!" the assistant said. One last time she spoke:

"I shall let him know, he will be glad of it. You owe it to him not to bear him a grudge, he was fond of you, as we all were. You were our employee—no, go now. Best of luck to you, Joseph."

She pressed his hand and then turned to her children as if nothing had happened. He picked up his little suitcase from the floor and went out. And then the two of them, Marti and Wirsich, left the Evening Star.

When they had reached the road down below, Joseph stopped, took one of Tobler's cheroots out of his pocket, lit it, and then turned around to look at the house one last time. In his thoughts he saluted it, and then the two of them walked on.

Afterword
by Susan Bernofsky

Robert Walser was not quite thirty in 1907 when he sat down in his Berlin apartment—a fifth-story walkup in a rear building at 141 Wilmersdorfer Straße in the Charlottenburg district—and began to write *The Assistant.* Two years earlier he'd come to the German metropolis to seek his fortune as a writer, following in the footsteps of his brother Karl, a successful illustrator and stage-set designer popular in the city's *beau monde.* Both of them, as natives of Switzerland, stuck out. First there was the accent, which to Prussian ears signified "bumpkin." Moreover, the two brothers seem to have shared a sense of humor as riotous as it was deadpan. There are stories about the two of them trapping the successful dramatist Frank Wedekind (author of *Spring Awakening*) in a revolving door and repeatedly shouting "muttonhead" at him as he spun round and round. And Robert is said to have walked up to literary giant Hugo von Hofmannsthal in a café to ask: "Can't you forget for a bit that you're famous?"

But unlike his charming brother, who specialized in entertaining actresses in tony restaurants, Robert never quite fit in Berlin society. The niceties of elegant social interaction eluded him, looking perhaps too much like hypocrisy, or a disagreeable pose. For reasons that to this day are not known with any certainty, he decided to enroll in a school for servants and spent the winter of 1905/1906 stoking stoves and waiting at table in a Silesian castle. Though he was already a published author—his first book, *Fritz Kocher's Essays,* had appeared in 1904—he seems not to have viewed his sojourn in Silesia merely as "research" for fictional work. (He did eventually write about the castle, but only a good dozen years later.) Instead he wrote, upon returning to Berlin, a semi-autobiographical novel about the grown children of a Swiss family, *The Tanners,* followed a year later by *The Assistant.*

Walser claims to have written *The Assistant* in a mere six weeks, as an entry for a competition sponsored by the Scherl publishing house—which promptly rejected it, no doubt at least in part because the entry was accompanied by a letter cockily demanding an 8,000 mark advance, a fortune in those days. The novel was then published in 1908 by Bruno Cassirer, who had brought out *The Tanners* the year before.

The Assistant, by all appearances, is set in Switzerland. We see the national holiday being celebrated on August 1 with the display of a large flag featuring a white cross on a red ground, and the characters speak, like their author, a Swiss-inflected German peppered with dialect expressions like "struber Gauner," "verschuggt" and "heimlichfeiß" (translated here as "the lowliest scoundrel," "ill-used," and "slyboots") all of which require explanatory footnotes at the back of the German edition. Unfortunately these subtle and not-so-subtle marks of difference and local color become invisible in translation, though I have attempted throughout to replicate the lilt and wiggle of Walser's style at the novel's lighter moments and the melodic soughing of the prose when he lapses into melancholy contemplation.

Curiously, the monetary unit changing hands throughout the novel is not the Swiss franc but the German mark. This odd discrepancy sent me running off to the Walser Archives in Zurich to consult the original manuscript, and indeed: the pocket money paid out to Joseph on Sundays is in the form of five-mark coins. The cognitive dissonance thus produced forces us to challenge our assumptions about the novel's setting. Perhaps its characters occupy, after all, some corner of the world that merely appears, by some coincidence, oddly Swisslike. Walser seems to be inviting his German readers to abandon any suspicions of provincialism they may be entertaining and instead attend to what is universal in his tale.

At the same time, *The Assistant* is at least in part an autobiographical novel. Walser himself worked for several months in 1903 as accountant and secretary to an ill-starred inventor named Carl Dubler who lived with his wife Frieda and four children (bearing the same names as their fictional counterparts) in a villa in the town of Wädenswil on Lake Zurich; the villa is still there, now minus its copper-clad tower. Walser himself is known to have worked from time to time at the Copyists' Bureau for the Unemployed in Zurich, and he gave his protagonist, Joseph Marti, his mother's maiden name.

The Assistant is the second of Walser's surviving novels, but in fact it was his third. Between *The Tanners* and *The Assistant*, he wrote yet another novel, also entitled *The Assistant*, that appears to have been quite different from the others, fantastical where the others are psychological and domestic. It recounted, he wrote in a letter to poet Christian Morgenstern, the adventures of a young man who sets off for Asia on a scientific expedition in the service of an unhinged intellectual whom Walser refers to as "the devil in a summer coat." Morgenstern read the manuscript and wrote an enthusiastic report on it for publisher Bruno Cassirer, but Cassirer declined to print it and at some point thereafter the manuscript was lost.

The final paragraph of *The Assistant* as published in 1908 was no longer the same as in the original manuscript Walser had submitted to the publisher. The ending appears to have been trimmed fairly late in the editing process, and whether Walser himself approved is impossible to say. Walser's long-time German editor Jochen Greven believes the cut was the publisher's decision. In my opinion, the original ending provides a more satisfying conclusion to, encapsulating the mood of the book's final pages in a poignant vignette in which the landscape that has been granted such powers of expression throughout the novel appears as lost in thought as its observer. Here it is:

When they had reached the road down below, Joseph stopped, took one of Tobler's cheroots out of his pocket, lit it, and then turned around to look at the house one last time. There it lay above him, silent in a wintry isolation, as if it felt cold. From the neighboring chimneys, delicate columns of blue-tinged smoke rose up, dispersing in the gray air. The landscape appeared to have eyes, and it appeared to be closing them, filled utterly with peace, in order to reflect. Yes, everything appeared a bit pensive. All the surrounding colors appeared to be gently and sweetly dreaming. The houses resembled slumbering children, and the sky lay, friendly and weary, upon all things. Joseph sat down on a rock beside the road and gazed back at it all for a long time. Fleetingly he thought once more of the woman, the children, the garden and all those mornings, noons, evenings and nights, the voices that for so long he had found so familiar, Tobler's voice, the smells wafting from the kitchen that had given him such pleasure, all this he now saluted in his thoughts, and then the two of them walked on.